Burnt Lungs &

Bitter Sweets

Virginia Betts

URBAN PIGS PRESS

urbanpigspress.co.uk

Shallow Grave in the River Gipping

Reeds, sharper than knives
fail to conceal
a fifty-year-old Finefare trolley
sunk to rust like a relic from another age;
insinuating hundreds of ordinary lives;
passing through a thousand pairs of busy hands;
carrying counter-sliced cheese
and tins of spam.
Before Marathons were Snickers,
and Spangles and Space-Dust littered the land.

To end here.
Unceremoniously dumped
by a couple of smacked-up punks
one night after a shopping spree
fifty years ago;
when I pushed him, and he pushed me,
just for a laugh,
and everything was free.

And seeing it rusting there,
its bones protruding, stark and bare
from that stagnant pool of filth,
I wonder what became of him;
and if he, too,
took the undignified slide into oblivion,
half-sunk in a shallow grave;
all that shining kinetic potential arrested;
dulled, and silenced
by time.

(Virginia Betts, from *That Little Voice*, Anxiety Press, 2024)

Contents

Thanks to James Jenkins and Bam Barrow for their belief in me; to Cody Sexton for the brilliant cover; to my family, and apologies to my mum if no-one speaks to her again after reading this book! Thank you as always to my son, Jacob, who champions everything I do with a smiley face.

Special thanks must go to my husband, Kevin, who (apart from being an NHS hero) must have due credit for helping me plot the outrageous fortunes of Hoagie and the gang, aided in no small way by The Wine Boutique on the Quay in Ipswich, which undoubtedly helped to fuel the fire!

Dead Swan (2024)

What a Waste (Ian Drury and the Blockheads)

They found a dead swan in the river today. I was there when it happened; I'd just cut across the skate park on my way to meet my man Dave on the riverbank when this minor drama starts to unfold. Like bloody Swan Lake, right there in real life.

I say my man Dave, but I'm not really sure if that's even his real name. We all call him Dave. It suits him. Anyone could be called Dave. Anyways, I could see he wasn't there, and this lot probably scared him off. Lots of shouting and 'ooing' about what they should do with the bird and how disgusting it was, and how useless the council are etc, etc. So, I thought I'd take a look.

I was a bit surprised at the small crowd it was attracting – it was bloody early in the morning and usually there's only a couple of dog-walkers who give me dirty looks when I go past in my tracksuit, without a dog of course. You've heard that saying, 'gone to see a man about a dog?' Well, that's me. Always seeing a man about a dog, but I haven't got a dog, see. Dave is usually the man, and the dog, well, the least said about that, the better.

Anyways, I thought they'd found a body in the river. It has been known. But it was just a swan. And when I saw it, I couldn't help it, but I thought of Hoagie. All them years ago. Poor bugger.

Way back, Hoagie and me, and sometimes Toggie, or even sometimes Jonesy used to hang about here a lot. I'm Toad by the way. Got big eyes, see. And my personality apparently. I remember one night, when we went on this raid of a supermarket. I think it was one of them ones that don't exist anymore like Finefare or something. We was so wasted! And we nicked a trolley and filled it up with snacks. Just kept doing it, anything we could lay our hands on, into this trolley it went. We was yelling and making a hell of a racket, but the little assistant was too scared to say anything. We whizzed it right out of the shop. Then me and Hoagie took turns pushing each other around in it. I wheeled him down here to the river and then I pushed him right in! What a laugh. Everything was a laugh back then.

Hoagie's real name was James Vincent Hoag. He got the right piss taken out of him for the Vincent bit. And the James bit. He didn't look like a Jimmy, so it just got shortened to Hoagie. We were the two musketeers. When he got a mohawk hairdo, I dyed mine green. I didn't dare go the full mohawk, but I fancied myself as a bit Johnny Rotten to his Sid Vicious, or maybe it was the other way round? I think we were singing 'Anarchy in the UK' as we raided that shop come to think about it.

Burnt Lungs and Bitter Sweets

Hoagie was nuts. I remember one time he picked a fight with this kid in the pub on the corner over his trousers being the wrong colour, and then he smashed a bottle and put it up to his face like he was gonna bottle him. But the kid's friend got hold of Hoagie and chucked him out. After punching him in the mouth full on. Hoagie found it hilarious. He said he wouldn't have to worry about his front teeth dropping out now 'cos this bloke had saved him the trouble. Hoagie was always on the script – methadone you see, makes your teeth rotten. Not 'cos he was giving up drugs, you understand. He just took that as well. Right laugh he was. Had the constitution of an ox. And he could drink you under the table too. Always the last man standing. The other two didn't have the understanding we had. Toggie's real name was Thorin and Jonesy was just always Jonesy. I don't remember his first name. Toggie went to jail for GBH and robbery, and Jonesy, well Jonesy went to work in a bank, I think.

That night by the river was a good night. One of the last times I saw Hoagie was by this river as well, quite a few years later. I'd cleaned up my act a bit and got a job. Don't get me wrong, I didn't join the bloody rat race. I was only packing stuff in boxes. But I thought if I got a bit of work and a bit of money, I'd get myself out of this dump. I mean, look at it. It's even worse now. In the cold light of day, it's a load of grey-block buildings, covered in graffiti, named after some famous poet. Always is, isn't it? Pretty name for an ugly piece of shit, as if the name will somehow improve it. Back then we had a bit of fun there though. But I never made any money 'cos I kept spending it. So, I'm still here. I just pack different boxes. I admire you mate, I said to Hoagie, that last time. Sticking to your principals. Not for him, working for some twat in a suit for a crap wage. Hoagie lived on his wits. He had twenty quid out of me that day, but well, that was Hoagie, what can you do?

So, when I see this swan, I look at it, floating all lifeless and bloated in that green mire and immediately my mind goes to Hoagie. Someone should clean up that river, they say. Look at the damage it's doing to the wildlife, they say. It's so unsightly, they say. I looked at its wings, folded one over the other. Bit like an angel. A fallen angel, dropped in that shitty, putrid river of green slime. Its beak was wide open and half full of green stuff. It probably choked to death on that. They say all sorts of things about swans, like they mate for life; they paddle furiously under all that graceful gliding across the surface. This one just looked exposed. Took its last breath amongst rusty bikes, used condoms and half-eaten Macdonald's. Probably somewhere in there is that bloody shopping trolley we dumped; a wire skeleton all covered in shit rusting and rotting away.

I wanted to pull the swan out. Not because I could save it; it was way beyond that. But because I wanted to give it back some dignity. All those bloody do-gooders and environmentalists around; all those people gawping, moaning about the state of the town. But the town's been like it for years. It's a dead bird at the end of the day. But it got to me. It got to me in a way I didn't think they'd understand. I don't understand it myself.

Burnt Lungs and Bitter Sweets

So, I went in, and I got it out, and I covered it up with my coat. And I just stood there looking at it, for what seemed like a long time, kind of protecting it, with everyone else's noise just fading into the background until someone in an orange jacket turned up and took it away.

Dave never showed, so I just went home. And for the rest of the day, I sat there, smoking and staring at the four walls. And I thought of Hoagie. It was quite a funny story really. He got chased by the police for something really stupid – nicking a pack of fags I think – and they chased him across that very river. But his trainers filled up with water and because he was so wasted as usual, he bloody sank and drowned. Stupid sod. It was in all the papers at the time. Just shows you can't escape forever. It'll get you in the end. He lay there for hours before anyone got him out. Poor bastard.

Virginia Betts

Dead Rats in a Bag

(1980)

Virginia Plain (Roxy Music)

'Kecks! Kecks!' Hoagie was yelling from the bottom of the ladder staircase in the split level flat. 'What are you doing in there? I need to get in.'

Kecks heard him yelling but she was intent on surveying her somewhat grey reflection under the fluorescent lighting. The tube flickered a bit. She noticed there were dead flies trapped in it. He kept calling.

'I'm up 'ere and I'm busy in the bathroom,' she finally answered.

Hoagie bounded up the ladder; skinny and lithe, he barely touched it with his feet. He stopped at the open door and stared at the vision of the gaunt and bony Kecks, standing there in her bra and a pair of pyjama bottoms, staring at her face. She turned when she noticed him.

'What you bin doing?' he said. 'You banging up now?'

'We've got to have a down day, Hoagie,' she said, ignoring the question. 'Get rid of the alcohol and shit out of our systems.'

'It's the *and shit* I'm worried about with you, Kecks,' he replied with a grin.

'I'm serious, Hoags. I need to stop. I'm not even 20 and I look 100. I've found a meeting and I'm going.' She picked up her black eyeliner.

'Like AA or somethin'?'

'Yeah, like that. I'm getting clean and I'm going sober.'

Hoagie burst out laughing. Then he saw that she was possibly serious.

'If you want then. I might join you,' he said.

'Would yer? Ok. But Hoagie, you'd have to leave your sarcasm at the door, yeah?'

'I can't promise that, Kecks. It's me, innit?' The grin again.

By half past six, Hoagie was sitting in the White Horse, on his third pint with Toad, who was sprawled over the chair, his skeletal frame taking up more space than was necessary.

'I'm serious! There was this guy there at the meeting, and he pulled out two dead rats!' Hoagie looked as if he might die laughing. 'Out of his bag! Not one, TWO! Like some sick magic trick. He goes, *I've got something comin' off me…sorry…I've got dead rats in me bag*. So naturally, I say, *really? Can I see?* 'Cos I'm so fuckin' high, see, and he says *yeah, course*. The guy runnin' it, well, you shoulda seen his face! He looks at me and then this guy, like, *fuck me, what have we got here?* He tries to salvage it. He says, *That's so good. You keep snakes, don't you? That's a great focus for you, having something to look after. It gives you a sense of purpose and responsibility. Something other than alcohol or using drugs. You love animals. That's good for you and for the animal.* But – I couldn't stop meself – I pipe up, *not for them rats it isn't!* And then they all laugh. Bloke in charge turns purple!'

'What did the rat bloke do then?' asked Toad.

Hoagie paused a micro-second, for the best theatrical effect. 'He opens up the zip of this adidas bag, and he pulls out a rolled-up plastic bag. Then he unrolls it and there is a dead rat! Right there! Then he unrolls another bit of tissue paper and pulls out another one!'

'What did it look like?' said Toad.

'Like it was asleep,' said Hoagie thoughtfully. 'It had its eyes closed and it looked all peaceful. Like some rat angel. It was pure white as well. They both were. Weird.' He took a swig of his cider. 'Then right, I made it worse, 'cos I said I went to see a taxidermy exhibition when I was a kid, and I was fascinated by the way things work. But I panicked and said, *not like I like dead things or anythin' and not choppin' up bodies, I'm not a psycho, I love animals.* The others were all fallin' about! Well, one woman was giving me odd looks, and tryin' to avoid lookin' at the rats. The bloke in charge of this AA meeting, or whatever it was, he was gonna burst! Then Kecks was sick on the floor.' He sipped his cider again. 'Got chucked out after that.'

Toad laughed. 'So, was Kecks pissed off?'

'God, yeah,' said Hoagie. 'She was spitting blood. She's wanting to get clean.'

'Why?' said Toad.

'God knows. Girl thing.' Hoagie shrugged. 'She said, *I can't stand it anymore, Hoagie. Get up, load up, sit around, drink. Your mates' round, raid the offy in that bloody old trolley. It's an endless cycle. I'm so sick of it.* Tha's what she said.'

'What did you say?'

'I told her she can do what she wants. But I'm all right. 'Nother one?' he indicated the empty glass.

'Yeah, all right,' said Toad.

Hoagie got up and began to head for the bar. Then he turned. 'Can you sub me a tenner, mate?'

'Yeah, all right. You owe me one though.'

And that was their relationship right there, thought Toad. Deeper and more lasting than any romance thing. Also, not as expensive and definitely less hassle.

A couple of nights later, Toad lay on his bed in his parents' house. He wondered if he'd still know Hoagie in 20, or 30 years' time. He couldn't imagine not knowing him, but he couldn't really imagine 20 minutes' time most days. He didn't want to be old, or not doing what they did now. Hoagie and Toad would always be mates, he thought. There were others in their little gang, but not as close. He wished Hoagie hadn't got a girlfriend. They'd planned to go out shopping the other day – their sort of shopping, the kind you don't need to bring money for – and Kecks had banned them, even though she could practically nick the whole shop and not get caught! He'd nothing major against her but trust her to get all twitchy about cleaning up.

As he dropped off to sleep, Toad began to dream. He dreamed he was sitting next to the river, waiting for Hoagie, and he thought he saw something in the water. He leaned forward, and he could just make out the pale face of a dead rat. He put his hand in to get it out, and it floated right up to the surface. Its eyes were shut, as if in a peaceful dream, and he tried to touch it. But as he did so, the eyes flew open, and it sank its tiny, sharp fangs right into his hand. He yelled out in his dream and wrenched his hand away, watching his red blood mingle with the muddy river water. When he looked again, he could no longer see the rat. Instead, he saw Hoagie's face under the water, and he woke up with a jolt.

Beads of sweat were on his forehead and back, and his hands felt clammy. He looked at his alarm-clock. It was an ancient one from childhood – a footballer clock with luminous green hands showing only 9 pm, despite the pitch-black winter sky outside. He lay still for a moment, considering getting up and going to see Hoagie, but then he heard a tremendous banging on the front door.

He had still not laced his trainers as he hurried downstairs to see what the noise was. His parents had beaten him to it.

'Hoagie! What the fuck?' he said.

'Kecks, man! Kecks!'

'I can't get any sense out of him,' said Toad's mother. 'Calm down James!' she appealed to Hoagie. 'He keeps saying something about Kecks. That's the girlfriend, isn't it?'

'Are you taking drugs, James, boy?' said Toad's father.

'You have to come with me!' said Hoagie. 'Kecks is in trouble.'

'Now just a minute…' began Toad's dad. But Toad was already out the door.

'She woke up from some dream – we'd both gouged out on the bed – and she screamed to high heaven. She said she'd dreamed some dark creature had hold of her arm and was pullin' her down into the ground – like, draggin' her off – and I had hold of her the other side and she tried to scream for help, but she didn't have a voice. Then she stopped making any sense, and she started shaking violently, and then she bloody foamed at the bloody mouth. Fuck, fuck! I think she's stopped breathing, Toad! Her eyes have gone back in her head, and she looks, like, blue.'

'You called the ambulance?'

'No! I can't – I'm loaded! And the room's full of gear and shit and – fuckin' hell! I'm not going to prison, Toad!'

'But what if she's dead?' Toad paused. 'Look, let's think. I know! Let's get her outside, and then we can call an ambulance from a phone box, and they won't even know she's anything to do with you. I've got change.'

Hoagie thought for a second. 'Good idea. I knew I could rely on you. Smart.' He seemed to calm down.

When they arrived, Hoagie hesitated on the doorstep. He was staying in a room on the top floor of a tall, thin, townhouse. Some do-gooder had found it for him after he'd told 'em some bullshit about a bad home-life. There were steps up to the front door and the rest of the place was full of people just like Hoagie. They were unlikely to notice if it was day or night, thought Toad. The patch of dirt, which might have once been called a small garden, was tangled with weeds as tall as a small child, and amongst the weeds and cigarette butts there was an old Finefare trolley and a rusting bike, minus the wheels.

'Come on!' said Toad, 'she might still be alive!'

'Don't think so,' said Hoagie. He looked wild-eyed; black hollows underneath, and staring, pinned pupils in the moonlight. His punk hair stood on end, yellow and black. He looks like a demented wasp, thought Toad.

Inside, they both stood staring at Kecks. She lay on the floor, still and blue-tinged, a trail of vomit from her mouth.

'I thought she was getting clean?' said Toad. 'She looks like she's been on the pin.'

11

Hoagie put his head in his hands and started rocking. 'It's my fault! I took the piss out of rat boy, and we got kicked out of the meeting and now she's on the floor!' Hoagie suddenly looked about 7 years old. Usually, he looked old for his years, but right now he looked skinny and vulnerable. Hoagie always knew what to do, but now he was lost. Toad felt irrationally annoyed.

'It's not your fault! She did it! Look, I don't want her to be dead. Let's stick to the plan, yeah?'

Hoagie was knelt over her. 'I can't hear any breathin' or anything.' Then he started some high-pitched wailing. Toad knew he had to do something urgently, so he punched Hoagie right in the jaw.

For a moment, Hoagie was stunned. Then he flew at Toad, and they started scuffling. Punches flew until they fell, wrestling, to the floor, tears of hysterical laughter streaming down their faces.

'Shit!' said Hoagie. 'Kecks!'

The two of them gathered her up. Toad took her arms and Hoagie the legs. She weighed less than a feather. They carried her out of the door and bumped her down the stairs, a foamy little trail of vomit spewing out from her mouth as she went.

Outside, they looked around. The street was dark and empty, and the only streetlight was broken.

'Put her in that trolley,' said Toad. They pushed her up the road, indicating how drunk she was with a roll of the eyes to a wary passer-by, until they reached the nearest phone box. Typically, it smelled of piss and had a smashed window, but at least it wasn't out of order. Toad said to leave her outside whilst he made the call.

'Done it,' he said. They both stood over Kecks, looking at her laid out on the pavement.

'Looks asleep,' said Toad.

'Yer know what? She looks like one of those fucking rats,' said Hoagie.

They heard sirens in the distance.

'Let's go,' said Toad. He gestured to the old trolley. 'Get in,' he said, and they legged it up the street and into the next one, Toad pushing the empty trolley at break-neck speed, Hoagie's hair waving in the wind, not stopping until they found themselves in a narrow alleyway, where Hoagie hopped out and pulled out his foil and lighter.

'Smoke?' he asked, dangling a tiny wrap under Toad's nose.

'Why not?' said Toad.

They stumbled out of the alleyway and lurched along towards the off-licence and late shop.

'Wanna go shopping?' said Hoagie. And he lifted Toad up and plopped him into the trolley. Then he screamed 'Aaaah!' and they charged through the front door, terrifying the tiny assistant who stood frozen at the till, as they charged around, singing *Anarchy in the UK* as loudly as they could, whilst stuffing Chewits, Spangles, Monster-Munch, Marathons, Kit-Kats, Mars bars, Pot Noodles and Space Dust into the trolley, along with bottles of Diamond White and packs of John Player Specials. Everything landed on top of Toad, and he yelped as the heavy bottles hit him on the foot. Screaming with laughter, they raced out, and once around the corner, Hoagie stopped and suggested they swapped places again. Then they headed for the river.

Virginia Betts

In revenge for the heavy bottles injuring him, Toad built up speed as they raced downhill. Then he let go, and the trolley containing Hoagie kept going straight into the shallow water, where it promptly fell over sideways and Hoagie tipped out. He was sat there in the putrid filth, splashing his hands about when Toad caught up.

Soon they were sitting on the bank, smoking the ciggies and eating Kit-Kats. Hoagie folded the foil into his pocket. He always kept the foil. 'Useful, that,' he said.

A few streets away, Kecks had been zipped into a black body bag and driven away.

'Hey, Hoagie,' said Toad, biting into his chocolate, 'Do you think Kecks made it?'

'Nah man,' said Hoagie. 'She was gone.' He paused. 'Them bloody rats!'

Problems With Paying

(1977)

Lipstick (The Buzzcocks)

Kecks met Hoagie just before Christmas, when she was a few days shy of her sixteenth birthday. She saw him eyeing her up whilst she was browsing on the ground floor of Debenhams. The large department store was still quite new at the time, and it was exciting to wander around the shiny eclectic displays. She spotted Hoagie in the gift section – you know, where they put miniature chilli sauces, and 'curry-for-one' Balti sets next to other pointless crap you eventually lost in the back of your cupboard. This year, gonk keyrings, travel connect 4, and novelty soap dispensers were on the shelves next to *Matey* and *Miss Matey* bubbles for the bath. Kecks liked the look of *Matey* in his cheerful sailor outfit, but it made her itch, perhaps providing the authentic experience of getting your private parts a bit too close to a sailor, she thought to herself with an inward giggle. She browsed the stationery section, sniffing all the fruity smelly rubbers, and trying out the cola lip-gloss, rolling it straight on to her lips before putting it back. It was a shopful of primary-coloured delights housing knickers next to nutcrackers.

Kecks was standing at the lippy counter when she noticed he'd continued to follow her through the store. He was older than her, that was obvious; she wasn't sure how much older,

15

but he was old enough to have left school, sporting his Mohican hairdo which was pink at that time. She looked at him from under her fringe, just like *Jackie* mag had advised, then she looked away. She thanked God that she'd put on her thick, black eyeliner and sprayed her hair into shape, adding a bit of glitter spray. She was wearing her second-hand black duffel coat, but she'd had to sneak it out in a carrier-bag because her mum had said it was scruffy and that people who wore them, like *punk rockers*, looked like bin-men and they were all on drugs. Once she got started, Kecks' mum launched her missiles of attack at anything and everyone even if they weren't connected. It went: *Kerry-Anne, you are NOT leaving this house looking like a scruff. Put on your nice coat. You look like one of those kids from the estate – all on drugs and sniffing glue. Like those Punk Rockers...* but by then, Kecks had usually switched off her brain.

Pretending she wasn't in the least bit interested in that older guy, Kecks asked the counter-assistant how much the lipstick she was holding cost. The saleswoman looked her up and down. Kecks wondered why make-up ladies always wore all of the products at once. The woman was pretty old – at least 30 – and her face was so plastered with the stuff it looked like she'd put it on with a trowel. She was orange and shiny and clearly believed she was a great advertisement for the brand, when in reality she looked like smiling might actually crack her face in half.

'It's £15,' said the woman. Kecks nearly fell over backwards. Boots 17 was only a couple of quid, if that. This one would cost all her Saturday job money. But Kecks didn't want to admit that it was too pricey, because then she'd be exactly what the woman thought she was – a kid. So, Kecks said, 'Is it tested on animals?'

'I don't believe so,' said Miss Pan-stick.

'Well, does it contain whale-fat?' asked Kecks, fishing for excuses.

'Ooh, I don't know,' said the woman, her fixed grin fading.

'Oh well,' said Kecks, in her poshest voice, 'then I couldn't possibly take it!' And she sauntered off. She thought about how her friends would have known instantly what she was up to. She was meeting her best friends in a minute.

Kecks glanced up again and noticed the punk-hair guy watching her. *Fuck off!* she thought. She was annoyed about the lipstick. It really was a cool shade of red mixed with black. She watched the make-up lady move up to the other end of the counter to serve a well-heeled woman in her fifties. *Lipstick won't help you much,* thought Kecks, uncharitably. And then something in her felt irrationally irritated. It was like those fat blokes who drove around in Porsches. Mostly old; usually bald. They looked shit, but they could afford the car. When you're young enough to look cool in a nice car all you can buy is a beaten-up escort. Or take the bloody bus. Or buy cheap, shit lipstick. So, on impulse, Kecks waltzed up to the counter, bold as brass, and put the lipstick in her pocket. Then she headed for the escalator at the back – and nobody stopped her.

She was waiting for her friends, feeling elated about her loot, when there was a tap on her shoulder. Her heart sank to her boots, and she turned. It wasn't security. It was that punk guy.

'Hi,' he said. 'I'm James Hoag. But everyone calls me Hoagie. I was impressed by your stylish shopping techniques,

17

and I wondered if you fancied coming out with me some time. We could always knock-off a jeweller's or execute a train robbery after, if you're up for the big league?' He winked.

Kecks was taken aback but tried to keep cool. 'I think I'm a bit young for you. I'm 16,' she lied. 'I'm still at school. Doing my A levels.'

'I'm only 19! Hardly a geriatric!' he protested. 'I haven't got any A levels. Or O levels. I couldn't be fucked really.'

Kecks had to admit, he had a winning grin. It lit up his whole face. A sudden recklessness took over. 'All right,' she said, 'I will come out with you. Where and when?'

'Meet you down the Spread Eagle at 8 tonight?'

'If I can get out I will, ok? Look there's my friends. I gotta go. See ya later.' She hid her smile – that grin of his was infectious – and she walked away, cool as you like, feeling him watching her but resisting the impulse to turn back.

'Who was that?' said her friend, Ally.

'Dunno. Some bloke,' said Kecks.

'Looks weird,' said Kelly.

'Yeah,' said Kecks. And off they went for chips.

Kecks had told her mum she was meeting Kelly and Ally in town later to go to the pictures. She'd tried on about 100 outfits and left them in piles, strewn all over her bed.

'Don't be late in, Kerry,' warned her mother.

'Won't! Bye!' shouted Kecks as she slammed the door. Her mum hadn't seen her final choice of outfit, thank God.

Kecks had never actually been in a pub on her own before. When she walked in, it was exactly as she expected. It was smoky blackness from ceiling to floor. Kecks, who had smoked a few of Ali's ciggies at the school gate before, had bought a packet to take with her. She had dared Kelly to buy some as well, but Kelly wouldn't. In the end she had bought Marlboro, in their red and white packet, because that was one of the brands she'd heard of, and she liked red. Now she was in the pub, though, she realised she had forgotten to bring a lighter, so at the bar she asked for a box of matches and a vodka and orange which was the first and only alcoholic drink she had ever had when she was out – at a youth club disco. God, she'd felt so self-conscious when Ally had got it for her, like she might be arrested or something. Then some kid had asked her to dance, and they'd ended up snogging on the field outside, with Kecks trying to think of a polite way to get his hand out of her bra and go back in, when Ally's dad had pulled up to take them all home.

She looked around for this guy Hoagie, but he was obviously late. He seemed the type who would be. Kecks suddenly felt a little bit intimidated, especially as her legs, in a very short tartan skirt, were attracting a lot of attention. This was not the youth club disco. She pulled her coat around her – a new one she'd bought today from a small boutique. It was sort of furry, and far too hot for being inside, but she felt a little safer being sightly covered up by it. She leaned with one foot up behind her on the wall and one elbow on a high table. She lit a cigarette, although she had to strike about 5 matches in the attempt, and she tried to appear cool. Her new lipstick left black-red stains on the cigarette, and she tried not to cough as she blew the smoke out from her rounded mouth.

Suddenly she heard a bit of a commotion coming from the corridor that a sign on the wall told her led to the toilets.

'You what? You haven't got the money? You piece of shit! You'll get the money now, or I'll fuckin' take it out of yer bit by bit!'

Kecks was desperate for the loo, and wanted to check her make-up, but she knew she would have to walk past whatever was going on. She went to the bar and bought another vodka. She downed it quite fast, and the room suddenly felt a bit uneven. And now the situation was getting desperate. She'd have to go to the loo.

As she passed them, she noticed that one fairly big guy, with what could only be described as mad hair and deranged eyes, was holding a small flick-knife at the throat of another guy, a slight, pale-faced and spotty boy. She kept her eyes down and went into the ladies' loo. The room was red with one bare lightbulb. It did not smell too great, and there was another, slightly toxic, chemical smell that she did not recognise. A skinny woman stood by the sink, bending over. She seemed to be snorting some powder up her nose, and when she stood up, her eye make-up ran in black streaks down her cheeks and formed little crudules near her chin. Kecks shoved at one of the stall doors and it swung open to reveal another girl sitting on the toilet, leaning back against the cistern with her legs splayed out in a Y shape. Her eyes rolled back in her head. Kecks tried the next stall.

When she came out though, she walked straight into the middle of a punch-up between the two guys whose exchange was so heated earlier. A fist hit her on the cheek and sent her flying into the wall.

'Get out of the way, stupid bitch,' growled the one who had the knife.

Kecks was rarely frightened, but now she was. She felt dazed by the punch, and completely out of her depth. She did not dare to move and simply covered her head with her hands.

'Fuckin' pay up for the gear, you fucker, or this knife is goin' in your head!' said the crazed bloke, who had punched her, to the other guy, whose friends seemed to have turned up to help him out.

Kecks screamed as one of them broke a glass and all hell broke loose around her. But just as suddenly, a huge hand seemed to lift her out of the epicentre and carry her to safety in the bar. It was Hoagie.

'Stay here,' he said.

He disappeared and Kecks could hear him shouting, 'What the fuck do you think you're doing to my date, you cunt?' Kecks peered around the corner just in time to see Hoagie head-butt the knife-bloke in the face. Blood streamed from his nose and seemed to stop the whole fight in its tracks. The other bloke's friends melted away as seamlessly as they had arrived.

'This bastard hasn't paid me what he owes,' said the knife-guy. I'm gonna cut his face open!'

'Look, Jez,' said Hoagie, 'I'd advise you pay my friend what you owe him now. Or get one of your mates to do it, because he does mean what he says.'

The small debtor shrugged, put his hand in his jacket and took out his wallet. His counted out some notes.

'That'll do,' said the knife guy, looking even more demented, 'make up for all your problems with paying.' He grabbed the whole wallet, and the wad of cash. 'Get the fuck out of here,' he said.

The other bloke started to say something, but Hoagie shook his head. The guy gave up and left, pushing past Kecks on the way out. Hoagie headed her way, but he brought the violent knife-wielding maniac with him.

'Hi, er – hey, I don't know your name!' said Hoagie.

'Kecks,' said Kecks. 'Maybe I should go home?'

'Hi Kecks,' he said. 'Please don't go! I am very sorry I was late, but I bought you some chocolate from the offy, and I tried to pay with my new card, but you know that machine where they zap the thing across? Well, the girl in the shop was new and she didn't know how to work it, and it got stuck halfway, and then another bloke said I hadn't spent enough to use it. So, in the end, I nicked it. Fuckin' flexible friend my arse. Here you go.' He handed her a Marathon bar. I hope you like nuts.'

His charming friend sniggered.

'I got these for you, you wanker,' he said, holding out a packet of spangles for his friend, 'but you don't deserve 'em. You tosser,' he said. 'This is Kecks. She's my date and you owe her an apology for punching her in the head.'

'Sorry,' said the friend, wiping his bloody nose. He extended his blood-streaked, filthy hand to Kecks, who looked at it in horror.

'Er, it's fine,' she said.

'Buy us a pint, mate,' said Hoagie. 'This by the way is Thorin O'Rourke. He fuckin' hates his name, hence I'm tellin' you it. He goes by the name of Toggie and as you can see, it int a good idea to cross him; but he's a nice bloke really, int yer, Togs?'

'No,' said Toggie. 'Pint then. And for the *lady*?'

'Vodka and Orange,' said Kecks. 'Please.' Fuck me, he was scary.

'Ooh, int she polite?' said Toggie.

'Fuck off,' said Hoagie. 'Sorry Kecks,' he said, whilst Toggie was at the bar. 'He's a mate, what can I say?' He lit a cigarette. 'Want one?'

'Yeah,' said Kecks.

'So,' said Hoagie, 'how old are you really?'

'I am sixteen, nearly,' she said, feeling her face turn pink. 'On Christmas Eve.'

'Shit! You like Jesus or something? Seriously, that must be crap.'

'Yeah,' said Kecks, 'I sometimes only get one present from my parents and family.'

'Tight fuckers!' said Hoagie. 'I'll tell you what, if you come out with me again after tonight, I'll get you a birthday present and a Christmas present.'

'Bet you'll nick them,' said Kecks.

'Pot callin' kettle black,' said Hoagie. 'Nice lipstick you've got on.'

She laughed. Toggie came back and plonked the two drinks on the table in front of them, splashing Kecks.

'Can you *not* bring him next time?' said Kecks.

'Cheeky bitch!' said Toggie. 'Your round next.'

The rest of the evening was trouble free, and as the barman called time, somewhere in her sluggish, intoxicated brain, Kecks vaguely remembered she had said she wouldn't be late home.

'S'alright,' slurred Hoagie, 'my mate Jonesy'll be along in a minute to pick us up. S'not late though. Thought you'd come back to mine.' He saw her face. 'It's all right, the boys will come too, I won't try anything on yer. I'm so pissed anyway. But we can have a smoke and a few more drinks. Got cider. Jonesy can give you a lift later.'

'Ok. Cool,' said Kecks. She might as well get into trouble for something rather than nothing. Although she wasn't keen on that Toggie.

Hoagie's place was on the top floor. At the entrance was a patch of grass, which was really a lot of overgrown weeds with a bike and a trolley tangled amongst them. To be honest, the flat itself was in a similar state. The walls and ceiling had a brown tinge and were coated with some sort of sticky film. There wasn't a square inch of floor to walk across without stepping on some dirty plate, or other bits of debris.

'Make yourself at home,' said Hoagie.

He introduced his friends as Jonesy – 'he's the driver', Toggie, 'you already know' and 'This is Toad – me best mate since school.'

Hoagie put on a record – the player sat on the floor in the centre of the room – and it spun into life with *I wanna be sedated*, then he disappeared and reappeared with some cider. Jonesy and Toad had contributed six packs of Special Brew. When they were settled, he asked Kecks if she'd ever 'done gear' or 'chased' before. Kecks had very little idea of exactly what he meant, but she wasn't about to say so and gave a non-committal nod. She assumed that when he rolled up foil round a biro to make a little tube, then heated up some brown lump on another piece of foil, it was just some fancy way of inhaling pot, which she had seen once at a party, and had pretended to smoke when it was passed her way. So, she said nothing and when it hit her, it hit her really hard. She fought back an enormous wave of nausea, knowing this was nothing she was familiar with at all, and then she sank backwards as if she would keep on falling forever, through the wall and into another dimension. She had no idea what time it was when she came round, but she sat up and was instantly and violently sick down her front. The boys were all lying on the floor around her, but Hoagie sprang to consciousness when he heard her vomit.

'You haven't done that before have you?'

'No,' she admitted. 'I thought it was good though.'

'Everyone's sick the first time,' said Hoagie, 'but you don't have to do it again.'

'Well, I might,' said Kecks.

Toggie sat up. 'Oi, mate, you owe me for the gear.'

'Put it on tick,' said Hoagie.

'Fuckin…what is it with not payin' for things today?' said Toggie.

'Ask Kecks about that,' said Hoagie with a wink, pouting his lips at her and blowing extravagant kisses, reminding her of a fish. 'Must be one of them days.'

'I've got to go home,' said Kecks. 'I live with my mum.'

'Toad lives with his parents,' said Toggie, 'Well, I say that, but he spends most of the time here. 'If your mum throws you out anytime, you might end up here as well!'

'Look,' said Hoagie, 'I'll walk you back. Jonesy's fucked.'

Kecks agreed, even though it was an hour's walk to her house. On the way back, Hoagie took her hand, and even though it felt funny, she didn't pull it away. They shared a ciggie and drank cider from the bottle as they walked. Kecks' feet were vaguely killing her, but the new drug she had smoked somehow managed to dull any sort of pain, physical or mental, into almost non-existence. And that was something Kecks really liked. She realised it was probably heroin, which her school warned all the kids about regularly. Well, she couldn't see what all the big fuss was about. The boys all seemed fine. And she was fine, apart from throwing up. But apparently that was normal. She probably wouldn't do it again though.

'Can I see you again,' said Hoagie, when they were outside her house.

'Yeah,' said Kecks. 'Yeah.'

Hoagie lunged at her in a sort of clumsy kiss. He bumped teeth with her a bit, but he didn't stick his tongue down her throat, like Andrew Davies did in the sewing cupboard at break.

'Well see yer then,' said Hoagie. He turned to leave, but then he spun round. 'What's your phone number? I mean, do you have a phone in your house?'

Kecks reached inside her tiny bag and pulled out her eyeliner. She wrote her parents' number on the back of his hand. 'Don't lose it,' she said.

'Not gonna fuckin' lose me hand, am I?' he said as he walked away before her mum saw him. 'We'll go to that club in town, yeah? The one next to the curry house, yeah?' he called over his shoulder.

She disappeared inside and he didn't hang around.

Halfway back home he realised he was feeling tired, and he had begun to sober up just enough for the walk to seem never-ending. He headed for the main road so he could get in a taxi, and, after covering his hair a bit with his jacket, he managed to look sober and sensible enough to persuade one to take him.

Once in the cab, Hoagie realised he had not brought his wallet. He confessed this to the driver when they arrived at his address.

'Right, you bloody little shit, I'm driving us straight down the nick then,' said the cabbie.

Hoagie was *really* not in the mood. His head hurt, his feet hurt, and his date had not only been crashed by Toggie, but he remembered she'd thrown up on herself and his rug. He tried to reason with the driver.

'I can pay you, but I have to go inside first, and my friends will pay if I haven't got it,' he said.

'Nah fuckin' way,' said the driver.

What is your problem, mate?' said Hoagie. 'I have my wallet inside.'

'My problem is you load of fuckin' smackhead punks who seem to have some sort of issue payin' for what they owe,' said the driver. Hoagie could tell he was about to go off on some sort of rant about smackheads and punks and probably bringing back hanging.

'I don't have any problem paying,' said Hoagie, 'but now I *do* have a problem with you and your fuckin' attitude.' He quickly opened the door and hopped out. He leaned into the driver's window, then he drew back his fist and punched him in the face.

'Keep the change, *mate*,' said Hoagie, and sprinted up the steps and into the house.

Virginia Betts

Radio Rentals (1976)

Young Offender's Mum (Carter USM)

In 1976, Diane Hoag counted herself lucky to have a television set. None of the neighbours had one. The amount of Green Shield stamps she'd saved would only get her a Parker pen and a golf ball. Her husband, Bobby, had just acquired the huge black and white box from Radio Rentals. Or so he said. She didn't like to ask too much about where he got things, but he said it was on hire and he'd show her the paperwork, so she pushed any nagging thoughts to one side and decided to enjoy it. In a couple of years, he told her, they'd upgrade to a colour one, but first they should get central heating as it was a right pain having to scrape the ice of the insides of the soaking windows every morning in the colder months. Her two sons, James and David were proper excited to have a TV of their own in the house in time for Christmas. Not that they were poor. Compared to some, say, that friend of James', Thorin O'Rourke and his family, they were doing all right. But Diane and Bobby had married young, and a telly was a luxury when food had to be put on the table and there was only one, often irregular, (she thought with a grimace), wage. Diane had not worked since James was born over 16 years ago. She'd been a secretary, but when she became pregnant, and married, she was sacked – well, 'asked to leave'. That's just the way it was. Bobby's work was sporadic to say the least, but finally Bobby Hoag had a good honest job at the docks, and they had a small semi in a reasonable area, bought on a mortgage with a down-payment Diane had inherited when her mother died. Now David was older, and getting towards secondary school, and James might have a job soon, Diane was thinking about going back to work. But what to do? And who would hire her after nearly 17 years as a housewife? Bobby said no-one would, and he weren't gonna have no bloody vesta curry for his dinner when he got home from a hard day at work. Work! That was a laugh! But she pushed these questions and thoughts away. Work was scarce for everyone and both boys still needed her really. The summer had been so hot that the all the grass had turned into straw; the heat had made tempers frayed; riots were breaking out everywhere and the people were one angry, sweltering mob. The streets were stinking and full of rubbish, there was a plague of fuckin' greenflies, and the power was always going off; but her most immediate problem was James.

James Vincent Hoag. Named after his maternal grandfather, but the dead spit of his father in every way, including the ability to stay out of work and permanently in trouble. She was worried about him. So much so, that she felt she neglected little David, who seemed to be able to get on with things quietly. James, though, he'd been in and out of trouble since he started school really. Fighting, stealing, swearing. He'd already received several clips round the ear from the headmaster and even the local police, as lately he'd been caught out nicking stuff from the paper shop. Only sweets and drinks, but he was getting older now and taking after his dad a bit too much. It was only by good grace that the victims of his petty crimes had taken pity on her, and no criminal action had been taken. But he was now officially a school leaver, and his last memorable act was to get himself suspended for dying his hair green and smoking behind the bike sheds.

But far more worrying was her suspicion he might be experimenting with drugs. This was something new to her, and something frightening. In her youth, half a pale ale seemed daring, and she'd hardly had time to experiment with anything before she was up the aisle and pushing a pram. Glue-sniffing seemed to be the latest craze sweeping the nation, according to the Daily Mirror. Dope-smoking another. And she was pretty sure that Jamie had tried something, as he often came home looking either sort of spaced-out or really hyped up, *and* some of her bloody Valium pills had gone missing. He also loved this new band called the Sex Pistols, who made what they called 'Punk Rock' music. He'd been to see them with his mate and come back soaking wet with lager and his t-shirt practically ripped off his back. To be truthful, she didn't mind the music. It was so full of energy and anger, and she often felt like that herself! You only had to look out the front door, and see the queues for the jobcentre, and the shit all over the streets, and the fucking politicians arguing up in their ivory towers, but doing sod all, when she had to get by on half a pound of mince between four of 'em and often suck on the bones of a meagre lamb-chop herself to save her husband and sons going hungry.

So, the rented TV was a bit of a Godsend this Christmas, she thought. Even if she had the feeling that Bobby Hoag had not quite told the truth about Radio Rentals…

Yes, her parents, James Vincent Featherstone and Mary Susan Featherstone, had warned her about Bobby Hoag. He was once known by his family as 'Little Bobby' because his father was 'Big Bobby,' but all that changed when Big Bob went to prison for stealing tools from his workplace. Honest-to-God, he'd steal anything – even stole lead off a church roof once. With him out of the way, Little Bobby gained seniority. But he also lived just outside the law sometimes. However, despite being warned, in the end Diane didn't have much choice, because on her wedding day she was already expecting James, and nobody decent had babies if they weren't married, although nearly everyone she knew was pregnant on their wedding day. So, she went ahead with a hastily planned marriage in the local registry office, followed by a quick drink at the Grinning Rat and a fish and chip supper. There was no honeymoon – couldn't afford one. She didn't see her parents after that, because her mother dropped down dead suddenly one Sunday, and her father blamed it on the stress caused by the existence of Bobby Hoag. So that was that. She had her family and she got on with it. Ignoring its dubious origins, she put her faith in the telly, hoping it would give James a bit of a distraction and encourage him to stay in the house a bit, where she could keep an eye on him.

But when they gathered around the telly on the 1st of December, her heart sank with regret at getting the set at all. For the show they watched was the Today show, with Bill Grundy interviewing none other than James' favourite band. It was supposed to be Queen, but they couldn't come, so the Pistols were asked to give him an interview. And boy did they give it to him. Jamie whooped with delight as they made Grundy, who seemed a bit pissed to be honest, look like a prize prat. He'd tried to goad them and make them look stupid, but it backfired spectacularly. Even she, an adult, could see that. And as sure as night followed day, she could predict trouble coming for her Jamie.

'What a fuckin' twat!' said Hoagie later, when he met up with Toad in the park, where they drank a can of special brew each and skinned up with some dope bought from Toggie.

'Fuck, yeah,' said Toad. 'Old Steve Jones really gave it to 'im. But the cunt deserved it. He was tryin' to hit on that bird in the back. Dirty old bugger. That Jones was right. And that Grundy can't say anythin' 'cos he was so pissed anyway. It's all over the papers: *The Filth and the Fury*. Brilliant. Shall we go and see 'em again? They'll be so big now. Won't be like that art college thing where we got spat on and jumped on, I don't reckon.'

'Yeah,' said Hoagie. 'I heard they might go to Holland or somefing. You can smoke weed there, like, in a café and it's not illegal.'

'Really?' said Toad, 'Cool!' He paused for a minute, beginning to plan the trip to Holland in his head. Then he remembered.

'Hoagie,' he said, 'Toggie said he can get us some better stuff. Some gear. You know, smack, like.'

'Ok...', said Hoagie. He thought about it. His mum was on at him to find a job or do the housework and his dad had said if he sat around doing fuck all he could soon fuck off.

'Well, I'm BORED,' he announced in his best Johnny Rotten sneering whine. 'It's so fuckin' BORING.'

'Yeah,' said Toad, also imitating a Rotten tone. 'I'm in if you are. Give us something new to do.' He gestured towards the shithole that was the kids' playground, where only last week some sick bastard had put a razor blade in the slide. 'Look at this place,' he took a long drag of the joint, then blew it out slowly. 'It looks like life.'

'Fuckin' philosopher now!' said Hoagie. 'You oughta cut down on that weed, mate. But yeah. It's shit, innit?'

Later, in the Grinning Rat, Toad had another revelation. 'Fuckin' boring,' he repeated once again. 'Why don't we form a band?'

'But we can't play anything,' said Hoagie.

'Yeah, we can! You can play guitar.'

'No,' said Hoagie, 'my brother has got a guitar, and I chose it as my instrument in music lessons for six weeks at school one time, but I can only play about six chords.'

'Tha's all you need!' said Toad. 'I can be the singer, Toggie can bang the drums and I think Jonesy can play guitar as well.'

'But you can't sing.'

'The Pistols can't really play or sing either,' said Toad, 'but it works, don't it? Then we can get loads of money and free drugs and girls.'

'I am an Anti-Christ-a; I am an Anar-chiste-a,' shouted Hoagie.

'I wanna DISTROY!' shouted Toad, and they rasped out the rest of the song, right to the battle cry:

'Get PISSED! DESTROYYYYYY!'

'OUT!' ordered the landlord.

The big drug deal was set for 9 O'clock pm at the Spread Eagle. Hoagie got there first, closely followed by Toad and also by Jonesy, who had agreed to try it and chip in some cash. Toggie was going to take the cash and meet his so-called dealer in the toilet, and then they'd split the gear and leave the pub one at a time, meeting up later to use it. Toggie had refused to tell anyone the name of the dealer. He said he didn't know his real name anyway on account of him being a 'professional, innee?' The three in the bar sat sweating and fidgeting, radiating shady business, when Toggie burst in.

'Fuck me!' he said, 'Don't look too fuckin' obvious will yer?' He lowered his voice to a comical stage- whisper. 'Have you got the cash?'

'Yeah,' said Hoagie. 'Is it enough? It's a bit cheap innit?'

Toggie took the money and counted it, then put it in his pocket. 'Yeah, it's right. Mine's a JD and coke. Back in a bit.' He disappeared out back.

When he reappeared, he beckoned them from the general direction of the toilets. They followed.

'Here y'are,' he said, and passed them each a tiny piece of cling film which wrapped a minute brownish lump.

'I int stickin' a needle in meself,' said Hoagie.

'Nah, mate,' said Toggie. 'We can chase it.'

'Like, smoke it?' said Toad.

'Yeah, I'll show yer back at mine,' said Toggie.

The lights suddenly went out.

'Power-cut,' said Toad. 'Time to go?'

Not long after, at Toggie's appalling flat, four skinny teenagers got high by inhaling Heroin off the foil, according to Toggie's instructions, and lay back in a near-unconscious state.

'It's fuckin'…,' slurred Toggie, tailing off, unable to form the words for his newly acquired sunny state of mind. And then Jonesy projectile-vomited all over him.

Burnt Lungs and Bitter Sweets

'Your sick's black!' noted Toad, who himself had a slightly green tinge to his face. He spat on the floor and then sank back into, and in his opinion right through, the threadbare carpet. He couldn't care less about anything as all his thoughts drifted; floated; evaporated as he become one with the floor and beyond it. It was the beginning of a lifelong and lasting love affair. In only a few months, smack was a central feature in their lives, when they could get it. Only Jonesy resisted, due to the black sick putting him off. 'I just don't like it that much, mate,' he said. But he was happy to smoke weed and his alcohol intake was legendary. So, their bond of friendship remained as strong as ever.

In Hoagie's house, things were less tranquil. It started when Diane Hoag had gone to Radio Rentals to ask when the first payment was due. They had never heard of any rental agreement, and it had taken all her acting skills to pretend she had made a mistake. It took fewer skills and less than three minutes to get the truth out of Bobby Hoag. He and his mate Trevor had stolen it from Rumbelow's. Like a hire agreement, but without the hire, he'd said. Or the agreement. The TV sets were in the back room, and as Trevor worked there, acquiring one was easy enough. Bobby had driven the 'getaway car' he told her, grinning. 'Cor that telly was bloody heavy though,' he said. 'Took four of us to get it out in the end.'

Diane was really pissed off. The charm of that grin had worn thin over the years of him turning up with food, electrical goods, booze and even, with Trevor's help, armchairs and a carpet from the local pub, and on this occasion, something snapped inside her. She grabbed a frying pan and hit Bobby on the head with it.

For a moment he was stunned and silent. Even Diane couldn't believe what she had done. He rubbed the top of his head and then a switch in his brain flicked.

'You bitch!' he hissed. 'I fuckin' married you, didn't I? I provide, don't I?' He suddenly went for her, punching her full in the belly. It wasn't that hard, but she doubled over, more winded and shocked than anything else. Both of them sat opposite each other on the dusty carpet, wondering again in disbelief at what had just happened, and then, quietly, she told him he had to pack his bags. His protests were loud and full of drunken expletives. But miraculously, he did pack a bag and leave. The last thing he muttered to her was that she ought to be grateful and no other fucker would put up with her and her brats. 'Got you a telly, didn't I? Ungrateful mare!' So that was the end of the Hoag's game of happy families. Soon after, Bobby Hoag was arrested.

Meanwhile, young James Hoag had taken to going out every night. He had started to look like one of the living dead, and his hair had become even more outrageous. And there was one more thing: she had noticed money going missing from her purse at an alarming rate. When David said his pocket money had disappeared, she knew it was James. Diane sat up late into the early hours one night, intending to have it out with him, but as the hours passed, she was becoming increasingly worried. As she was picturing him lying in a ditch, unconscious and hit over the head, or with a needle sticking out of his arm, there was a knock on the door. David appeared at the top of the stairs.

'Who's that? Is it Dad come back?' he said.

'You stay there. I'll go and see,' said Diane. She put the chain on and opened the door a crack. A policewoman was on the doorstep. There was a car parked in front of the house, and although it wasn't very clear, it appeared there were two people in the back.

'Mrs Hoag?' said the policewoman, 'Can we come in for a moment?'

Diane was feeling dizzy with fear. She let them in.

'Is it my son, James? Is he in trouble? Is he…is he dead?' She did not want to hear it. But then a large policeman, with blood dripping from his nose climbed out of the car. He was holding a familiar skinny boy with broad shoulders by the scruff of the neck; a boy who looked just like a puppy with huge paws who eventually might grow into the full size for his frame. He dragged him down the path and up to the front door.

'Does this little rat belong to you?' he said.

Hoagie was kicking and spitting like a cat, fighting with every inch of his scrawny body as the policeman held him aloft by the neck of his t-shirt.

'He's been arrested, Mrs Hoag,' said the policeman. For being drunk and disorderly. And he, er, he punched a police officer.' He coughed and swiped his hand under his bloody nose. 'But we also think he may have been using illegal substances.'

'Oh, I don't think he'd do that,' said Diane, knowing in her heart that he probably had. 'Did he have any drugs on him?'

'We can't find any drugs on his person, but he has some, what we call 'paraphernalia' on him. Unfortunately, it's happening a lot round here. However, we can release him to your care but you'll need to come back down to the station with me so I can do a bit of paperwork. Due to his age, you know.' The policeman looked around. 'Is there a Mr Hoag?'

'As far as I know, he is also in custody, said Diane, with pursed lips. 'Well, I'll just have to come and sort it out. But I'll have to get my younger son dressed as there's nobody to look after him.' Her mind raced about what sort of drugs. Heroin? What all them punks used. Heroin held terror of almost mythical proportions. In her mind, it was like a big, shapeless shadow that enveloped and sucked the life out of its victims like a vampire. Once you tried it you were forever in its claws, immediately addicted, your life in ruins.

'But mum! They are fuckin' picking on me because of my hair and my clothes!' said Hoagie indignantly. He was determined to give his side of the story.

'Shut up, Jamie,' she said. 'All right,' she said, turning to the policeman, 'we'll come with you and sort it out.'

At the station, whilst he sat alone with his mum and his brother was looked after by a policewoman with a bag of sweets, it all came out. He'd been out on the town with Toad and Toggie. Yes, they'd done a bit of gear, some mandies, and a whole lot of booze, but he left some of that bit out of the story to his mum, and she couldn't bring herself to ask. He admitted he was a bit pissed and then he recounted the whole story.

At the end of the night, he'd run out of money, so instead of taking the bus he decided to walk home. And that was when it went wrong. He had got halfway up the big hill, and nearly to his house, when a cop car drove up alongside him. They made him put his hands on the car and they searched him. Although he had nothing on him, and he'd committed no obvious crime, they decided they would take him down to the station and conduct a proper search and some questioning. After half an hour, he was released without charge.

So, he got nearly home again, halfway up the hill, and once again they picked him up, drove him back to the town centre for a repeat performance and then let him go, to walk all the way home again. He had miraculously kept his patience, although he may have used a bit of bad language. Who could blame him? Once again, he'd been released, and once again he'd begun the lonely and cold walk up the hill.

He had been aware of some pissed old bloke swaying along behind him and although he felt a bit unnerved, he'd kept his cool until the bloke sauntered up behind him and tapped him on the shoulder. Hoagie had swung round, ready to punch the bugger.

'What the fuck? Oh my God! Dad, it's you! What the fuck are you doing here?'

'They just let me out as well. Got yourself into a bit of trouble have yer?' said Bobby.

'Police brutality.' said Hoagie. 'I'm being picked on.'

'Not surprised, the way you look.'

'Shut the fuck up,' said Hoagie, defiantly. 'You can't talk! You've been in the nick for pinching a telly!'

'Well, I'm out,' said Bobby, 'And you can cut the swearing, or I'll box your ears.'

'You're pissed,' said Hoagie.

'So are you,' said his dad, 'and you're underage.' He paused. 'Look, I won't say anything. Here y'ar. Have a drink.' He passed over a bottle of vodka which he had concealed beneath his coat. 'Warm you up. You oughta put a coat on.'

Hoagie swigged it cautiously and they sat on a wall together, drinking vodka at some time midnight. They'd talked about a few things and then came the part of the story he left out when he told it to his mum. His dad had suggested they go 'on the rob' together with his mate, Trevor. Trevor could sell anything on, you see.

'But Dad, said Hoagie, 'they just let you off!'

'Oh, come on! It'll be great!' said his dad. 'Father and son enterprise. They *have* let me off, you're right. See how easy it is to beat the fuckers.'

No, Hoagie didn't mention that little episode to his mum, but he told her he'd met his dad going up the hill, and his dad had been sympathetic about him getting stopped. He told his mum they'd walked up the hill together. But what had actually happened is that they had continued to drink as they walked up the hill, plotting the robbery as they went. His dad didn't tell him where he was staying that night, and Hoagie hadn't really thought about asking.

But when they had parted company, he'd been nearly home, and it had happened again – the same smarmy policeman had picked him up. And this time he'd lost it and punched the bastard square in the middle of his smug grin. So then, of course, they'd had a reason to charge him with drunk and disorderly, and assault on a police officer. And they tried and tried to pin him down for drugs, but they just couldn't. He had to admit he'd used drugs before, 'for personal use' but he had nothing on him and it had been a few hours, so all they could really find was a urine sample that suggested opiates – 'yeah mate I'm on codeine and paracetamol for a bad tooth,' a piece of foil – 'yeah I was starvin' so I had a kit kat,' and a lighter and giant Rizlas – 'yeah, so? I smoke rollies, it's cheaper. And the big ones last longer.'

'Bastards!' agreed Hoagie's mum, although she wasn't entirely sympathetic towards her son. She would ask him about the drugs later. She definitely would. However, he was blood, and the police hadn't ever done anything much to help her or Bobby, although God knows Bobby didn't deserve much help. But she paid a fine and took Hoagie home. She did give him a bit of a slap, much as she'd had to do to Bobby Hoag over the years. She wasn't about to be frightened by these men of hers. And Bobby wasn't her problem now. Even she didn't ask where he was staying. She didn't want to know. Perhaps, she thought, she could turn Jamie around a bit now she had him to herself? Now her no good husband could no longer try to get him involved in his schemes to pinch stuff, which he'd been trying to do since Jamie could fucking walk.

But it wasn't over there. Two weeks later, Bobby Hoag came banging on the door at 2 am, holding a small tv set and shouting and carrying on until someone called the police for the disturbance and he was carted off screaming, 'But it's legit! I definitely got it from Radio Rentals this time!' and because of the disturbance, the neighbours called the police. And because of that, and the trouble with her eldest son, she had a visit from the bloody social services. She could have just told them to fuck off. But she thought that if she was polite, they might see it for what it was and leave her alone. However, it was difficult to hold her tongue in the face of the patronising questions, and it got her into a bit of a muddle. I mean, they stood there, smoking like chimneys in her living room, looking like old hippies in rags, asking all sorts of shit. Should she say she was on friendly terms with her soon-to-be ex-husband, or should she be strenuously denying his very existence? She lost her cool a bit. 'You should look at the home life of Thorin O'Rourke!' she'd told them, bitterly. Now there really is cause for concern there. I reckon they're all bloody in-breds!' It hadn't helped that at that moment James came home, accompanied by none other than Thorin O'Rourke and the gobshite he called Toad. It was bloody obvious they were all as high as kites and James Hoag was not about to keep his cool when he noticed what he considered to be nosey fuckers in his house. He got right up to them, right in the face of one of them, laughing manically. The upshot of this meeting was that, after Hoagie had lashed out and then thrown up on their shoes, her youngest son was removed from her care for three weeks until they were satisfied that home was a safe environment for him to be in. It was terrifying experience David would never forget, and one which certainly soured the brotherly bond.

In an attempt at re-constructing some sort of family life, when David was returned, Diane took her two boys on a trip to the boating lake, like she used to do when they were small. She watched from the bank as her two sons argued over who would row. Hoagie, as everyone now called him, a beanpole with spiky hair and a ripped t-shirt, on the cusp of manhood, had snatched the oar and was standing in the middle, using it like a punt pole, whilst the smaller and stockier David, still a smooth-skinned boy, tried to wrestle it off him. The other oar had somehow slipped into the water and floated just out of reach, threatening to sink and be lost to them. David gave up trying to get hold of the remaining oar and sat back down, defeated. The little boat simply spun in circles until Hoagie decided enough was enough.

'Don't do it!' shouted Diane, watching him begin to overbalance as he tried to reach out and grasp the sinking oar, but her voice dissipated on the wind. Hoagie tipped forward with one last lunge and then he toppled into the green water. He splashed around with the most enormous fuss and then he suddenly stood up holding the oar aloft, his grinning face draped with green, slimy weeds.

'Got it!' he yelled. The boat careered chaotically towards the shore, the boys didn't hit each other over the head with an oar, and for the first time in a while, Diane Hoag felt there might be a glimmer of hope on the horizon.

But the storm clouds were gathering.

They had all squeezed into Toad's bedroom for their first band practise. Toggie had drumsticks but no drums, so he was making do with Toad's chest of drawers for now. Jonesy had a guitar and Hoagie had one too. After a bit of a scuffle over who would be the singer, it was decided that Toad and Hoagie would share the job, but Hoagie needed to play the guitar because he knew some chords and Toad didn't. Hoagie had borrowed his brother's guitar and sat strumming it tunelessly.

'What should we call ourselves?' said Jonesy.

'The Addicts!' said Toad.

'Nah, mate! There's already a band with that name. From Ipswich,' said Hoagie.

'What about Needlepoint?' said Jonesy.

'What about fuck off that sounds like a fuckin' old lady's sewing group?' said Toggie.

'I thought it was all right,' said Hoagie. 'Like it *sounds* like sewing, but it's really about shooting up dope. Like it's *ironic*, innit?'

'Fuckin' *ironic,* my arse,' said Toggie.

'You don't even know what it means,' said Hoagie.

'Be fuckin' *ironic* when I punch you in the nose won't it?' said Toggie with a grin.

'I think that might just be a co-incidence,' said Jonesy.

Toggie looked as if he was about to jump on Jonesy, so Hoagie quickly said, 'shall we worry about the name later and play somefing?'

Jonesy started playing the opening riff to *Pretty Vacant.* Then he stopped.

'Why did yer stop?' said Hoagie.

'I only know that bit,' said Jonesy.

Toggie rolled his eyes.

'Why don't we make one up?' said Toad. 'I, er, I wrote some lyrics.'

Toggie sniggered. 'Can you ach-ley write?'

'Nah, let's hear it,' said Hoagie.

'All right,' said Toad, and brought out a torn scrap of paper.

'Is that Holly Hobbie paper?' said Hoagie.

'It's my little cousin's writing set paper,' said Toad. 'You can sniff it and it smells of fruit as well.'

'Less 'ave a sniff,' said Hoagie.

'And me,' said Jonesy.

They all stuck their noses on Toad's piece of paper.

'I can't smell nothin',' protested Jonesy.

'You fuckin' girl tossers,' said Toggie. 'Give that here!' He snatched the paper and began to read it out.

'Radio Rentals, Radio Rentals, I don't own nuffin, I'm goin' mental. Radio Rentals, Radio Rentals, my life's on hire, I'm goin' mental. I'm so bored, I'm so tired, there's nuffin to do when your life's on hire. All I want is a rent-free space to live my life and get off my face. Radio Rentals Radio Rentals…Fuck me this is a bit shit, innit?' He had a quick sniff of the paper and pulled a face. 'Apples, innit?'

'It's all right I think,' said Hoagie. 'We can do somefing with it.'

'Yeah, Fuckin' burn it,' said Toggie.

'Just 'cos you can't do it,' said Toad.

Jonesy started playing a riff. 'Radio Rentals, Radio Rentals,' he sang. 'Yeah, it could work.'

'Let's use some of our favourite songs and also put in some of our own,' said Hoagie.

'Try and learn more than three chords won't yer,' said Jonesy.

'Fuck off,' said Hoagie.

'Let's do some gear,' said Toggie. 'Are your parents definitely out, Toad?'

Once they were high, the band practice disintegrated, but a new plan was hatched.

'You know we said we'd go and see the Pistols?' said Toad, they *are* going to do Rotterdam. Next year sometime. Who's in?'

'Not me, mate,' said Jonesy. 'No money.'

'Nor me,' said Toggie, 'I owe Big Adam. Got this on tick and owe about three weeks.'

'Fuckin' hell. I wouldn't wanna be you. But I'm in,' said Hoagie. 'I can get a bit together.'

45

'Well, I have some *news,*' said Toad. 'I won an art competition, and I won money!'

'How?' said Hoagie. 'I didn't know you could draw?'

'I can,' said Toad. 'I saw this thing on the back of my sugar puffs pack. Look.' He pulled out a ripped piece of card. 'It was this – I filled in the form, but this was the rules.'

Hoagie looked at the card. 'Honey Monster art competition: wow us with your paintings and drawings and maybe you could win a £100 prize! What the fuck! Did you win a hundred quid?'

'Yeah, I did,' said Toad. 'I sent in that picture of Johnny Rotten singing that I drew in school. Mr Talbot said it was good and me mum kept it, so I sent it in, and I got first prize!'

'Oh my God! Yeah! I remember that one! Oh yeah, that *was* good,' said Hoagie. 'I actually thought you traced it.'

'Why didn't you tell us before now?' asked Toggie.

'Cos I thought you'd want me to spend it all on gear,' said Toad.

'Very honest,' said Hoagie. 'And we would, wouldn't we?'

'Yeah,' said Toad. But now, I can go and see the Pistols. And I can still get us some gear.'

'Fair enough,' said Toggie.

'I'll get some money from me mum and me brother,' said Hoagie. 'I know where they keep their savings books, and I can forge their signatures.'

When the building society called Diane Hoag because they spotted 'an anomaly' in the signatures, she knew immediately what had happened. Her son wasn't really bothering to hide his drink and drug use anymore. There had been quite a few incidents that she was already trying to forget.

Sliding the bolt across the outside of his bedroom door, she did feel a little guilty. He hammered on it and screamed at her – he hated her; he'd never forgive her; she was such a bitch. His stamina for protesting was impressive.

'Mum, you have to let him out!' whined David, too young to understand why his big brother was locked up as if he were a prisoner.

'It's for his own good, David,' said Diane. 'I'll unlock it to put food in for him and things. Better a prisoner here than Chelmsford nick. He'll eventually get tired of all the shouting.'

She was right. It did go quiet. But when she unbolted the door to give him some food, the room was empty. The window was flung wide open and in place of Hoagie on the bed was a piece of paper with a drawing of two fingers making the V sign.

By the time Hoagie and Toad boarded the ferry to Rotterdam to see the Sex Pistols gig, Hoagie was living in his own place, found for him by some do-gooder homeless youth charity, when he spun them a hard-luck story about how hard his home life had been and how he was sleeping on his friend's couch after his mum had told him to sling his hook. That last bit at least was true. It had taken a while, but she had finally had enough of him. Now he had a place where he and all his friends could do what they liked. Thank fuck for the do-gooders and thank fuck for the grim upstairs split-level room above the weed-tangled yard, with the bike and the trolley as permanent features.

'I might even rent a telly from Radio Rentals,' he said to Toad, who hooted with laughter.

'Nah, mate,' said Toad, 'just get your old man to nick one from Rumbelow's. Wherever he is.'

Jubilee (1977 - 1978)

God Save the Queen (The Sex Pistols)

 'You're sweating,' said Toad, as they stood in the line to go through customs and board the boat. 'Why are you sweating?'

'I'm not,' said Hoagie.

'You are, and it's not even hot in here.'

'Shut up,' said Hoagie, gritting his teeth.

Toad shut up for a minute. But it was very noticeable that Hoagie was beginning to sweat even more as they approached the front of the line. He pointed it out again.

'You are sweating. You look like you're up to somefing. Are you?'

'Am I what?'

'Up to somefing?'

Hoagie got hold of Toad by the arm.

'Listen you twat,' he said, 'Shut the fuck up and I'll tell you when we're on board. Just look normal. All right?'

He noticed the officials begin to give him some odd looks. Shit, that was all he needed, to be on their radar.

'Nerves,' he said, indicating Toad with a sideways nod and rolling his eyes. 'He doesn't like the water. I'm doin' some deep breathin' exercises with him and steadyin' him, like.' He grinned at them.

Toad made some elaborate fanning motions with his hands. 'Yeah. Dizzy,' he said. 'It's like a fear of flying, only with boats.' Hoagie kicked him in the shin.

They got through the customs and their bags were left undisturbed, so they both made their way on board the boat to the Hook of Holland. This was it. They were off to see the Pistols in Rotterdam.

'And you know what?' said Hoagie, 'We can go over to Amsterdam by train while we're here. Make the most of it.'

They headed for the bar area. After they had sunk a pint of lager each, Hoagie visibly relaxed.

'You've stopped sweatin' now,' said Toad.

'Yeah mate, thanks for pointing it out,'

'So, what was the problem?'

'I've got Valium in me sock,' said Hoagie.

'Shit!' said Toad, looking round instinctively to see if anyone heard. 'Shit! We might have got pulled over!'

'What, when we were boarding a boat? For Valium?' said Hoagie. 'Don't be soft. Might have got it taken away though. But we didn't, so we can enjoy our trip over.'

'Better make sure we use the lot before we land,' said Toad.

'Dock,' corrected Hoagie. 'But I can put it into me bag and they won't look. After all, it's Holland.'

'Where'd you get it?' said Toad.

'It's prescription,' said Hoagie.

'Who is it prescribed to?'

'It's me mum's.'

'Oh yeah, my mum has that,' said Toad.

'I think all mums do,' said Hoagie. 'I'll get us another beer.' He ordered two more lagers. 'It's Dutch lager,' he said, 'tastes like cat's piss.'

'Oh no, it is not piss,' said a voice from behind them. 'It is your first time to the Netherlands, is it?'

Hoagie turned to face a very tall, lean-faced blond man with a beard. 'Yeah, it is,' he said, 'so what?'

'You try to look hard,' said the Dutch man, 'but I think you are very innocent.'

'Fuck off, who asked you?' said Hoagie.

'I don't mean this as an insult,' replied the man, 'and I like your punk hair. It's very cool. I am Martijn.' It sounded like 'Mar – tan' to Hoagie, the way he said it, and when he extended his hand, Hoagie took it very tentatively.

'Look,' said Martijn, and he lifted up his tank top to reveal a Pistols 'Never Mind the Bollocks' t-shirt.

'Bloody hell, mate,' said Toad, 'I thought you was gonna flash at us!'

'What?' said Martijn.

'Never mind him, Mart…Mart… Martin,' said Hoagie.

'Just call me Marty,' said Marty. 'The vowels are difficult for the English to pronounce.'

'You going to see the Pistols?' said Hoagie.

'I am going home,' said Marty, 'but yes, we are going to see them in Rotterdam. Why don't you come and sit with my friends and me,' he indicted a small, shiny table, where a group of young people were sipping from small shot glasses. They gave a small wave at Hoagie and Toad.

'It's Jenever,' explained Marty, 'It's like a type of Gin.'

'I don't like Gin,' said Toad.

'I think you'll like it if you like strong alcohol,' said Marty, 'it's a proper drink, you might say.'

'Wass it called again?' said Hoagie.

'Jenever,' said Marty.

'Well, you lot'd be all right at the Pistols gig,' sniggered Hoagie, 'gobbing every time you speak.'

'I like your humour,' said Marty. 'Call it Geneever.'

'Why do you fuckers all speak good English?' said Toad, when they were sat at the table.

'We learn it as soon as we start school,' said one of Marty's friends.

'We don't even learn proper English at school,' said Hoagie. 'And this is fuckin' good stuff.' He downed his second one.

'You might want to go easy,' said Marty. 'It's very strong.'

'Well, I reckon we ought to put our stuff in our cabin while we can still see,' said Hoagie. 'Come on Toad.'

'Why are you called Toad?' said one of the girls.

'Seriously?' said Hoagie. 'Come on, Toad, obviously this shit impairs yer vision if she can't see why you're called Toad.' They headed for the stairs. 'Catch yer later,' he said.

'There's a disco later,' said Toad as they headed down to the cabins.

'Yeah…' said Hoagie distractedly, '22, 23,24, ah, here it is.' He put the key in the lock and they burst through the door.

'Bags the top bunk,' said Toad.

'Christ! Prisoners get more space in a cell!' said Hoagie.

'Better get used to it, 'cos that's where you'll be,' said Toad.

'Fuck off!' said Hoagie. 'You, you mean – you'll be a prison bitch.'

'Wanker,' said Toad and clipped him across the back of the head. Hoagie returned the blow and they scuffled for a minute, like kids.

'Let's go back to the bar,' said Hoagie.

'Just a minute, 'I'm hanging me stuff up!'

'What the fuck? Where?' said Hoagie, 'and since when did you hang stuff up? Come on! Last one back to the bar is a wanker who has to buy me a drink!

'Eh?' said Toad, but Hoagie was already gone.

The disco was now in full swing. Some fellow passengers, mostly English, were drunk and jumping around on the small dancefloor, and others hung around the bar, or at the tiny tables. Some glared in disapproval at Toad and Hoagie as they bounded noisily in, but no-one refused to serve them more lager.

'Is it me, or is the water gettin' higher?' said Toad, 'like we're goin' up and down a lot more?'

'It's a bit stormy out there,' said Hoagie.

'I feel a bit sick,' said Toad, and just as he said it a young girl with orange hair shoved past them in a hurry and was promptly sick in a bin.

Toad turned a shade of pale green.

'Get outside on the deck,' ordered Hoagie.

'You said it was stormy!' protested Toad. 'I might fall over the side! The wind might blow me and…'

'I think we oughta go back to the cabin and lay down then,' said Hoagie.

'Hoagie!' shouted a familiar Dutch voice. 'Drink?'

Hoagie looked at Toad, whose face was still tinged with green.

'Aw, come on,' said Hoagie, 'It'd make us feel better! It's like hair of the dog I reckon.'

They went over to the table.

'Not many left are there?' said Marty, 'All dropping like flies! Last man standing, I think. Cheers!' He held his shot glass aloft and then handed one to Hoagie.

'Cheers!' said Hoagie. 'What do you say in your language?'

'Proost!' said Marty.

'Sounds German!' said Hoagie.

'Swine Hund!' said Toad in a ridiculous accent.

'We are Dutch, not German,' said Marty.

'Sounds all the fuckin' same,' said Hoagie. 'Prost mate,' he said as he knocked it back. 'I'm the son of the son of a sailor's son, me!' he said with a swagger. But almost immediately the nausea swept over him like a tidal wave. 'Oh. Fuck,' he declared. And, leaving Toad to just stand there, he bolted for the toilet. Toad looked awkward, shifting from foot to foot in silence.

'He cannot handle it,' said Marty. 'Look at the horizon now! It has disappeared!'

Toad glanced queasily at the horizon as the boat seemed to rise up, and then plummet. He clutched his stomach and tried to swallow the bile that was also now rising up, but it was too late. He threw up right in Marty's grinning face.

'Oh shit!' he said, "I am so sorry,' and, with his guts gurgling, he too vacated the bar swiftly and headed for the cabin, where he suspected Hoagie might have retreated to.

Burnt Lungs and Bitter Sweets

Having forgotten the room number, he banged on every door on the way until he heard Hoagie's muffled voice from within. 'I'm fuckin' in 'ere. 25! It's not locked.'

The sight that greeted Toad was not a pleasant one. It was Hoagie's arse in the air, as he was bent double over the cabin toilet heaving into the bowl. And just as suddenly, he switched to take a seat on the throne and proceeded to evacuate the contents of his bowels from the other end.

'Hurry the fuck up!' said Toad, as he heaved into the upright ashtray.

'I can't! Ahh it's like fuckin' food poisoning,' moaned Hoagie, 'It's literally brown rain!'

'Ohh,' groaned Toad. They swapped over positions. It continued like that for a while.

'Will it ever end?' whined Toad.

'Dunno,' said Hoagie. 'Shall we have a smoke and see if it helps?'

'Anything,' said Toad.

They lit up. 'It doesn't help,' said Toad, and flew into the tiny toilet, falling over Hoagie's feet and again not bothering to close the door.

'Why don't you go down into the lower decks. I've heard that you feel better if you go down into the bowels of the boat,' said Hoagie.

'Don't say fuckin' bowels!' moaned Toad and was sick again. 'He stripped off his trousers.

'Have you shit your pants?' said Hoagie.

'No!' said Toad, 'They just feel too tight. Fuck this. We need two toilets!'

'Go down to the bottom of the boat,' said Hoagie, taking Toad's place and shouting over his shoulder in between retching. 'Nother bog down there.' He retched again.

'All right!' shouted Toad. 'Don't lock it!' he called as he left.

An hour later, the storm seemed to have calmed down, and with it the all-consuming nausea. Hoagie, on his knees with his backside still sticking out of the cubicle was exhausted. To be honest, he'd forgotten about Toad and his whereabouts; all he really cared about now was getting some sleep. Still in his sweat-soaked clothes, he crawled towards the bunk beds and heaved his weary body up onto the top buck where he passed out completely and started snoring.

He was awoken by a commotion outside the cabin and frantic banging on the door. He sat up and banged his head on the ceiling.

'Fucking let me in, you arsehole!' shouted a voice.

Hoagie was confused, and then he realised: he had locked the cabin door. He looked at his little alarm clock – 5 am, declared the red neon numbers! He swung himself down from the top bunk and went to let Toad in.

'You fuck!' said Toad. 'I was out there in me pants! This old lady just hit me! Why did you lock it?'

'I don't remember lockin' it!' protested Hoagie. 'I've had a lovely sleep. See! I bet I was right about the bowels of the boat. Bet you felt better straight away.'

'Not fuckin' really!' shouted Toad. 'I've sat in the corridor in me pants all night. I did bang, but I couldn't make you hear, and then this old lady came out and told me to shut up or she'd hammer on my head, and then I must have conked out, cos the

56

next thing you know, she was next to me saying it's disgusting, and she hit me with her bag or somefing!'

'Oh, I thought I dreamed about some banging noise,' said Hoagie. In me dream, someone was killin' a spider with a shoe.'

'You fucker!' said Toad. 'Next time YOU can go to the bowels of the fuckin' boat.'

'Well, we have to get off the boat in about an hour, and it stinks in here, don't it?' said Hoagie. Let's get our stuff and go to the bar again.'

'Wait,' said Toad, 'have you got any painkillers? My head is banging.'

'I've got that Valium,' said Hoagie. 'I don't really want to take it through customs the other end either. Shall we just take it?'

'Jesus, how much have you got?'

'Only four,' said Hoagie. 'Three for me and one for you!'

'Fuck's sake,' said Toad. 'I just need some paracetamol.' But he didn't fancy going through the customs check with the knowledge that there was still Valium in Hoagie's sock, even if they were pretty relaxed in Holland. 'Oh, go on then,' he said, 'p'raps it'll sort me head out.'

They were wild-eyed by the time they got on the train to Rotterdam from the Hook of Holland, but they fell asleep until the announcement said something in Dutch.

'What did he say?' said Toad. 'Deja what? All that fuckin' gobbing and growling!'

The traveller seated behind them leaned forward. 'He said it is the end of the line for this train,' he told them. 'This is Rotterdam.'

'Looks like the arse end of nowhere,' Hoagie said when they arrived in the city centre. However, they managed to get to the youth hostel they had planned to book into without incident, following the street map Hoagie had pinched from the newsstand at the station. It wasn't too far to walk. They only had a small rucksack each and Hoagie said they ought to take it with them rather than leave it. Neither of them liked the look of the hostel much.

'Why don't we go to the gig and then get a train to Amsterdam tonight,' said Hoagie. What's the worst that can happen? We have to sleep on a park bench or something? There's some sort of B and B I looked at in the travel brochure thing and it looks better than this dump.'

'Will there be a train?'

'Yeah, they run quite late, and anyway the gig finishes by 11,' said Hoagie. 'If we get on the train, we can head over to Amsterdam earlier than we planned and the city is open all night there. We can hole up in one of them dope cafes and get stoned.'

'We could just go tomorrow, 'said Toad, 'like we said.'

'Maybe,' said Hoagie, but I reckon we'd get somewhere better in Amsterdam and it's more fun I reckon. And we'd get longer there, 'cos we won't be there in the late night otherwise – we'll have to catch the train back to get on that pissin' boat again.'

'Let's just get to the gig and see,' said Toad. 'It's fucking cold, I know that.'

'Yeah – that temperature thing on the clock says it's minus 9 or something. I think that is pretty cold.'

The venue was fairly close and by now it was time to go for a drink and head on over. Hoagie and Toad spotted a few other people looking exactly like them, so they followed in that general direction, stopping off to get tanked up in a tiny bar first.

'Is this it?' said Toad, 'It looks like a right dive.'

'Brilliant!' said Hoagie. 'Eksit. Oh yeah! Eksit – Exit – I get it. Small innit?'

'Be packed then,' said Toad.

There was a lot of pushing, shoving and spitting already as they squeezed in, packed tightly like sardines in a can. The bar was already in full flow and Toad and Hoagie headed that way, clutching a fistful of guilders. If there was going to be fighting and shoving, it was better to be pissed and then they wouldn't feel it. They had been drug searched on the way in, although not very thoroughly. Hoagie and Toad had nothing on them, but there was plenty of opportunity to buy inside the club. Toad bought speed, although he had no idea if he'd been ripped off or not, and they were getting revved up for the gig, giving the support act hell, when some skinny punk covered in blood, with spiky black hair, bumped into Hoagie, who told him to, 'Watch it you fucker!'

The kid turned to face him. He had a face like a rat: narrow, with tiny eyes. 'You what?' he said.

Hoagie pulled himself up to his full height and squared off his broad shoulders, which belied the rest of his very skinny body. He gave the punk, who was uncannily similar to him to look at, his most menacing stare; his bravado helped by the fact that he was quite high.

'I said watch it, fucker,' he said. Emphasis on that last word.

Without thinking, the punk kid threw his pint straight in Hoagie's face and then he smashed the glass and brandished it at Hoagie. Toad was trying desperately to get Hoagie's attention, as if he had something very important to say, but Hoagie brushed him aside. He jumped up and head-butted the kid right in the face. Blood streamed out of the kid's nose and from Hoagie's forehead, though he could hardly feel a thing. There was a small crowd forming around them. Then just as suddenly, the spotty, geeky kid chucked the glass down and gave a manic cackle, lunging forward at Hoagie.

'You fuckin' tosser,' said Hoagie. 'Want some more?'

The punk kid suddenly pulled out a knife, and Toad gasped, trying to pull Hoagie away but the kid drew the knife slowly and deliberately cross his own chest, drawing blood. Then he turned and headed off into the crowd, cackling like a crazy man.

'Who was that stupid tosser?' said Hoagie.

'That's what I was trying to tell you,' said Toad. He pointed to the stage. The tosser was on it, holding a guitar. 'That's only bloody Sid Vicious!'

'What? That wanker? Where's Glen Matlock?' said Hoagie.

'His gone innee? Sid Vicious! Right here! And you headbutted him and called him a tosser – and lived!'

'Well, I'm a bigger tosser, int I?' said Hoagie. 'Or something like that anyway.'

They surged with the crowd, who pogoed and spat as was the tradition. But as the gig was coming to a close, Toad said it might be a good idea to get out before Vicious came back off the stage and nutted Hoagie back – or worse.'

'Yeah,' said Hoagie, who was drenched in blood and sweat, with wild eyes. 'Also, we can get the train to Amsterdam and carry on with the party.'

So, they made a run for it, caught the train and arrived in the middle of the night at Amsterdam Central Station, where the party did indeed seem to be continuing.

'Where's the party at?' Hoagie asked a random stranger.

'English?' said the stranger, and Hoagie nodded. 'Turn left and you will soon find everything you need.'

'Thanks mate,' said Hoagie and he and Toad headed for the core of the red-light district.

'Jesus fuckin' God!' swore Toad. 'Look at that! I mean, I've read about it, but when you see it with your own eyes!'

'Not that pretty, are they?' said Hoagie.

'Who cares?' said Toad. 'I'm not lookin' at their faces!' His eyes bulged even wider than usual.

The neon lights blazed, and the women mouthed kisses and beckoned them from every window. They had the faint twinkle in their eyes, like they were amused by the small skinny boys with the spiky punk hair.

'You want to go in? You want business?' said a big bloke with a moustache.

'Nah, mate,' said Toad.

'I will if you will,' said Hoagie.

'Nah, we might catch somefing,' said Toad. 'Might get killed by that big one and her pimp as well. Look at then fuckin thighs!'

'There's a bar over the road, other side of the church,' said Hoagie. Let's go in there out of the way.'

'Or a coffee shop,' suggested Toad.

'I don't want a fuckin' coffee,' said Hoagie.

'They call 'em coffee shops, but they sell dope,' Toad reminded him.

'Oh! Oh yeah! That's different,' said Hoagie. 'Yeah, let's try that one.'

They ate hash brownies and smoked some joints in a little café called Mellow Yellow.

'What happened to him?' a woman asked, pointing to Hoagie.

'Oh,' said Toad, 'he nutted Sid Vicious.'

'Yeah, right,' said the woman.

'No, he did,' protested Toad, 'called him a tosser too.'

The woman looked disinterested.

'Is there somewhere to stay near here?' asked Hoagie, 'like a hostel or B and B? Cheap, like. Or maybe free…'

The woman laughed. 'There is a bench in the park,' she said, 'It is always free.' But then she pointed towards the door. 'Alternatively, go back to the station, then keep walking straight on. You need to get to Rembrandts Plein,' she said. 'You'll find something around there I am certain.'

The cold hit them as soon as they stepped outside, and the wind cut through them. They stood shivering, contemplating how far it was and how you used the trams. People carried long strips of card that looked like tickets, but where did they get them? Then, they had the same idea together as their eyes alighted on the bike leaned up against the posts. It was unchained. Without thinking, they hopped on – Toad peddling and Hoagie up front on the handlebars, giving directions. They swerved chaotically through the streets.

'Watch out!' shouted Hoagie.

'What for?' shouted Toad.

'Stop!' yelled Hoagie, 'The canal!' But it was too late. Toad slammed on the brakes and Hoagie went flying.

The bicycle crashed to a halt and Toad fell crumpled to the pavement. He hauled himself up, hearing yells from Hoagie. 'Where are you?' he yelled.

'I'm here!' Toad looked down and there was Hoagie, flailing around in the water.

'What the fuck are you doing down there?' said Toad.

'Taking a fuckin' bath, what do you think? Just get me fuckin' out,' said Hoagie.

Toad extended his arm and Hoagie gave it a jerk, nearly pulling Toad in with him. "Serves you right if you fell in,' he said, but he let Toad pull him up.

'Are you all right?' said a passer-by.

'Yeah. Had a bit too much to drink,' said Hoagie.

'Hey,' said the passer-by suddenly, 'hey, that's my bike! Hey Bram! My bike!' Then he shouted a lot of things in Dutch, and a huge young man, who stood almost 7 ft tall appeared beside him.

'Fuckin' run!' shouted Hoagie.

'Have we lost them?' cried Toad, as they stopped to catch their breath.

'For now, but I think we oughta duck inside somewhere,' said Hoagie.

'Here?' said Toad.

'Jubilee,' read Hoagie, 'Tattoo Parlour. Really?'

'I will if you will,' said Toad.

Inside the tattoo shop it was dark and the walls were black. If you can imagine every stereotype of a tattoo parlour you have ever seen or thought of, this was it. After some careful deliberation it was decided that Hoagie should pick a tattoo for Toad and Toad choose one for Hoagie. Being sober would have helped them make rational decisions when deciding on permanently inking a part of their body, but unfortunately, they were not sober.

Hoagie decreed that Toad should have an axe on his left arm. The tattooist made a start.

'Where do you want yours?' said Toad.

'On my arse!' slurred Hoagie from the table, and then he seemed to nod out, almost falling asleep on the spot.

'Well, what does he want?' said the other tattooist to Toad while he was being inked. Toad beckoned her close and whispered something in her ear. She giggled.

'Are you sure?'

'It's fine!' slurred Toad. 'It's on his arse anyway, whose gonna see it?'

'Ok,' she said.

'Fuckin' hell that hurts!' said Toad, 'I'm glad we had plenty of stuff for an anaesthetic earlier.'

When the tattoos were done, they paid up the last of the money and realised they had none left to pay for somewhere to stay now.

'It's getting light soon,' said Hoagie, who was still lying on his front. 'We might as well head for the station and catch the train to get the boat. Good job we kept our bags and the tickets on us. We can kip at the boat port or whatever it is. How's my tattoo looking anyway?'

Toad peered at Hoagie's backside. 'Oh. Oh shit,' he said.

'What?' said Hoagie.

'Oh, nothing. Er, looks a bit sore, that's all.'

Toad went over to speak to the tattooist. 'It's the wrong way up!' he said. 'I mean, the arrow – it's pointing the wrong way!'

'Well, I can't do anything about it now, can I?' she said. 'Best not tell him.'

'Yeah,' said Toad, 'How often do you see your own arse anyway?'

The boat trip back was uneventful, as the two of them slept in the bar most of the way, using their rucksacks as pillows. But when they came through the baggage hall, Hoagie was surprised to see his mum and his brother waiting to greet them. Their faces both looked serious and drawn.

'What the hell are you doing here?' he said.

'It's dad,' said David.

'What about him,' said Hoagie, 'No-one has heard from him in ages.'

'He's dead,' said Hoagie's mum.

They didn't go to any funeral – Hoagie's mum said he'd moved in with some woman and left town. She only heard about it from her hairdresser – after the funeral. Apparently, he'd died of a heart attack. Pff! Just like that. It was all just really weird, and Hoagie pushed it to the back of his mind, reasoning he hadn't seen his dad for ages anyway. His mum wouldn't let him stay with her, on account of David being in the house, who might get hooked on drugs by some sort of osmosis. Hoagie sat around with his friends getting stoned on anything he could get his hands on, often staring at the walls of his flat as the seasons changed.

He'd barely noticed when Christmas had come around again, and he had little to show for the time that had passed, except perhaps for a few more scars on his lungs and a bit more ink on his body. The carol-singers had started up; he had no money to give them and no money for any more trips away with Toad and anyway, any money they ever got their hands on was always blown out in a halo of smoke or swallowed in liquid or pill form. He barely saw his family and every grey day sort of blended into the next one, with some highs and lows here and there. They all consumed more Heroin than ever, but he had not succumbed to the needle yet; he didn't intend to, but perhaps it would inevitably happen one of these days. When they went out during the daylight hours, it was usually for 'shopping', either for drugs, or the sort of shopping where you didn't use money. Quite often, Hoagie went shopping because it was the only highlight of an otherwise dull day. There were quite a few new shops springing up in town though – he thought he'd have to check out that new department store one of these days. What was it called? Debenhams. You never know, he might find something interesting there.

Lines and Lanes (1978)

The Sound of the Suburbs (The Members)

 'Do you know what?' Hoagie suddenly piped up as he leaned back in the saggy yellow sofa, 'People are fuckin' weird.'

'I agree,' said Kecks.

'You always fuckin' agree with him,' said Toggie, 'can't you have an opinion of your own?'

'Fuck's sake, Toggie!' said Hoagie.

'Yeah,' said Toad. 'Leave Kecks alone.' Although secretly Toad agreed. And disagreeing with Toggie was always a slightly dangerous thing to do. Toad shifted a few imperceptible centimetres away from Toggie. You never knew if he would turn. But he also knew that Hoagie would appreciate him standing up for his girlfriend, so he was on relatively safe ground.

'We appear,' said Jonesy, 'to have reached an agreement stroke disagreement impasse.'

'Look,' said Hoagie, who had his hand protectively on Kecks' thigh now as she slouched beside him, 'isn't anyone actually gonna ask why I think people are weird?'

'Maybe we don't ach-ue-ly fuckin' care?' said Toggie.

'I do,' said Toad.

'All right,' Toggie gave a deeply dramatic sigh and then poked his fist in the shape of an invisible microphone into Hoagie's face. 'Why do you think people are weird, Hoagie?'

'I was in the swimming pool the other day, right,' began Hoagie.

'What the fuck? Why?' said Toggie.

The others rounded on Toggie and pelted him with cushions. 'Shut the fuck up and listen!' shouted Toad and Jonesy together.

'Mind my face!' protested Kecks, but they were now all looking expectantly at Hoagie.

'So right,' he went on, 'there's two of us in one lane – '

'Aye, aye,' winked Toad.

Hoagie gave him the arched eyebrow. 'As I was saying, before I was so rudely interrupted several times, there's two of us in one lane, and I am a bit faster than the other bloke, so I says, how about you take the left-hand side and I go on the right, then I can overtake if need be? Reasonable, yes?'

'Makes sense,' said Kecks.

'And I don't exactly take up much room, do I?' said Hoagie, now warming to his theme.

'Skinny as a rat,' agreed Kecks.

'So, right, this fuckin' old tosser goes, No, you have to swim in a circle. It says it there on the sign. Clockwise in a circle. Up one side and down the other. It's very clear. I couldn't believe it! So, I says, Yeah, but there's only two of us, mate, and I'm skinny and you're…sorta slim as well, and I won't bash into yer, but we can go at our own pace. Anyways I'm getting' out in a minute. But he says no, then he proceeds to get right in the middle of the lane and wherever I try to go to get past he swerves over the other way to block me. What a twat! But why? I mean, I smiled. I wasn't rude. If there'd been, like, four people in the lane, then it makes sense, but just two skinny blokes going up and down? What the fuck? People are weird. Isn't just me, is it?'

'Nah, mate,' said Toad. 'It isn't just you.'

'Thought not,' said Hoagie, as he shoved his face down towards the glass coffee table; the remains of his line disappeared up his nose. 'Tha's better,' he said. 'And since you asked, Toggie, I was at the swimming pool because I like swimming. Good for yer, innit?' He rubbed his nose and sniffed.

'I'm bored,' said Jonesy suddenly. 'Shall we go into town?'

'Can't be arsed,' said Toad.

'Oh, go on!' said Kecks, 'We can go in your car can't we, Jonesy? I'm fed up too. All anyone cares about is the bloody football right now.'

'But why go out?' said Hoagie. 'There's nothing in town that we haven't already got here.'

Kecks put on her bleeding-heart expression. She somehow made her eyes look huge in her delicate face. Like Hoagie, she was as slim as a whippet, and since she'd been with Hoagie, she had somehow diminished further. Maybe she was taking too much stuff, thought Toad, feeling momentarily sorry for her. Hoagie had picked her up in Debenhams when she was messing around with make-up. She's just a kid really, he thought to himself. About 15 when he met her, and they had been inseparable since. Hoagie wasn't much older himself, but he seemed years older than Kecks. Hoagie seemed to really like her, which annoyed Toad for some reason, but you could never really tell with Hoagie. However, Toad knew that they didn't have any food in the house and that would be the deciding factor for Hoagie.

He was right.

'I am fuckin' starvin' though,' said Hoagie. Toad chalked up an inner victory, knowing where this was heading. 'I want a chicken sandwich. Have we got a chicken sandwich?'

'Go and look, you lazy cunt,' said Toggie.

'Oi, this is my place,' said Hoagie, 'fuck off getting so arsey!'

'So, get up and look if there's anything in YOUR fridge,' said Toggie.

'Kecks, go and look and see if there's any bread. And chicken,' said Hoagie.

Kecks got up. 'There are 3 slices of bread; all green,' she shouted. There's something that looks like chicken in the fridge, but I'm not sure if it's ok.'

'Right. That settles it. We're goin' out,' said Hoagie. 'Fire up the escort, Jonesy!'

Toad was amused. Kecks had got what she wanted, but Hoagie had managed not to lose face. Out of all of them, despite Toggie's psychotic menace, Hoagie was the leader. He was nicer than Toggie, who might knock your teeth out at any given moment, and he only resorted to violence when it was absolutely necessary and fair. Hoagie could take out Toggie any time. Toggie was bigger, but the bigger you are the harder you fall, they say. Make no mistake, though, Toggie was really nasty. One day, thought Toad, he'd end up inside for murder or at least GBH. And probably over a bloody Marathon or spilled pint. No, Hoagie was nicer. Unprincipled, but nicer. Jonesy, well. Toad didn't always know why Jonesy was there. He didn't say much, though he never seemed afraid of anything, but with Jonesy you sort of knew where it was going to end. He'd just grow up. Still, he had a car.

Himself? Who knew. Toad didn't really know who he was or where he was going. But right now, he liked life. He lived at home rent-free (although that would change soon, he knew it). He got to hang out with all his friends, and they could get high whenever they liked on whatever they liked. But he wasn't an addict, and neither was Hoags. Toggie could take it or leave it too, and as for Jonesy, he drank like a fish and smoked a bit. That was all. Toad wasn't so sure about Kecks, though. She looked fuckin' ill these days. He'd mentioned it to Hoagie just the other day.

'Your girlfriend looks ill,' he'd said.

'She's naturally pale,' said Hoagie. 'And she likes that black shit round her eyes.'

'She using?' asked Toad.

'Well, yeah. Duh!'

'Yeah, but I mean, like properly into it, like bangin' up?'

'Nah, don't think so.'

'Ok,' said Toad. And that was the end of that.

All five of them piled into Jonesy's clapped-out escort. You could always hear it coming from a mile away because of the blown exhaust. Rusty doors creaked as they slammed shut. No seatbelts in the back, not in those days, but Hoagie, who was in the front without question was told to belt up, which caused hysterical giggles from the three in the seat behind.

'You're squashing me, Toggie,' complained Kecks.

'Sorry, Kecks,' said Toggie, unusually chivalrous. That's the thing. You never knew where you were with Toggie. 'I'll move up, shall I?' Then: 'I could crawl up Toad's arse if you like?'

'I wouldn't do that if I was you,' said Hoagie, from the passenger seat.

Jonesy fired up the engine and they skidded uncertainly away.

'Jesus, Jonesy!' shouted Toad. 'Have you passed your test, mate?'

'Yeah! I had three lessons and passed first time,' Jonesy was indignant.

'Shows,' commented Kecks.

'Try not to kill me,' said Hoagie. "I am, after all, in the danger seat.'

'Clunk-Click,' said Toad. 'Put a seatbelt on every time you take a TRIP.'

'Haven't heard that one before,' snorted Toggie.

'Where we going?' said Toad.

'Food,' said Hoagie. 'There's one of them new big superstores outside town. Solar or something. Less go there.'

'I've been there with my mum,' said Kecks, 'and it's like a giant warehouse. It's got loads in it. You have to load up your trolley like normal, but it's massive. Not just food, like – everything!'

'I'm already loaded up,' said Toad.

'Fuck's sake,' said Hoagie.

The car shot along the suburban streets and Jonesy took a left toward the store. 'Which lane am I supposed to be in?' he said, his voice taking on a slightly higher pitch.

'Dunno,' said Hoagie. 'NO! Dammit! LEFT! Shit! SHIT!'

In the mirror, a blue light began to flash.

'I'll speak to 'em,' offered Toad.

'No way!' said Kecks. 'I'll speak to them.'

'Show 'em your tits,' said Toggie.

'Fuck off, Toggie,' said everyone.

Jonesy pulled over and wound down the window. At least Jonesy didn't have hair that was too stupid, thought Toad. He was more Steve Brookes than Sid Vicious.

'Good afternoon, sir,' said the cop.

'Afternoon,' said Jonesy. 'Sorry, was I speeding? My speedo is a bit dodgy.'

'No sir, but you changed lanes and cut me up. And you went through the lights on amber. I've got a prisoner in the back of my van, and you nearly gave him a heart attack.'

'Doesn't amber mean get ready and go,' said Jonesy, 'like in the races?'

'No, sir,' said the policeman, 'it means stop.'

'Oliver Castle!' said Hoagie.

'Sorry, sir?' said the policeman.

'Oli! You were at our school! Done well for yourself, in't yer mate?'

'Er, James Hoag?'

'The one and only!'

The young officer looked at Hoagie. He looked at Hoagie's friends in the back. 'Well, yes, hello James,' he said. 'Aren't you Thorin O'Rourke?' he asked Toggie.

'Might be,' said Toggie.

'Yes, he is!' said Hoagie. 'Year above.'

'Well, well,' said Oliver Castle. 'Yes, I think I have heard your name about, Thorin, now I come to think about it.'

Toggie sank down a little lower in the seat but retained a belligerent stare.

'Hey, Oli, I mean Officer,' said Hoagie, 'remember when we was kids and we raided the post office. Ha! Bet you never thought you'd be a copper then? Mind you, you made us take all the sweets back. See, I've got a photographic memory, me. I remember everything from school.'

PC Castle looked a shade paler. 'Well, it wasn't really that long ago, was it?'

'Nah mate, I mean way back,' said Hoagie. 'You used to come round my house!'

PC Castle turned his attention back to Jonesy. 'I would ask you to step out of the vehicle, sir, but it's a fairly busy road. If you'd just show me your licence, please.'

Luckily, Jonesy had it with him and passed it through the window. PC Castle inspected it closely.

'I got lost,' said Jonesy. 'We are trying to get to Solar to get some shopping, and this lot in the back keep shouting at me go this way, go that way! I got a bit confused with all the instructions and I got in the wrong lane. I'm ever so sorry.'

The officer handed back the licence. 'Today, I am just going to give you a warning. Be more careful and always plan your route before you go out anywhere. Ok then,' he shot a parting look at Hoagie and then a sideways glance at Toggie, who glared back, 'Mind how you go.'

'Thank you so much, Officer Oliver!' said Jonsey.

They kept what might pass for straight faces until the officer had departed, then they cracked.

'It's Charly the cat! It's bloody Charly!' said Hoagie. 'Always plan your route before you go somewhere! Always tell your mummy before you go off somewhere!' miaow, miaow, miaow!' He did a passable impression of the safety advertisement.

'Mind how yer go,' said Toad.

'Shut up!' said Jonsey. 'Let's get to that shop now before another one comes along.'

The new store was huge. 'Told you,' said Kecks, 'this is the future.'

'It's all in straight lines,' said Hoagie. 'Bit bright though. And everything is beeping all the time.'

'Wait 'til you see the booze bit,' said Kecks.

The alcohol lanes were impressive, but at the moment they had chains over them.

'Must be too early to sell it,' said Hoagie.

'Like that's gonna bother me,' said Toggie. He had already put a hat on when they exited the car, and now he pulled it down low over his brow and reached in to grab a couple of bottles.'

'We came here to get grub,' said Hoagie, who was beginning to sweat with hunger.

Toggie had put the bottles in his coat.

'What if there's cameras?' whispered Kecks.

'Hence the hat,' said Toggie. 'And I can run.'

'They aren't installed yet,' noted Toad. 'It's too new, look.' He pointed at the security cameras above. 'Wires and stuff. These ones are dummies.'

'Fine,' said Hoagie. 'But let's just get the food and piss off. I am starvin' and soon I am going to kill someone and eat them. Split up and grab what you can and put some in the trolley – without drawing attention to ourselves – and go to the till and pay for those bits. And no-one is allowed to ride in the trolley in this shop.'

Toad, who had already hopped into the baby-seat area of the trolley, hopped out again.

They went round together, putting the bare minimum, like bacon and coke into the trolley, and stuffing whatever else would fit into their coats and trousers.

'Fuck. Where's Kecks?' said Hoagie when they got to the till queue.

'I reckon she's looking at clothes,' said Toad. 'I'll find her.'

'Oi, mate,' said a greasy little man in a tracksuit, 'Get in line!'

Toad, who was about to depart to find Kecks, tried to make eyes at the man to warn him off, but it was too late. Toggie was in his face. He squared right up to him. 'We was here first and if you don't fuck right off out of my line, then I will rip your fuckin' ears off and shove them down your oily throat,' he whispered in the man's ear. The little man looked at Toggie right in the eyes. He took in the hair, which gave Toggie at least another five inches in height. He took in the mean shoulders and the twacked-out stare. And he moved to the back of the queue.

They paid for the bits in the trolley and headed back to the car. Toad came rushing up behind the others. 'I can't find her!' he said.

'Shit,' said Jonesy, 'where did I park the fuckin' car? This place was half empty when we arrived!'

'Over here!' they heard Kecks shouting. She was already at the car and loading something in the tiny boot.

'How did you get it open?' asked Jonesy.

'You forgot to lock it,' said Kecks. 'Good job people are honest!' she winked at Hoagie. 'What did you get then?'

'Few bits,' said Hoagie. 'Toggie nicked some whisky, we paid for some bacon and stuff, and I dunno what everyone's got in their coats.'

'Take a look in the boot,' said Kecks.

The boot seemed to glow like a treasure chest. There were four bags inside: clothes; food; bottles; toiletries. 'I even got bread,' said Kecks.

'Did you have money, Kecks?' asked Hoagie.

'Nah, I just filled up my trolley and then I sent the till boy on an errand to find something I forgot. And oops, I just kept walking, right out of the shop.'

'No cameras yet,' reminded Toad.

'What? How? Kecks!' said Hoagie.

'Must be the tits,' said Kecks.

'Respect,' acknowledged Toggie.

'Can we piss off now?' said Jonesy.

'Kecks,' said Hoagie, 'Did you get chicken?'

Virginia Betts

Getting Burned (1979)

White Punks on Dope (The Tubes)

'Well!' exclaimed Kecks, as she slammed the door, shaking the house to high heaven. 'That shoe-repairman is the single most miserable bastard on this earth. I asked him if he could put a simple metal heel on my high boots – you know, the ones I wear to go out – and he said I'd pounded the nail in by walking on it when it had already fell off. Even though I weigh fucking nothing! Basically, my boots are fucked, he says.'

'Oh him! Yeah,' said Hoagie, 'I took my DMs to him last week for a new sole. I said, *ay, ay mate, can you perform a miracle? My boots are sick, and they need to be spiritually HEALED, and given a new SOUL.* He didn't crack a smile. He said they'd gone right through so 'e couldn't mend 'em.'

'It's bloody pessimistic,' said Kecks. 'Why can't he just repair them because THAT'S HIS JOB! Shoe man of doom! I have never known ANYONE have a job and so obviously not want to do it.'

'Cept for Toad,' said Hoagie. 'He got a job at the Wimpy last month, and he finds nearly every reason not to do it. Did the bloke do your boots in the end anyway?'

'Oh, yeah,' said Kecks, distracted suddenly, 'But not without a whole load of rigmarole. He even burned his bloody fingers with the machine and then tried to blame me for making him have to get too close to the shoe!' She paused. 'Hey, is Toad in tonight? Shall we go?'

'How much money you got?' asked Hoagie, 'I haven't sold much shit this week so I'm short.'

Hoagie liked hard gear, and to keep this habit going he sometimes had a nice little side-line dealing stolen scripts and pep-pills to bored middle class housewives. Kecks worked, but he was more than generous with her, and they always shared his drugs. Hoagie's habit had not, at this stage, made the transition from smoking to needle, not in those days; although Toad suspected that Kecks might have dabbled, as she always looked sick lately and had taken to wearing long sleeves all the time. Hoagie assumed it was a fashion thing, to which Toad, who had raised the subject recently, had simply grunted in response.

'I hate you dealing,' said Kecks, breaking Hoagie's thoughts. 'I've got enough money to go out 'cos me mum gave me some. Less go out and make Toad wait on us!'

'All right. Wear the boots,' said Hoagie, 'now they're done.'

'Nah, I think I'll wear the other ones,' said Kecks.

By 7pm, Hoagie was starving.

'Come ON, Kecks!' he growled, as he stood waiting by the door.

'Nearly ready!' came a muffled reply.

Kecks appeared suddenly, wearing black, as usual, with fishnet tights and high boots. She had black hair, eyes, and nails, and wore her old school shirt and tie.

'You got your nose pierced!' said Hoagie.

'Yeah, Kelly did it,' said Kecks. 'Does Toad know we're coming?'

'No! It'll be a lovely surprise for 'im,' said Hoagie.

79

They arrived at the Wimpy and waited to be seated. In the background, Hoagie spotted Toad carrying plates and a tea towel. He immediately caught Hoagie's eye and looked alarmed. Hoagie nudged Kecks on the way to their table. 'Time for some freebies I reckon,' he said, and then he noticed something else which interested him even more. He nudged Kecks again.

'Toad's got a Girlfriend,' he whispered. 'Look!'

Sure enough, Toad could be seen talking frantically to a blonde woman, who kept rubbing her hands up and down his arms and shoulders. He was giving the nod over to Kecks and Hoagie, obviously explaining that he knew them, but also obviously not wanting *her* to know them.

'Dark horse, that one,' said Kecks.

Hoagie was never quite sure of how Kecks felt about Toad and vice versa. Kecks was usually ok with most people, but she was a bit prickly around Toad, and Toad was oddly possessive of Hoagie at times. They sort of tolerated each other. Their friend, Toggie, of course, was usually rude to Kecks, but then he was rude to everyone, so at least you knew where you were. Even so, Hoagie was a little hurt that Toad seemed not to want to own up to his friendship tonight.

'Less 'ave some fun,' he said to Kecks.

The girl Toad had been talking to came over to wait on their table.

'Can I take your order?' she asked. Her voice had a brittle, whining quality to it.

'A Kingsize with cheese, and an Egg Bender, both with chips please,' said Hoagie, and while she took it down on her notepad, Hoagie sized her up. She was about ten years older than Kecks and probably quite a bit older than Toad too. She was busty in the beige uniform, which gaped at the buttons and stretched down over her rounded hips. Her face was a shiny, pan-sticked affair, with glittering black eyeshadow and spidery lashes. She could barely hold the pencil due to her red acrylic talons. But there was something in her that Hoagie could instantly recognise; something that told him instinctively she belonged with his kind of people. He knew what appealed to Toad: the hair, bleached almost white, fell in a shaggy crop over her high cheekbones. Together, with Toad's green and black spikes and his studs they would look like his idols: Sid and Nancy. If they lost the uniforms, of course.

'You know my friend, Toad, don't yer?' said Hoagie.

'Er...yeah,' said Wimpy's answer to half of the famous punk duo.

'Oh yeah,' said Hoagie, 'I've known him for years. I'm James Vincent Hoag. But friends of mine call me Hoagie?'

'Hi, Hoagie,' said 'Nancy' (rather presumptuously thought Hoagie), 'I'm Becca.'

'This is Kecks!' Hoagie almost shouted, 'So you can be Bex and Kecks!'

'It's Becca,' said Becca. 'But hey, yeah, hoping to be a friend if you're, er, *Toad's* friend.'

'Tell you what,' said Hoagie, 'if you throw in some free drinks tonight, you'll be a friend even quicker,' he laughed, but he wasn't really joking.

'Ah, I can't do that,' (did he detect a slight American twang there?) 'but I can give you some extras with your mains?'

'I bet you can,' laughed Hoagie again. Kecks coughed.

'Tell you what,' said Hoagie, 'why don't you come over to our little place when you two finish up and we can keep the party goin' tonight?'

Kecks kicked Hoagie under the table and when he looked at her, she gave a slight shake of her head. Hoagie ignored her.

'Er,' said Becca, 'er, well I'll have to check with Peter, I mean, Toad. But I guess…'

When she had gone, Kecks kicked off at Hoagie.

'What the fuck do you want to invite her over for? I've got to get up early and I really ought to put my head in at home with my parents at some point. Also, we don't know her! What if she's straight? She could cause loads of trouble, comin' to the house.'

'She seems to be at it with Toad, so I seriously doubt she's a clean-livin' God-squad type! I've got in-built shit detectors and a nose for one of 'us'. I know people. And I can tell you with confidence that she seems to be all right,' said Hoagie.

'You fancy her,' said Kecks.

'What? No way!' protested Hoagie. 'I just wanna wind Toad up. Peter! Ha!'

'I never knew that was his name,' said Kecks.

'No-one does,' said Hoagie, 'he's been Toad ever since he's been about 3!'

'Suits him,' said Kecks.

They were halfway through the burgers when they heard a great commotion coming from the kitchen. Someone was screaming blue murder.

Toad came running out and grabbed loads of cloth napkins off the nearest table. He rushed back into the kitchen and there was a sound of water gushing out of taps turned on full pelt. Then he appeared and made his way over to Hoagie and Kecks.

'Becca got her hand burnt with oil,' he said. 'I grabbed loads of cloths and wet them, then I sorta wrapped it up like a bandage. I ran it under the taps first, but then I thought that might calm it down a bit. But it's ok. It's just surface stuff. Happened to me in Home Ec once when I was making a fruitcake.'

'Why did you put hot oil in fruit cake?' said Kecks.

'What?' Toad looked confused. 'Oh, I didn't. I put my hand on the wire bit in the oven.'

'Oh,' said Kecks.

'So, she's not all disfigured then? We could take her to the hospital?' offered Hoagie.

'I think she's fine, but they're sayin' she should go to A and E in case it needs some proper burns treatment,' said Toad.

'Well, tell her we can take her,' said Hoagie. 'You was comin' round after anyway.'

'Were we?' said Toad. 'Ok. But you haven't got a car?'

'We can ring Jonesy from here?' suggested Hoagie.

'I'm out with Toggie and some other people,' said Jonesy on the other end of the restaurant phone line. 'I'll have to bring him 'cos I was givin' him a lift home.'

Hoagie winced at first, but then he thought it might be even more of an opportunity to wind Toad up.

Eventually, they all piled out of the Wimpy. Hoagie and Kecks first; then Toad, with his arm round Becca, who had half her arm wrapped in a wet tablecloth. They climbed into Jonesy's car.

'I'm ok,' she insisted, 'but I have to get my kid before we go to the hospital.

Everyone immediately froze.

'You have a kid?' said Hoagie.

'Yeah,' said Becca. 'She's 7. She's with my little sister at mine right now, but I can't expect Jen to stay around for hours without knowing what's happening. And Hayley, that's my kid, she needs to know where I am.'

'7!' exclaimed Toggie, 'how old are you?'

'I started young,' said Becca.

'This is Toggie,' said Hoagie. 'He's never one to hold back.'

'Tell you what, said Jonesy, 'why don't we get your kid and then I can take you to the hospital. The rest of them can take your kid home and watch her whilst you get seen, and then I can come and get you later. Then we can party on.'

'Erm, but I don't know you,' she said doubtfully.

'You know me,' said Toad, 'I can watch her.'

'Well…all right,' said Becca.

'She looks like you,' said Hoagie, not really sure what he should say about the kid, who now sat on Becca's lap in the somewhat crowded car. He couldn't deal with kids really. What the fuck was Toad thinking of?

'Yeah,' said Becca. 'She looks like her dad more, but honestly, he's not been around since I was pregnant.'

'Why didn't you have an abortion?' said Toggie.

'Toggie! Shut the fuck up!' said Toad.

'Yeah but, sorry, how fucking old are you? You must have bin up the duff at like 12 or somefing?'

'I was 17,' said Becca, and I was in for an abortion, but the doctors sort of shamed me into changin' my mind. You're fuckin' direct, I'll give you that. If you must know, and I have no idea why I'm telling you this as I only just met you, but they said I was old enough to know what I was doing, so I felt bad about it. I had never even had sex before though.' She paused for a moment, then added, 'I was actually born in the States, and there's even more of an attitude there.'

'Hey, I thought I could hear some accent,' said Hoagie. 'I'm like the Punk Professor Higgins, me!'

'Who?' said Toggie.

The kid was half asleep on Becca's lap but Kecks suggested perhaps they had better shut up about it all.

Back at Hoagie's place, the kid, Hayley, sat on a cushion, staring at Toad.

'Stepdad, ay ay,' said Hoagie. Toad gave him a look.

'Fuckin' let's boot up then,' said Toggie.

'There's a kid 'ere,' said Hoagie.

'So what?' said Toggie. 'The mother looks like she'd know all about it. Must be some junkie if she's in with Toad. Better be if she's in with us.'

'Why don't yer have a look at these magazines?' Kecks passed the kid copies of *Just Seventeen*, *Cosmopolitan* and *Love-in*. 'Fuck's sake, Hoagie, these are all torn about! You bin usin' bits for roaches?' Hoagie didn't answer. 'Come and sit over here and have a read.'

'Can I cut the people out and dress them?' asked the kid.

'S'pose so,' said Kecks through gritted teeth. Seeing Hayley's face fall, she added reluctantly, 'Yeah, ok, I've read them ones.'

'It don't seem right to have gear. Let's wait 'til the mother's back at least,' said Hoagie. 'Skin up, Toad.'

Toad obliged. 'She does do it mate, so she wouldn't mind,' he said, taking a drag of the joint and passing it on to Hoagie.

'I'd rather she said that it was all right,' said Hoagie.

The telephone in the hallway downstairs rang at that moment. 'Pick up for us, Jonesy,' said Hoagie.

Jonesy duly ran downstairs, and they could hear his muffled voice speaking for a moment. Then he re-appeared. 'She's ready to be collected,' he said. 'You comin' with me Toad?'

'Er,' said Toad.

'She's your girlfriend or whatever,' said Hoagie.

'Yeah,' said Kecks, 'you should go, but on the other hand, I don't think she'd be best pleased if the kid was left with a bunch of strangers. I think she left her with us because she knows Toad.'

'Did you actually know she had a kid then?' asked Toggie.

'Yeah, I've met her once,' said Toad.

'You sad bastard,' said Toggie, sneering, 'you should give that sort of thing a fuckin' wide berth.'

'You can fuck right off mate,' said Toad, standing up and moving towards him with his fists clenched.

'Yeah, go easy Toggie,' said Hoagie, seeing the warning signs flash in Toggie's eyes. He turned to Toad with his hand on his arm, holding him back. 'He's just wasted, mate. Anyone can see that this Becca is all right, and I am a very good judge of character. Never get it wrong, me.'

The heat died down as quickly as it arose, and Toad declared he'd stay and watch Hayley with Kecks and Hoagie whilst Jonesy picked Becca up from A and E.

'Is my mum coming now?' said Hayley, in a sleepy voice.

'Yeah, kid,' said Hoagie.

Pretty soon, with the first signs of dawn on the horizon, all of them were sitting back in Hoagie's flat. Kecks sat with her legs draped over him on the worn sofa whilst he sorted out some gear; Jonesy sat on a stool, smoking a joint and drinking a beer; Toggie was flat on his back on the floor and Toad sat next to Becca on a beanbag, paying a great deal of attention to her bandaged hand and fetching and carrying drinks for her. Hayley was dozing amongst the magazine cuttings; Kecks had covered her with a blanket whilst Jonesy was out collecting Becca.

'You do gear, don't yer, Bex – Becca – don't yer?' said Hoagie? 'Cos, here you go, have this one on me,' he passed the foil and lighter. 'After yer troubled night and all.' The others raised their eyebrows and Toggie was about to protest, but Hoagie put up his hand and made a dramatic sweeping gesture. 'Well look at us now!' he said. 'This is where we were supposed to be before you went and burnt your arm, Becca. Bit late, but welcome to the party. Any friend of Toad's is a friend of mine. You're all right, you are.'

Becca began to heat the heroin on the foil, and it was nearly ready when Hayley, who must have woken to hear her mother's voice, came running in holding pieces of magazine.

'Mummy! Mummy! Look what I've made!' She put her hand right in the foil.

'Oh shit!' cried Becca, as the child began to scream in pain, the sticky substance covering her fingers like molten tar. The kid cried out, 'It's burning! It really hurts! Get it off me!'

But Becca did not clean it off. She instinctively knew, as did everyone else, that the hot heroin would break up into little pieces and be lost, and what a waste that would be. "Shh, darling,' soothed Becca. 'We have to wait 'til it's cool, then we can peel it off in one go and save it. I know it hurts, sweetie. Do you want mummy to sing to you?'

The kid switched from piercing screams to a whimpering sound, sobbing almost silently into her mother's shoulder until, at last, she fell silent.

In a short time, the substance was cool, and Becca was able to peel it off her daughter's fingers and put it straight back on the foil.

'But really,' she added, 'we could just shoot it up? I've got works; we could share?'

It was a rare thing to happen, but Hoagie could do nothing but stare at the scene, speechless.

'Maybe you better take Becca and Hayley home, Toad?' he suggested, finally. 'It's been a long night.'

Toad, who seemed a shade paler than usual, stood up. 'Yeah,' he said, 'I'll take you home. Jonesy, can you give us a lift, mate?'

'Sure,' said Jonesy.

'Well, fuck me,' said Hoagie when they'd gone. 'Seems like I'm not always right about people after all.'

Good Behaviour (1983)

White Wedding (Billy Idol)

'So, James,' said the psychiatrist, 'you told me in our last session that you couldn't think of one single event that might have led you to your current predicament; nothing that might explain your addictions and the decline in your behaviour which has brought you here. And yet you have just told me that your girlfriend died of an overdose a few years ago at the age of around 20.' He sighed and took off his glasses. 'Do you think that this incident might have had some impact on you?' He looked Hoagie in the eyes directly and raised his eyebrows expectantly.

'Nah, mate, not really,' said Hoagie, defiantly. Hoagie would rather have died than admit to this old tosser that the death of Kecks was the single most traumatic event in his life, apart from being taken to prison, of course. It was the turning point that had taken him from light to dark; from foil to needle. Everything had changed.

The psychiatrist was speaking again. 'Well, you see, James, the thing is, we have been seeing each other once a week for several months now, and we don't seem to be making any real progress.'

Hoagie grunted.

'But,' the psychiatrist went on, 'If we want to make an application for a reduced sentence on the grounds of good behaviour, I have to make a report, a *full* report, which shows there is some sense of remorse for your crimes. If you see what

I mean. We don't want to be *behind bars,* so to speak, forever, do we?'

'*We* aren't behind bars, though, are *we?*' replied Hoagie. 'I am.'

'I was just speaking figuratively, inclusively,' said the psychiatrist.

'You was speaking *condescendingly,*' said Hoagie. 'If you see what I mean.'

The psychiatrist turned a brilliant shade of magenta. 'Shall we continue?' he said.

'You can do what you like,' replied Hoagie, 'but you ain't pinning my current *predicament* on something that happened years ago. And I don't want to talk about that anyway.'

'Mr Hoag,' said the Psychiatrist, 'think about it. It will help your case. It is more than likely that this incident in your past could have triggered many of the issues that followed.'

'I'd like to go back to me cell now,' said Hoagie.

Back in his cell, Hoagie's cellmate was busy sharpening the handle of the toilet brush to a point. He'd obviously hidden his quota of razor blades in the soap, and he'd made a fine job of re-purposing the handle. Now he was just finishing it off by filing it on the brickwork.

'What'ya doin' that for?' asked Hoagie.

'It's me weapon,' said the cellmate, who was called Patrick, but known as Prick. 'I might get into a fight and need it. I've managed to set up a thing with some smack comin' my way, but I might need this. You in?'

'Nah,' said Hoagie.

'I thought you was a junkie?' said Prick.

'Ex-junkie,' said Hoagie. Although that wasn't strictly true. Prison was better than anywhere for sourcing smack. However, he wasn't about to let on to this weasley little bastard. Hoagie had seen his type before and in prison you trusted no-one. Some of the older and more seasoned inmates got the younger ones hooked so they could control them and use them. This little prick thought he was in with the big league, but really, he was just being used and Hoagie wasn't having any of that. Hoagie didn't know it then, but by the time Toggie was banged up for a much longer stint years later, the heroin problem was supposed to have been eradicated. But by then the synthetic drugs, like spice, were coming in and that was worse. Then they hit up new inmates just for fun, watching them going around like zombies and cackling like demented hyenas. There'd always be something.

'Oi, mate, 'said Hoagie, 'do us a favour, will yer? Can yer just piss off for a bit?'

His cellmate didn't hesitate to leave. Hoagie had a way of looking at him that said, *don't mess with me*, even though he seemed all right really, most of the time.

When the little twat had gone, Hoagie got to thinking. The psych had really messed with his head today; made him say things he'd never said before, and he didn't like it. He thought again about that night. They'd never put him in the frame for Kecks' death because he and Toad had dumped her in the street. They'd raided a late night offy and got so high that he'd ended up in the river. He was still really pissed off with Kecks. They'd all used smack, but the stupid cow had started banging up and hidden it from him pretty well. The night she died, that's what she must have done – and they'd smoked it too, so no wonder!

The funeral was *so much* fun. Loads of music Kecks hated and bible stuff that weren't anything to do with the real Kecks. The boys had all gone; had to sneak in at the back as they weren't welcome. Kecks' mum was a complete hypocrite. She'd hated Hoagie from the moment Kecks met him, kicked her out when she was 17 because she guessed about the drugs, so Kecks had moved in with him full-time. Now she blamed him for her death. Hoagie was having none of that. Kecks had done it to herself, she could do what she liked. *But she was only 15 when you met her. You introduced her to it all.* Shut up, Shut up, voices! It wasn't my fault, it was her. Bloody head shrink.

A few weeks after she'd died, he'd injected for the first time, and after that there was no going back. He made quite a bit of money dealing, and now he needed to make even more. That was when it got a bit more serious. All the gang, Toad, Toggie, even Jonesy, had to nick and sell just to keep up with it all. Toad still lived with his parents, so he had quite a good, steady supply of cash – as long as he took small amounts irregularly, no-one really noticed. And they gave him money too. So, it was ok for a bit. Until Hoagie lost it in a pub.

It started when the bloke with the wrong trousers came in. They were pink and Hoagie, probably thinking about Kecks' loathing of the colour, took an instant dislike to him. He edged up beside him and started taking the piss a bit loudly about his pink jeans, deliberately bumping into him and spilling a bit of cider over the offending garments. And it would have been fine, but the guy decided to be brave and called him a *fucking junkie loser*, so Hoagie nutted him. He gave him his due, the pink jeans guy got up and punched him in the face, but Hoagie was mad, and strung out, and sick of everything that day, so he broke a bottle and went for the guy, stabbing him in the side with it. As the guy lay bleeding on the floor, Hoagie was picked up by the scruff of the neck and booted outside; two big bouncer types tried to hold him, but he bolted for home, and it was only later he realised he had dropped his wallet, and someone had called the police.

The guy didn't die, but he wanted to press charges, and when the police came knocking, Hoagie was hauled off. That was the beginning of his acquaintance with prison; he spent a short time there, but his sentence was then suspended on account of his drug addiction. He could not help it because he was ill, they said. It really was his get out of jail free card. He entered into a methadone programme, and went to those stupid meetings, (like the one with the dead rats that he blamed entirely for Kecks' death), and he still scored secretly at the same time. But it didn't last. This latest episode was because someone had tipped them off that he was dealing heroin. No-one could really get him on dealing as much as he did, because he'd managed to get rid of a load on Toad, but nevertheless, there was enough in his flat to make dealing questionable and use undeniable, so here he was in prison properly. And he really did want to get out.

The more Hoagie thought about getting out on good behaviour, the more the psyche's words made sense. Perhaps, he thought, Kecks' dying really did mess him up so badly that it led him here. There was definitely some mileage in it. Next time he'd tell the old wanker a bit more.

So, the next time he saw the psychiatrist, he began to pour his heart out with more conviction, obviously missing out the part when he and Toad dragged her outside and left her beside the phone-box, and the psychiatrist was genuinely interested and made lots of notes.

'Mr Hoag, I can file my report at the end of the week, and I will be recommending that you are no longer any danger to yourself or others and are eligible for parole,' he said, 'although naturally there will be some conditions.'

'Thank you,' said Hoagie, wondering if the conditions would be acceptable to him.

On visiting day, Hoagie was surprised when the guard said, 'you've got a visitor today.'

'Bloody Hell!' said Hoagie when he walked into the hall. Sat at the table was a small, prematurely middle-aged woman with a perm. It was his mum. He hadn't seen her for quite some time.

'Heard you were in trouble,' she said, 'so I thought I'd come and see you.'

'Right,' said Hoagie, not sure how to react.

'I can't understand why you ended up in here,' said his mum. 'You were always a good boy until you went to that school and met that Thorin.'

'I bet Toggie's mum has said exactly the same thing to him,' said Hoagie.

'Well, James,' said his mum, 'they say you might be getting out, and I thought I'd make it up to you a bit, after all this time. I thought,' she hesitated, 'I thought you might need a place to live, so I thought you could come and live with me.'

Nothing appealed less to Hoagie. 'But I've got me flat,' he replied.

'No, James, they had to let that go.'

'What about all me stuff?' said Hoagie, appalled.

'I've got it safe,' said his mum. 'Now, they said they needed someone to vouch for you, and keep you on the straight and narrow, so I thought that could be me. That way you'd get out earlier.'

'But mother,' said Hoagie, knowing she disliked this formality, 'you washed your hands of me some time ago, remember?'

'Well, you turned out like your dad,' she replied. 'Good for nothing, though with him it was the booze. But James, I feel bad I slung you out. I just couldn't cope with it all. Stealing from your own mum's purse!'

'Mum, I'm clean. No more drugs. I'm out on good behaviour, you know.' He winked.

'You sod!' she said and smiled for the first time that day.

'Mum, do you remember when I was little, and dad came back from the pub with his mates – and they'd nicked all the carpets and the two armchairs from the pub lounge! Put them in the back of Terry's van and drove home!'

'You remember that?' said his mum.

'Yeah!' said Hoagie, 'I was impressed. But I remember you chased him up the stairs and kicked him right in the arse!'

'I made him take 'em all back too,' she said. 'I might be little, but I am not afraid of nothing.'

'You're bad, mum,' said Hoagie.

'Clipped you round the ear a few times too, haven't I?'

'Yeah,' said Hoagie, 'didn't help though, did it?'

'No,' she replied, tartly. 'But when he started tryin' to get you involved, and…' she hesitated, 'and other things, he had to go.'

'But he *died*, mum!' said Hoagie. 'When he left, when you *kicked him out*, he had nowhere to go! And what do yer mean, *other things*?'

'Those bloody punk records! Them Sex Pistols and them Buzzin'cocks, or whatever,' she said, expertly avoiding the subject of Hoagie's father. You thought you was that Rotten one. Or was it the Vicious one?'

'Mum!' persisted Hoagie, 'he *died*.'

'It was a heart attack, James. It was genetic.'

'Comforting,' said Hoagie.

The bell rang for the end of visiting time. Hoagie's mum tentatively kissed him on the top of the head, a gesture he seemed to remember from long ago, before she could no longer reach, then she left, turning once to wave at him before she disappeared beyond the large doors. 'See you soon,' she had mouthed. Hoagie put his head in his hands. It would all go wrong, he thought to himself.

Coming out was weird. Like being re-born or something. He had been given back the things he'd had when he went in – an old watch; two gold rings; a torn shirt; his black jeans; a pair of ox-blood DMs; his wallet; a badge with 'Anarchy' on it; some leather fingerless gloves and a studded belt. He looked at his reflection in the rusty toilet mirror. He looked pale but strangely healthier in his complexion. Although he was still slim, his drainpipe jeans were too tight, and he had to ask his mum to bring a pair of tracksuit bottoms. It was true that although he had still managed to find drugs in prison he was no longer, he knew for sure, an 'addict'. He had genuinely been drug-free for a few weeks when he reached his date of release. He stared at his reflection. The light was grey and dull and the face that stared back looked tired of life. He was still young, but he felt ancient. He had no money, no prospects, no chance of getting hold of any drugs for a while and he was going to live with his mum. When he was 19, he'd run around snarling, 'Naaaow Fuuuutya!' Now it seemed he'd fulfilled that prophecy. He'd been told he would be fine; he'd find gainful employment; that things were on the up. 'England's fuckin' dreamin,' he said to himself and walked out of the toilet and towards his new life. He had a feeling it would be pretty similar to his old one.

The taxi driver had been surly; Hoagie could feel him judging him. His mum had made a valiant effort – chatting about the weather and politics, but Hoagie knew it was because she found silence uncomfortable and being with him, coming from the nick, even more uncomfortable. He wondered what she had told her neighbours about where he'd been. When they arrived home, she'd strung up banners that read 'Welcome Home,' as if he'd been abroad or something. Perhaps that was what she had told the neighbours? He went straight up to his old room. It was just as he'd left it when he left home. Or rather when he'd been asked to leave home. His old posters stared back at him, and he saw that most of his stuff from the flat was here. He reached for one of his records and put it on the turntable. '*Shot by both sides*,' the lyrics rang out at him. He took it off abruptly and went downstairs.

'Mum,' he said, 'can I borrow a small bit of cash? I want to go and get some hair dye, then I wanna call Toad.'

'I don't know…' she said, warily.

'Mum, I am clean. I am going out for 10 minutes to get some hair dye because I look like a rat's arse. I am not going to buy drugs. I don't know anyone who could get me any drugs because I have been away. Please can you lend some money to me until I can get some of my own.' He tried to keep an even tone.

'Oh, course I can, James. Just…don't be long eh? I'll worry,' she said.

'Mum, I haven't lived at home since I was 17!'

'Well, no. You gave me so much trouble, James. And I had to think about David.'

'Where is David?' said Hoagie.

'I told you,' said his mum, 'David is away studying. He got in at Trent Poly. He'll be around soon to see you though.'

'Oh good. I haven't seen him for ages! Bloody Trent? Long way from here!'

'Not really that far. Except I don't drive. But I expect he just wanted to get away from here, you know, after everything.' She looked at him sadly.

'Can't blame him for that,' said Hoagie, not rising to the bait. 'Fuck all to do here. Nah, good for him. He's done well.' Hoagie was looking forward to seeing his little brother after all this time.

'He has. And so can you, James,' she paused. 'James? Do you have to go dyin' your hair again? It looks all right. You look… you look normal for once.'

'Yeah,' said Hoagie, 'That's the fuckin' problem.' He left and headed for the local shop to get some bleach. And who should he run into? Toad.

'I was on the way to see you!' he said. 'Heard you was out. Guess the fuck what?'

'What?' said Hoagie.

'Jonesy's only gettin' fuckin' married innee?'

When they got back to Hoagie's mum's place, Toad sat on Hoagie's bed while Hoagie put the bleach on his hair. Whilst it was turning from his natural brown to blond, Hoagie got the full story.

'He met this girl – Leela. Only met 'er about three months ago, but she's up the duff, see – '

'For Fuck's sake!' Hoagie nearly choked.

' – and she's about twenty-six,' continued Toad. 'Mind you, she's quite fit.'

'Wass she like then?' said Hoagie, his head wrapped in tinfoil and cling film, with drips running down his cheeks.

'Jesus! That stuff stinks!' said Toad. 'Well, my mum likes her.'

'Why has she met your mum?' said Hoagie.

'She's at her church or somefing,' said Toad.

'Jesus!' Hoagie was astounded at how fast things had moved on without him. 'Iss all gone wrong without me to keep you lot on the straight an' narrow. Jonesy's getting married to a god-squad and he's gonna have a kid. Shit.'

'Yeah, but also, you know he got himself on one of those youth training things a while back? Well, he's got a job and he's gonna be trained to be an accountant, like.'

'Fuckin' boring!' said Hoagie. 'We need to sort him out.'

'Won't do much good. The wedding invites are already sent out. Could be a good piss up though?'

'Jesus,' said Hoagie. 'Where's mine then?'

'I reckon your mum's got it. Or p'raps he didn't think you'd be out.'

'Perhaps,' said Hoagie, 'the wife-to-be didn't want an ex-convict at her big day more like.'

'Well,' said Toad, 'you can be my plus one.'

'Fuck off! I'm not a fuckin' queer!' said Hoagie.

Toad gestured towards the cling film and dye on Hoagie's head. 'You sure about that?' he said.

'You can fuck right off!' said Hoagie, diving on Toad.

Hoagie's mum came running up the stairs. 'You'll break the bloody bed!' she shouted. 'And what the hell have you got on your head?'

'Shit,' said Hoagie from the bathroom. 'Shit, shit, shit.'

'What?' yelled Toad who was in the bedroom playing Hoagie's 'Astro Wars' game machine.

'Look,' said Hoagie. He appeared in the doorway. His hair was still damp, but it was clearly going to be a vibrant shade of orange.

'S'alright,' said Toad, shrugging. 'You used to have it yellow and black. John Lydon's hair is orange, even if he int Rotten no more.'

'Yeah, but it wasn't supposed to BE orange. It was supposed to be white,'

'Yeah, but who wants to look like fuckin' Sting? Orange looks good,' said Toad.

'But it is a sort of yellowy-shit-orange. Like obviously when the fuckin' dye's gone wrong,' moaned Hoagie.

'Well, put another actual orange over the top,' said Toad. 'I might do mine orange as well. I'm fed up with black.'

'You're not havin' the same hair as me!' said Hoagie. 'Specially if I go as your 'guest' to Jonesy's wedding.'

'Shit! Orange hair will really piss off the new Mrs Jonesy!' giggled Toad.

'And Mrs Jones senior,' said Hoagie. 'She has always hated me.'

'Do you think Toggie is going?' said Toad.

'She hates him even more,' said Hoagie. 'But Jonesy wouldn't dare leave him out in case he got a brick through his window. Still, Toggie might not go,' he considered.

They both looked at each other.

'He will,' they both concluded simultaneously.

The night before Jonesy's wedding, Hoagie organised a stag do with himself, Toad, Toggie and, of course, Jonesy. They'd meet at the Gold Hind, then do a crawl, stopping at every pub until they got to the Spread Eagle. It would be just like the old days.

'You can come back to mine after,' said Toggie. 'I've got a video game machine. Space invaders and Pac-man.'

'Where did you get the money for that?' Toad had asked.

'Some of us fuckin' nicked it from the fish shop,' said Toggie.

'What – how?' said Hoagie.

'Nobody said anything,' said Toggie. 'Nicked me coat an' all. From Debenhams. Just put it on and walked out.'

'Fuck me,' said Hoagie. 'Look, I thought we'd end up at the Black and White Club at the bottom of Toad's mum's road, then the curry house next door. I s'pose after that we could go and play your stolen game machine.'

Jonesy had said he didn't want to be too late in on account of his wedding the next day, but they had all jumped on him and beat him up good-naturedly until he reluctantly agreed to the plan.

It started off quite well. But by the time they had reached the town centre, Jonesy was a bit the worse for wear, Toad having spiked his drink a few times to liven the party up. In the Spread Eagle, Toggie disappeared for ten minutes and then returned all jumpy and hyperactive.

'What are you on?' said Hoagie.

'Whizz,' said Toggie.

'Can you get me some?' said Hoagie.

'Got us all some,' said Toggie. 'But you have to pay me first.'

'No thanks,' slurred Jonesy.

'I'll have his,' said Toad. 'But he has to buy it. He's working.'

They didn't make it to closing time. Toad got into a fight and got them all kicked out.

'Club then,' said Hoagie.

The Black and White Club was, in Toad's words, a bit of a dive. The four of them strode in like they were in the Wild West and about to rough up the saloon bar. The music was good – ska, punk, David Bowie – pretty much all of 'their' music got played at the Black and White and with the eclectic clientele – multi-cultural, mixed-gender, wide age-range – pretty much anything went. And even though it *was* a dive, they all rubbed shoulders peacefully as they all got off on the same music and 'outsider' vibe. A range of dance styles from Pogoing to waving around like a dandelion might have left some fearing for their lives, but it was rare to have the same kind of fights as in other late night drinking establishments. Most people carried knives, but few people used them in the Black and White Club. And when the club shut at 2, many happy revellers usually spilled out into the curry-house next door. The boys were well-known at the club and in there they all felt like kings, even the increasingly drunk Jonesy.

'Mate!' said a voice behind Hoagie, and a huge hand slapped him on the back. 'Long time no see! You've put on weight.'

Hoagie turned. It was Big Adam. Big Adam had been his dealer before Prison. Big Adam was an Ex-Marine, and he was huge and terrifying; even Toggie was a bit scared of him. It was a total drag running into him here.

'All right?' said Hoagie, 'Yeah, I've been away.'

'I know, mate,' said Big Adam. 'Come and see me out the back in five and I can sort you out.'

'Nah, mate. I'm clean,' said Hoagie.

'Yeah, right,' said Big Adam. 'Round the back in five.' He vanished into the haze of smoke and dry ice.

'Fuck,' said Hoagie out loud. He thought about what he could do. There was really nothing for it but to meet Big Adam, buy some gear and then just sell it to someone else and leave with the others. As far as he could tell, they were all off gear, even Toad possibly, and he thought it was probably cheaper and healthier to stay that way. Also, he had to because of his release conditions and the methadone. 'Fuck,' he said again. He went to find the others.

'Solidarity,' said Toggie. 'We'll all go. 'I'll buy it off yer. For a cheap rate of course.'

'I'm not going,' said Jonesy.

'You fuckin' are!' said Toggie. 'Look, you've just gotta stand there.'

They all went out the back and sure enough there was Big Adam, ready to do the deal. Hoagie handed over the money.

'All of you,' said Big Adam, 'I'm sure you don't want to leave your friends out, Hoagie,' said Big Adam.

Hoagie was about to protest, knowing that it would do no good, and he'd inevitably end up buying for four people, when Toggie suddenly did something very reckless. He jumped straight up as if he'd been fired from a cannon, and he head-butted Big Adam right on the bridge of the nose. Blood began to pour from Big Adam's nose, and he dropped the heroin as his hands flew to his face. Toggie did not miss the chance, and whilst Big Adam was defenceless, he grabbed the stuff and pocketed it, then he punched Big Adam hard in the gut, and again in the face. He had blood down his shirt from his own head where he had nutted Big Adam, but he hardly noticed it as their blood merged and he shouted, 'Run!'

By the time Big Adam had recovered himself, the four were away up the hill and halfway to Toad's mum's house.

'We can't let my mum see us like this,' said Toad. 'Anyway, my dad won't let you in.'

'Less go through the park,' suggested Hoagie, 'cos he might come after us with his mates. We can cut through to my mum's and go there. She won't mind. He'll expect us to go to my old flat and he doesn't know where my mum lives.'

'I feel sick,' said Jonesy.

'Shut up,' said Toggie. 'Let's go.'

They climbed over the park railings. It was quiet in the park, and empty apart from the usual alcoholics and junkies who also climbed over to use the park as a haven of misbehaviour.

Toggie sat down on the memorial fountain. 'Come one then,' he said, 'Let's not waste this stuff.' He started to cook it up.

'Here?' said Hoagie.

'Yes here,' said Toggie. Where else? Mine's too far, we can't go to Jonesy's cos of his missus, and we can't go to yours or Toad's cos you both live with your mums! I don't think your mums would be happy to have a bunch of smackheads bangin' up in the bedrooms, do you?'

'I'm not doing it,' slurred Jonesy. 'I never did that with it anyway.'

'Aw, come on Jonesy,' said Toggie, 'this is your last night of freedom.'

So right there, in the middle of the park, in the middle of the night, four friends lamented Jonesy's last night of freedom by shooting up smack. For Jonesy, it was the first and only time he ever would. He was violently sick immediately and passed out on the statue.

'Put him on his side and cover him with my coat for a bit,' said Toggie. 'Fuckin' wuss.' Toggie dabbled in everything constantly and seemed to be indestructible.

For Toad, it was one time in a line of many, and many more to come. Years of use would follow.

For Hoagie, it was the moment you might say he became an addict once more, although he wouldn't say so himself.

They woke up shivering and still sprawled on the steps of the statue's pedestal as dawn began to rise.

'Shit! We'd better get out of here!' said Hoagie. It's the fuckin' wedding day!'

Toggie nodded over to Jonesy, who was still sleeping, with an evil grin. 'Got some rope,' he said.

Toggie, Hoagie and Toad sat with angelic looks on their faces as Jonesy came racing into the church and ran up the aisle, stopping with an abrupt skid at the altar beside his future brother-in-law. The organist struck up immediately and the bride, who had been waiting for Jonesy to get there, entered on her father's arm. She glanced over at the three young men at the back, drew in a sharp intake of breath at Hoagie's orange hair, and scowled at them.

'She don't look pregnant,' said Hoagie, far too loudly.

And then Jonesy became a married man.

'So, how did you get untied?' Hoagie asked Jonesy at the evening reception, as it briefly crossed his mind that he'd not been invited to the formal daytime meal and he was starving.

'You fuckin wankers!' said Jonesy. 'This old lady came along walkin' her dog and screamed. Bloody dog ran off and everything. She must've called the police 'cos they arrived and untied me. They put a bloody sack round me. I was in the cells! Nearly charged with indecent exposure and missed me own wedding! But Leela came and bailed me out. Her mother is NOT best pleased. It was nearly all off thanks to you bastards! Luckily no one knows about the bloody drugs. *Luckily* I never got tested, because the coppers assumed I had just got drunk on me stag do and that I had bollocks wankers for so-called friends!'

'Aw, no harm done, then,' said Toad.

'Fuckers!' said Jonesy.

The bride and groom had been given quite a few gifts which were duly displayed next to the cheesy pineapples on sticks; some gifts were in little white envelopes.

'What's this?' said Toggie, holding up a wire whisk.

'Sex thing?' said Toad.

'Oh my God!' said Hoagie. 'It's a Mounlinex Magimix! *Moulinex makes things simple; Moulinex makes things nice – and that includes the price*. He parroted the advert in a sing song voice, with a grin. 'My mum's got one of these!'

'Christ. Time we went,' said Toggie.

Toggie had brought a carrier bag and the three of them had helped themselves to as many bottles of wine and beer as they could manage. But afterwards, Hoagie discovered in the morning, he'd also helped himself to several little white envelopes from the present table. He'd gone to see Toggie immediately. Jonesy was unpleasantly surprised to see Hoagie on his mother-in-law's doorstep the day before he was leaving for his honeymoon but was thrilled to receive the cheques and cash that he had thought had gone missing.

'We can't thank you enough,' said Jonesy's mother-in-law. 'I must admit, I misjudged you, er, James, isn't it?'

'Me too,' said Leela, 'Thank you so much. We didn't actually know what we had been given but there's so much here! We thought the envelopes must have got swept up when they cleaned up or something, but YOU found them!' She hugged him awkwardly.

'Anytime,' said Hoagie. 'Yeah, I saw them on the floor and put 'em somewhere safe so I could bring 'em round this morning. And I'm very sorry for our little prank on the stag night. I was against it myself, but you know how boys are when they've had a few.'

'Boys will be boys,' said Leela's father.

'Have a nice holiday,' said Hoagie, as he left them. 'I expect it'll be yer last one for a while.' He gestured towards Leela's stomach and patted his own. She blushed.

Hoagie went back to Toggie's flat. Toad was already there.

'How was I to know that most of the gifts would be useless cheques?' said Toggie.

'Well, luckily, something can be salvaged from this,' said Hoagie. He held up a white envelope. 'Leela's dad was so grateful to me for finding the cheques, he gave me a *hundred quid* as a reward! Oh, and I also kept back a couple of envelopes which were cash. They won't even know they had them.'

They sat at the table and divided the money between them.

Checking in and
Checking Out (1983)

Blue Monday (New Order)

 Hoagie lay back on the sun-lounger and peered over at Toad, who lounged beside him, from behind his black shades.

'Cheers!' he said, raising his large all-inclusive glass of Tequila Sunrise.

'Cheers!' replied Toad. 'Hey, do you think Toggie will mind? Yer know, us booking without telling him?'

'He had the money, same as us,' said Hoagie. 'He wasn't there when we booked.'

'Yeah,' went on Toad, 'but we didn't really give him the choice did we, 'cos we didn't invite him, did we?'

'Well, it was spontaneous, weren't it?' said Hoagie. He paused. 'Look, to tell the truth, I didn't fancy bringin' him. It's the risk factor innit? I couldn't put up with, well, yer know. Like the stag night – when he nutted Big bloody Adam. You just never quite know what he might get us into. He'd insist on carryin' somethin' through the bloody customs and want to score as soon as we got here. I can't risk bein' put inside again.' He sighed.

'Yeah,' said Toad, 'He's a right pain in the arse. Still…'

Hoagie adjusted his umbrella. Then he lay back and picked up the dog-eared paperback. He was reading one called *Rita Hayworth and the Shawshank Redemption* by Stephen King.

'Make a good film, this book,' he said to Toad.

'Huh?' said Toad, who was sipping another Tequila, with a foil umbrella in it.

'Don't suppose you can bloody read,' said Hoagie. 'I said, it'd make a good film this here book. It's about a prison escape.'

'Who wrote it?' said Toad.

'Stephen King.'

'Oh, I don't like horror,' said Toad. 'Or reading.' He went back to his Tequila.

'It's not a horror,' said Hoagie, 'I just said! It's about a prison escape.' But Toad had put his Walkman on.

Hoagie had read a lot in prison, enjoying the act of reading more than he'd ever done at school where it was really boring books, and you were forced to read the crap by boring teachers who spent most of the time sitting on the desk, drinking coffee and waiting for the bell or their next fag break. If he was ever in the classroom that was – he was more than often kicked out to stand in the corridor. This book had been suggested to him by his support worker for some reason. *You'll like this,* she had said. Hoagie had been told he had to join some methadone programme, but he was off the gear, so all he had to do was check in once a week to be tested for a while. So, he had this week to have a holiday and to be honest they were a bit crap at keeping tabs on him. If he had said he was ill, nobody checked except his mum. Still, he was fine to join the programme anyway and get the methadone. Better than nothing in hard times, he thought.

In the book he was reading, a prisoner outwits everyone and escapes down a tunnel which he had hidden behind a poster of Rita Hayworth. Hoagie liked to fantasise, and he liked women with red hair, although he didn't fancy prison again. He was very glad indeed he had not included Toggie in the bargain bucket trip to Ibiza, bought with the stolen wedding money and his reward for 'finding' the rest of it. The only other time he'd been abroad was a trip to Rotterdam to see the Sex Pistols with Toad, and then they'd gone over to Amsterdam. Christ al-fuckin-mighty! That was an eye-opener. They weren't that old either, maybe 18 tops, although Hoagie had already left home, and Toad's mum thought Toad was staying with him. Hoagie had funded the trip by stealing stuff from Woollies and selling it to his mates, and Toad had come up trumps by winning a cereal packet art competition! Best timing ever! What the hell had he painted? Hoagie couldn't remember, but he knew it was good. Good old Toad. He'd paid most of it. They had caught the ferry. 'I'm the fucking son of the son of a sailor's son,' Hoagie had boasted. Fuck me, he spent most of the trip hangin' over the bog. He'd even managed to bring his mum's Valium with him, hidden in his socks, and nobody checked.

He'd done the same this time, but the Valium pills were legally prescribed to him now, to help him sleep, as he was doing so well being clean. There was enough alcohol to keep him going anyway, and he felt in control. Toad was enjoying himself too. Maybe he was off drugs? Who knew? What better way to recover than a bit of sun and a load of booze? As far as Hoagie was concerned, everything was looking sweet.

'Ay, ay!' said a familiar voice.

Fuck, thought Hoagie. 'Toggie!' he said.

'Surprise, you fuckin' pieces of shit,' said Toggie, amiably. 'Your mum told me where you was, so I thought I'd fly out and join yer. Sold my space invaders as well, so I'm loaded. In more ways than one.'

'Er,' said Hoagie, 'we had to grab the deal last minute, so no time to tell yer.'

'Yeah,' said Toggie, 'your mum said. But here I am, yer wankers and guess the fuck what? The happy couple are only down the road a bit. By bus, or taxi.'

'What?' said Hoagie.

'Yeah,' said Toggie, 'Jonesy and Mrs Jonesy are in a quieter bit, yer know, on account of Leela bein' a bit up the duff I reckon.'

'I don't think you can be a bit up the duff,' said Hoagie.

'Yeah, right,' Toggie looked puzzled. 'Anyways, whatever, we can all go over and see 'em can't we? Surprise 'em. All of us together again. Fab four. And bloody *Yoko*.'

Hoagie was astonished. 'I don't think Jonesy will want us gate-crashing his honeymoon,' he said. 'He's gonna be an accountant or somethin',' he added, as if this was relevant.

'Yeah,' said Toggie, 'so he'll be glad to have a bit of fun first then, won't he? Last fling for him before he gets *really* boring.'

'I think he had enough of that on his stag night,' said Hoagie.

'Bollocks,' said Toggie loudly, making a couple of holidaymakers turn and glare at his newly green hair and tattoos. 'That is what a holiday is for. Besides,' he lowered his voice and leaned in, 'I met a bloke last night who knows where we can score.'

Fuck, thought Hoagie. He nudged Toad, who took off his Walkman and then stared in disbelief as the tinny echo of Iggy Pop vibrated from his sun-lounger.

'Toggie,' he said.

'The one and only,' said Toggie.

Fuck, thought Toad. But, as he always said, he was a mate, so what could you really do?

In the restaurant, three amigos stuffed bread rolls and bottles of wine into their pockets, daring the other diners to say something. They were quite a sight, with their torn shorts and boots on bare feet, Hoagie's orange hair and old Pistols shirt; Toggie's green hair, and Toad with his black spikes and Ramones vest, stained with Tequila Sunrise. They swore and they stole, and they returned to the buffet at least four times. Hoagie was getting quite an overhang on his stick-like frame already, 'like Olive Oil got pregnant,' as Toggie put it.

'What shall we do now?' said Toad.

'Toggie has a plan,' sighed Hoagie.

'Yeah,' said Toggie, 'we're goin' to see Jonesy and his missus at their shag palace.'

'It's down the road,' said Hoagie.

'Ok,' said Toad. 'Will he mind?'

They managed to find a taxi which would take them, by putting hoodies up over their hair, and Hoagie put on a posh voice. Toggie and Toad giggled in the back, although Toad was still wary of Toggie.

'Fuckin' hell!' said Hoagie! How much do you think Leela's parent forked out? This Palm Court Place is a bit nicer than ours.'

'Yeah,' Toad chimed in, 'her parents are like them, oh yer know, them ones on the telly, think they're all la di da. I forget the series.'

'Let's go and find 'em,' said Toggie, with no plan at all, clearly.

The receptionist was obviously startled by the entrance of three drunks, with multi-coloured hair, striding in.

'Can I help you,' he said in a heavy accent.

'Yes,' said Hoagie in his posh voice again, 'we are looking for our friends, the newly-weds, Daniel and Mrs Jones. We believe they are staying here, and they invited us over.'

The receptionist looked sceptical. 'I am not sure I can help you gentlemen,' he said. But Toggie had started to walk towards the back, where he had spotted a fountain cascading into an enormous pool, and he could hear the faint sound of a bingo-caller. The others, ignoring the receptionist's weak protests, followed him.

'Twenty-two, veintidós, zweiundzwanzig,' said the caller.

'Yes! House!' screeched a woman's voice.

Simultaneously, Hoagie spotted Jonesy, in a Hawaiian Shirt, jumping up into the air and slapping the screeching woman on the backside, telling her to 'get the fuck up there and get the money!' They ran over to him.

'What the fuck are you three doing here?' said Jonesy.

'Surprise!' said Toggie.

'Oh no. No, no. Oh Leela's gonna love this,' said Jonesy.

'Knew she would,' said Toggie, and he pulled up a chair. Then he pulled up two more. By the time Leela returned, they were sitting together looking as if they had been there all the time. Her face fell.

'What the fuck, Dan?' she said.

'I didn't know. I swear,' said Jonesy.

'I'm goin' back to the room,' said Leela. 'Let me know when they've gone. Very nice to see you and everything, but I'm on my honeymoon, I'm pregnant and I'm tired.' She rose from the table.

'Aw, come on Leela,' said Hoagie, '*Mrs Jones*,' he crooned, batting his eyelashes at her.

In spite of herself, Leela smiled.

'What do you lot look like?' said Jonesy to his mates, who now seemed to definitely be staying around. 'All that neon hair and old shirts and stuff. It's a new decade in case you haven't noticed. Has been for a while.'

Toggie stared at Jonesy very intently. 'Well at least,' he said, 'my hair doesn't all lift up in one go with the wind 'cos it's sprayed so hard in that stupid flick thing. If there was a nuclear bomb goin' off, like everyone's so twitchy about, your hair'd be the first line of defence. Nothin'd shift that!'

'Fuck off!' said Jonesy. This is me new look.'

'Oh well,' said Hoagie. 'He's a married man now, Togs.' He winked at Leela. 'So, Leela,' he said, rolling the sound of her name around in his mouth. 'Leela, Leela, Leela. Is that a real name then?'

'Actually, my name's Lisa,' she said, 'but my sister couldn't say it when we were kids and it got changed to Leela, and I kind of like that better. Less common. More…exotic.'

115

'Knew it wasn't a real name!' said Hoagie.

Leela was very wary of Hoagie. She'd heard tales of him from Jonesy, who was never involved in the exploits, so he said, and she knew he was into drugs and had been in prison. Leela had smoked joints, and she liked her booze. But Jonesy had hinted that this little lot were into hard drugs. Leela didn't judge anybody, but she really didn't want them around now she was making a family life with Jonesy. To be honest, she was a lot pissed off that she was pregnant and couldn't drink as much. One glass, she reasoned didn't hurt, but the usual amount was probably not a good thing. It had put a stop to her fun. She was still smoking the odd ciggie but apparently that was not a good thing either and she'd seen a woman with a bump getting filthy looks from other people on the bus. So, she supposed that would have to stop too. And then there was the ridiculous stunt they'd pulled on the stag night. But Jonesy had said it wasn't Hoagie's fault about going to prison as he'd been unlucky. So maybe he wasn't a terrible person. He looked like he might be able to have fun anyway. Jonesy had only been meant to be a bit of fun, not turn into a husband. Still, she could do worse. That's what her mum had said. And he had good job prospects, and he was trying hard. She hoped he wouldn't be wound up by these clowns over what he might be missing. She reasoned it would be better to put up with them and then keep them away once they were back home and busy. Perhaps they'd move to another town? Yeah. That would be best. When they got out of her mum's house, which would be soon, hopefully.

'Who's up for a party, then?' said Hoagie when the bingo was over. 'How are we gonna spend that cash you won?'

'We're not, said Leela, 'and I can't really, can I? Danny can go?'

'Oh, no, it's ok,' said Jonesy.

'Pussy-whipped already!' said Toggie.

'Aw, come on, Leela,' said Hoagie. 'I can look after yer and we won't be out late.'

Leela looked at her husband, who did look somewhat torn.

'Ok,' she said. 'Just the one and then we can go back to the room. I do fancy a bit of music. Maybe a dance?'

'Are you sure, Leela?' said Jonesy.

'The lady says yes,' said Hoagie.

'Hey ho! Let's Go!' Toad, Hoagie and Toggie chanted together and took off towards the reception.

'Oh, no…hang on… The club is downstairs,' called Leela.

'Ah, nah,' said Toggie. 'We already have a little place in mind. Have you got yer wallet, Jonesy?'

The Paradise Club did not live up to its name in looks, but it certainly had a pulse. It was smoky, and dark and a chaotic confusion of lights flashing in time to the beat. They went down a narrow passage which widened out into this inferno of noise and straightaway Toggie vanished. He reappeared soon after alongside the others at the bar looking very pleased with himself.

'Scored!' he said.

'Scored what?' said Hoagie.

'Coke and whizz,' he grinned.

'What the fuck?' said Hoagie.

'Give us some money and meet me in five in the bogs,' said Toggie.

'I'm in,' said Toad.

'Oh, fuck. Oh, all right,' said Hoagie. 'Is there any proper gear?'

'Thought you was clean?'

'Mostly,' said Hoagie. 'On second thoughts, best not. I'll go for some speed to keep us goin'.'

'Yeah, cleaner innit?' said Toggie. Get us goin' for the night. And it doesn't fuck you up as much.'

'I prefer somethin' a bit smoother,' said Hoagie, 'but I'm in.'

After they had bought and snorted their respective purchases, the three of them returned to Jonesy, who was nursing a can of special brew, of all things, and sitting alone in a booth next to the flashing dancefloor. He nodded towards it.

'Look at Leela,' he said. 'She's away dancin' and I don't know if she should.'

'Ah leave her,' said Hoagie. 'She's pregnant, not dead.'

'Yeah, but it in't right, is it?'

'She's getting' a lot of attention,' said Toggie, with a glint in his eye. 'If she was my wife, I'd lock her up, mate.' He took off like a madman towards the dancefloor and barged a couple of kids out of his way. Then he proceeded to jerk his body all over the place, as if he was having a seizure. Hoagie noticed that a couple of the dancers began to copy him.

'Bin up North to that Hacienda place in Manchester, inn 'ee? said Toad. 'Tha's where 'ee picked up that spazzy dancin'.'

Hoagie just nodded. But then he noticed that Leela had left the floor and was over at the bar talking to a couple of olive-skinned, blonde-haired guys, who seemed very interested in her. Jonesy was getting steadily more pissed, and although

Hoagie was quite wired, he thought he'd keep a little eye on the situation. He waved at her. Then he went over.

'Hi, Hoagie,' said Leela.

'You alright?' said Hoagie.

'Yeah, I'm just talking,' she said. 'I haven't been out on my own for ages.'

'You're not on your own now,' said Hoagie.

'I'm fine,' she said, with annoyance. 'Piss off will yer?'

'Pissin' right off,' said Hoagie. But he kept watching from the other side of the bar, until suddenly he was taken roughly by the arm and dragged onto the dancefloor. It was Toggie, and he was pogoing up and down, and jerking and flapping all over the place. He'd been joined by Jonesy, who had succumbed to a bit of whizz and was emulating Toggie's every move.

'I knew he had it in him!' shouted Toggie.

'What?' shouted Hoagie as he bounced about amid the startled crowd.

The music slowed down and became a hypnotic pulse of synthesised rhythm.

'I like this stuff,' said Jonsey, and then he passed out on the floor.

'Fuckin' hell,' said Toggie. 'Help me drag him out the way.'

They got Jonesy back to the booth, where he slumped down into the sticky, stained red velour seat.

'Get him back to his room,' said Hoagie. 'I'll go and find Leela.'

'Where is it?' said Toggie.

'What?'

'What room is it?'

119

'I dunno, he's probably got his key in his pocket. Check,' said Hoagie.

'Ah yeah, here it is,' said Toggie. The two of them hauled Jonesy's near-unconscious frame upright, then Toggie said he could manage if Toad could help him.

'We'll all crash in their hotel room,' said Hoagie, 'and we can go back to our hotel tomorrow. Ours is too far. Can you manage, you arse?'

'Yeah,' said Toggie.

'Well, be careful with 'im,' said Hoagie, 'he's gonna have a kid. Why the fuck did you let him have drugs for? You know he's a fuckin' lightweight.'

'He can drink me under the table sometimes,' said Toggie.

'Whatever. He doesn't get high though, does he?'

'He does if I'm around,' said Toggie, grinning. 'Er, mate, have you got money to get a cab? He can't walk, can he?'

'Have this,' said Hoagie, producing some cash, 'and fuck off. I'll knock in a bit. What number?'

'2001,' said Toggie. 'A fuckin' space oddity!'

'Fuck off!' said Hoagie. 'Find Toad – look he's over there – and fuck off.'

When Toggie had left with Toad, Jonesy propped up between the two of them, Hoagie looked around for Leela. He couldn't see her. 'Fuck,' he said, out loud. He went to the bar. No Leela. He pushed and shoved all round the noisy, sweaty club. No Leela. He went outside. Still no sign of her.

Hoagie started to sweat. In his wired, whizzing state, he began to imagine worst-case scenarios. Leela being gang-raped; Leela being sold into slavery; Leela at the bottom of the warm bath of the sea, surrounded by jellyfish.

Just as he was reaching a crisis of paranoia, wondering how he'd explain it to Jonesy, he spotted her, still with the two guys, trying not to be pulled into a sand-buggy.

'Ah come on, babe,' he could hear one of them say, 'come for a ride down to the sea,'

'No, no I can't,' she was protesting.

Hoagie's blood rose like fire from within and he strode over, bigging up his slender frame as much as he could, and roaring as he went, 'Oi you fuckin' tossers!'

With his orange hair and ripped shirt, and the crazed look of a heroin deprived junkie cranked up on a speed-fuelled flash, he looked like he'd escaped from the looney bin.

The blokes, all tanned and Wham-flicked hair in white vests, turned as if to front up to him, thought better of it, and made to run for the hotel; one of them got away, but the other met with the square end of Hoagie's fist. He reeled backwards and fell to the ground.

'Come on, you stupid cow,' said Hoagie, taking Leela by the hand.

Leela meekly and gratefully followed, and they walked slowly back to the hotel.

'I feel a bit faint, James…Hoagie,' she said. 'Can we get a drink of water somewhere?'

Hoagie looked around wildly. The whole place was still buzzing. 'That little café, now,' he ordered.

They sat silently at the outside table as the warm wind fanned Hoagie towards certain sobriety.

'I'm sorry, Hoagie,' said Leela. 'Thank you for rescuing me. I think they spiked my drink.' She started to cry.

'Fuck's sake,' sighed Hoagie.

'I was just carried away with it all. I mean, I won't be able to do this much longer, will I? Perhaps never! Fucking hell,' (Hoagie had never heard her swear much before, he thought she went to church for God's sake) 'Why the fuck did I get pregnant?' she went on. 'We're only in our twenties. We should be out dancing and getting pissed, not washin' terry bloody nappies!'

'I think they do disposable ones now,' said Hoagie.

'Fuck!' said Leela again. 'I fuckin' hate my life. I can't do it. I like Danny a lot, but he was supposed to be my boyfriend. Like, a fling thing, a date or two, maybe get engaged, like me mum and dad. Shit. Shit. Now I'm stuck with it all. I've had to leave my job, Danny says he's gonna earn enough to keep us and we can get a little flat. And he's gonna get a little car and one of those car-phone things…Oh my god! And my mum is gonna look after the kid, and I can go back to work in an office. FUCK! FUCK! My life is over. I've never even tried any other drugs like you have.' She buried her face in her hands and sobbed uncontrollably.

'Shut the fuck up, you spoilt cow,' said Hoagie. 'You want to be like me? You don't know you're fuckin' born.' Then, more gently, 'Look, Leela. You got what you got. It's not that bad. Jonesy is the straightest of all of us. He's done a bit of nicking stuff, and he likes to get pissed. He's only done gear once, when we got him pissed on the stag night 'cos we was fucking runnin' shit scared from Big Adam the fuckin' mental dealer after Toggie nutted him, and he is pretty much as straight as a die. Don't tell him I told you that about the gear by the way. Look, it'll be all right. Dry your fuckin' eyes – not on my shirt – dry your eyes and let's get back to your bloody hotel, where, incidentally, we are all crashin' tonight 'cos your *husband* is fucked and we can't be arsed to go back to ours.'

They walked slowly back in silence and did not speak until they reached the wedded couple's room.

'You won't tell him, will you?' she said, 'you know, what I did…and what I said?'

'Nah, what's the point?' said Hoagie.

Leela stood on tiptoe and kissed Hoagie on the cheek. She made to do it again, but he turned as she did so, and they banged teeth.

'Ow! Fuck!' he said. 'Get in there and go to bed.'

'Where are you going?' she said.

'I've just got something to do,' said Hoagie. 'I'll knock in a bit. Three knocks. Don't go to sleep yet.'

Hoagie wandered back down to the hotel reception, where he had spotted the two guys, one nursing a black eye. He thought he'd have another word.

In the late morning, all of them sat having breakfast in Leela and Jonesy's hotel.

'Thanks for bringing Leela back safely, Hoagie,' said Jonesy, nursing his hung-over head. Hey, there's a lot of running about this morning,' 'I wonder what's happened?'

'I'm gonna ask,' said Toggie.

He came back all excited.

'Some guy od'd last night,' he said. He literally checked out, right here in reception!'

'Really?' said Hoagie. 'I'm not surprised. There's a lot of spiking in these sorts of places. You have to be so careful. Anyways, we'd better get back to our hotel.'

Leela eyed Hoagie suspiciously, but his face was impassive.

'Yeah, leave the honeymooners to it I reckon,' he said, and gave her a wink. 'No doing anything I wouldn't do, eh?'

'Ha!' spluttered Toggie. 'That don't leave much.'

Burnt Lungs and Bitter Sweets

Vincent (1983)

The Passenger (Iggy Pop)

Most people suffer from post-holiday blues, but Hoagie was suffering from post-holiday blackness. And it was now December, so it was well post-holiday, and there was no upward trajectory in his mood. To be precise, it was December 23rd and tomorrow was Christmas Eve, a date he was always a bit jittery about since it was a reminder of a birthday. Not Jesus for Christ's sake! Kecks. But Kecks was gone. Had been for a few years. His latest drugs Counsellor had told him to try to look at things positively. Saved on buying two presents every year since, he'd said. That didn't go down to well. But it was positive anyway.

He was currently watching a repeat of *A Fine Romance* on his portable telly because he couldn't be bothered to get up and change the channel. This morning he'd had gone to the chemist for his Christmas drink – methadone at the counter with his mum standing over him like a bloody hawk. 'Cheers and Happy Christmas,' he'd said. That hadn't gone down too well either. The methadone had. Although it was never an adequate compensation for the loss of his best friend. Heroin that is, not an actual friend. He was chilled. He was calm. He was clean and serene.

Bollocks he was.

He was sitting in his childhood bedroom, still with his Ramones and Pistols posters stuck to the wall with Sellotape, because the wallpaper behind them was a different colour so it looked crap if they were removed, and he was waiting for his brother, David to return from Uni, (even though in his opinion it weren't a proper Uni), where he would soon be sleeping in the room next door, whilst his mum pretended that Santa was coming. Then, on Christmas day, his mum's boyfriend, Alan, would drink sherry in the kitchen, laughing, and then they would squeeze round the tiny dining table in the lounge diner and his mum would pass food through the serving hatch and they would all get sloshed, and he'd try to keep smiling whilst inside he was dying.

Not that he had anything against Alan. Alan was all right. Straight as a die and always brought whiskey with him. Maybe she'd marry him? Then she'd probably want Hoagie out. Well, it was time he went again really. Alan was a better deal than his dad was. His dad was dead too. Perhaps, Hoagie thought, everyone who had anything to do with him died? He himself seemed to go on and on. Bullet-proof. Perhaps if he slashed his wrists? Stop, he thought, noticing he was slicing across his right wrist with his left thumb nail. Negative spirals. He'd been told by the counsellor he had to keep a tracking diary of his activities and thoughts to stop him focusing on drugs and negativity. It was surprising how many thoughts he had in both areas when he wrote them down. When he told the truth that was. Get out of the spiral by doing something else they said. Anything else. Once the thought of smack wormed its way into his head though, it was pretty difficult to think of anything else. Because as soon as someone says, 'try not to think of that,' you can't stop thinking of it. Try it. See?

At that moment, the phone rang. Hoagie charged downstairs to answer it. Perhaps this was the 'something else' he was looking for.

'Hello?' he said.

'Hoagie, mate!' It was Toad.

'Mate,' said Hoagie, 'wass up?'

'Nuffin. Just sittin' 'ere.'

'Why do you sound all echoey?' asked Hoagie.

'I'm in the downstairs toilet,' said Toad.

'What? How?'

'It's an extra-long lead, so I dragged the phone from the hall into toilet and jammed the door shut so I could talk in private,' said Toad.

'Okay…' said Hoagie.

'So, yeah, there's this mate of mine, Lee, we call him 'Honest Lee', geddit? – and he's got some stuff he needs to shift, like. Trainers, Nike wear, stuff like that,

'Go on,' said Hoagie, inwardly groaning at the terrible gag about the name.

'And he needs some help to move it. We get paid, like,' said Toad.

'Sweet. How much?'

'A hundred. Fifty notes each.'

'Sweet,' said Hoagie again, 'So, what exactly does it involve, and when does he want us to do it?'

'Tonight,' said Toad.

'Fuck off!' said Hoagie, 'Tonight?'

'Yeah, it has to be tonight. See, a few geezers have been sniffin' round his lock up, and he needs to get it out of there and move it to the one the other end of town. He thought, if we did it on Christmas eve-eve it'd be a time when most people were either in, or in the pub, and the people'll be distracted by it being Christmas and stuff,' said Toad.

'All right. It'll be better than sittin' around here another night. But me brother is coming home today, so later?'

'You still clean?' said Toad, 'cos I've got some great gear.'

'Yes. I am still off smack,' said Hoagie, 'thanks for reminding me though, I hadn't thought about it in, oh, at least ten minutes.'

'Are you allowed to smoke weed?'

'Yeah, why not?' said Hoagie. Why not indeed? And yes, it may be sad and desperate that the only thing he could think of that remotely interested him was a dodgy favour for a bloke with a stupid name, but sad and desperate he was.

'Got that too,' said Toad. 'Weed, I mean. Seven thirty at the Rat?'

'Yeah, all right,' said Hoagie.

He'd just put the phone down, when it rang again.

'Hi,' said a woman's voice the other end. It was Leela.

'Hi, Leela,' replied Hoagie. 'What can I do yer for?'

Leela laughed. Then she started sniffling.

'You grizzling?' said Hoagie.

'No, I'm all right,' she replied. Then she started wailing.

'What the fuck's the matter?' said Hoagie. Women crying. Always terrifying.

'Oh, I'm so fed up,' said Leela. 'Danny's away on this course thing in London, and I feel horrible. I'm so big and I'm really nervous I might go into labour when he's not here and…' she became incomprehensible as she dissolved into more howling.

Hoagie was freaked out. But not as freaked out as he was at her next question.

'Hoagie, will you come and keep me company tonight until he gets back at 10?' she said.

Hoagie could think of nothing much he'd like less, except perhaps prison.

'Ah, Leela, if you'd have rung ten minutes ago… but I've got to do a mate a favour tonight,' he said.

She began wailing again. 'Oh please, Hoagie! I can come with you even,'

'Ah, shit,' he said. He *hated* birds wailing, and then he had to be careful – Leela was Jonesy's wife. Perhaps he could just sit with her and have a pizza or something until it was time to go on the job with Toad and this bloke 'Honest' Lee.

'All right,' he heard himself agree. I'll come round about 4, but I have to go again by 7.'

'Oh! Thank you so much! Danny said you would,' said Leela.

Bloody Jonesy, thought Hoagie, I'll have words with him when he's back.

So, by 4pm, Hoagie was on Leela's sofa, squeezed up next to her with her massive pregnant bump, watching TV and munching on a pizza. So far, she'd jabbered on about fuck all and then, in the ad break, she'd showed him her belly, where you could see the kid inside move around! It made Hoagie feel quite queasy.

'Why don't you tell them to pick you up from here?' said Leela, with a mouthful of pizza, and shedding crumbs all over her enormous bump.

'Yeah, I could do,' said Hoagie.

'Actually, I'm feeling a bit weird,' said Leela. 'Can I just ride out with you, just so I'm with someone? I'm so cooped up in here and I haven't been out for ages. And I told Dan you wouldn't let me out of your sight… I could try to call him at his hotel…'

'Look, Leela, I'm not sure…'

'Oh, Pleeese, Hoagie,' she said, flapping her eyelashes at him and nudging up.

Now of all the women he'd ever known, which wasn't that many to be fair because, let's face it, you don't have much time or inclination for relationships when you have a dedicated heroin habit, Leela was one he had a bit of a grudging soft spot for. She was so God-damned vulnerable-looking, pretending to be all hard, but she wasn't. She was all soft, dark, sweet-smelling hair, like a Timotei advert, swishing and flicking it around. She wouldn't look out of place on the back of a cart, eating a flake. And then there were the eyelashes. Give Bambi's mum a run for her money. He'd had to rescue her once and here they were again, only a few months later and Jonesy had entrusted him with his heavily pregnant wife while he was God-knows-where.

'You can come with us, but you'll have to stay in the van,' he said. We won't be long – just gotta move some stuff from one place to another, get paid, then you and me will come back here and I'll stay 'til Jonesy gets in and that's it. And you are not to tell him you came out with us, right?'

'Ok,' she said, meekly. So, Hoagie called Toad and told him to tell Lee to pick him up at Jonesy's place. He didn't mention Leela coming with them.

The white transit drew up outside. Hoagie and Leela went out together.

'No way,' said Lee. 'No way is she comin' with us.'

Now nothing annoyed Hoagie more than being told what he could and couldn't do. He looked this Honest Lee up and down. He was a bit of a runt of the litter type. A chancer who had probably got hold of some hot merchandise, got nervous and wanted shot of it pretty quickly. Hoagie gave him one of his looks that spoke volumes.

'Yeah, mate, she is comin' along for the ride,' he said. 'Or the whole deal's off.'

The runt was about to say something, but then he thought better of it. He needed help to shift the goods, and he needed to move it all tonight. And this geezer with the hair, although he wasn't a big bloke, looked like someone you didn't argue with for some reason.

'Get her in the front seat then,' he said. 'I suppose it will look more legit if there's a bird in the front anyway.'

'I can't get up there,' said Leela.

'Toad, get out,' said Hoagie. 'Give us a hand getting Leela in.'

The two of them, Toad and Hoagie, got hold of Leela's arms, and attempted to hoist her up into the passenger seat.

'Fuckin' hell!' said Hoagie, 'It's like tryin' to push a bloody elephant into a mini! Leela, try to help yourself a bit.'

'I am!' she whined.

'Push her by the arse,' said Hoagie. 'One, two three, up.'

But once up there, Leela was wedged in so tightly it looked like she'd never come out.

'Can you put the seat back a bit,' she said, 'my bump doesn't fit properly. I can't put the belt on.'

'Jesus Christ!' said Honest Lee.

Hoagie slid the seat back with a thud. 'We can go in the back,' he said to Toad.

Lee jumped in and started up. 'Right, we're going,' he said. 'She has to stay in the van.'

They set off.

When they reached the lock-up, which was nothing more than a garage really, the boys jumped out and started unloading boxes and throwing them in the back of the van. Leela sat patiently until they declared they were all done, and they climbed back in and set off for the other 'warehouse' on the other side of town.

But they had been going less than a couple of minutes when Leela suddenly let out a massive screech.

'Jesus Christ!' exclaimed Lee, struggling to keep control. 'What's the matter? Hey what the hell? Shit! Oi, you two in the back – your bird here has pissed herself!'

'You stupid twat!' said Leela. 'My bloody waters have broken! I'm in labour!'

'For fuck's sake!' said Lee.

Fuckin' hell!' said Toad, 'Are you sure?'

'Yes I'm fucking sure!' said Leela. 'I have to go to hospital.'

'Babies don't come for ages,' said Lee. 'My missus was in labour for about two days. Then they had to suck it out with this sucker thing. Looked like a fuckin' Martian; cone head thing.'

'Ventose,' said Leela, 'and thanks.'

'All I'm sayin' is we can at least get the stuff to the drop off,' said Lee.

'I don't think so,' said Leela. 'My family has kids like shellin' peas.'

'Put her in the back,' suggested Toad, 'and she can lay down on them blankets.'

'Them blankets are coverin' up the gear!' said Lee.'

'I fuckin' knew this would be a nightmare,' said Hoagie. 'Look, why don't we put her in the back, but we'll have to go to the hospital on route.'

'Deliver the gear first,' said Lee, 'then the hospital. But we'll put her in the back.'

They pulled up in a layby and hauled Leela out of her seat. Hoagie and Toad supported her to get to the back of the van, which Lee had already opened up, and they helped Leela crawl in and find a place to stretch out amongst the boxes and crates of hot goods.

'You can get in with 'er,' said Lee to Hoagie. 'She's your bird.'

'She's not my bird, she's my mate's wife.'

'Whatever, mate! You brought her, you can get in.' Lee puffed his stocky little frame up to look like he meant business.'

'Look, you can pay me now,' said Hoagie, 'and I'll get in. Otherwise, I'm not helping the other end, right?'

Lee pulled out two 20's and a 10. 'Tha's yours. Now please, just get in and we'll be on our way.'

They set off again.

'This seat is damp,' moaned Toad.

'Just move up!' said Lee. 'There's no need to take up all the bloody seat.'

'I liked the back better,' said Toad. 'Obviously not now though.'

They could hear a bit of moaning coming from the back. Then there was a little knock on the dividing window.

'Oi,' said Hoagie, 'I think we have to go to the hospital now. I think the baby might come out otherwise. She's took 'er knickers off in here!'

'Ay, ay!' said Toad.

'Trust me, mate it int pretty,' said Hoagie. 'We need to get to the hospital first. Then we can ditch this stuff in peace.'

'Sorry!' moaned Leela.

'Fuck's sake,' said Hoagie. 'You can't do much about it though, can yer? When is the bloody kid due?'

'Oh, I'm overdue,' said Leela. 'That's why Jonesy wanted someone with me.'

'You didn't tell me you was ready to pop!' said Hoagie.

Lee suddenly swerved and pulled up in a layby again. He leapt out of the van and was round the back, yanking the doors open. 'Get out!' he ordered. 'There's a phone box here. You two will have to get out and call an ambulance from there. I'm not having a bird droppin' a sprog in the back of my van.'

They got out.

'Sit here on this bit of dirt,' said Hoagie to Leela, 'and I'll call the 999.'

He went into the phone box, which smelled of the obligatory fags and piss. A memory from 10 years ago briefly flooded his brain and for a moment he was frozen. Then he noticed that the phone was hanging off its wires.

'For fuck's sake!' cried Hoagie. He ran out to say something to Lee, but as he did so the white van pulled away with a screech of tyres.

'Shit! Shit!' cried out Hoagie.

'What?' said Leela.

'Fuckin' phone's out of order!'

'What are we gonna do?' wailed Leela. 'I can't give birth by the side of the road!'

'I dunno,' said Hoagie, 'I'm gonna fuckin' kill that Lee. And Toad. And fuckin' Jonesy! Let me think.' He rubbed his temples. This was turning into the worst day ever. 'Perhaps I can flag someone down.'

'Yeah!' howled Leela. 'Flag someone down!' She clutched her stomach and groaned.

Hoagie ran to the side of the road and waved frantically, miming a pregnant belly. Several cars sped up.

'Look! One's stopping!' said Leela.

'Thank fuck!' said Hoagie.

The car pulled up alongside them. It was a police car. Hoagie began to sweat.

'Can I help you, sir?' said the cop.

'Yeah, mate,' said Hoagie. 'We were in me mate's car, only he's driven off, see, but my, er, me wife's havin' a baby and we need to get her to the hospital.'

'You don't have very good friends, do you?' said the policeman.

'No. You're telling me,' said Hoagie.

'Don't I know you?' said the copper. He peered at Hoagie.

Hoagie knew he recognised him! He'd had dealings with this one before. 'Nah mate,' he said, 'I've just got one of them faces.'

The young policeman looked at him very closely. Then Leela came struggling up to the car.

'Please,' she begged, 'can you give us a ride? Or call an ambulance or something? I don't want to have it out here!'

The policeman went pale.

'I think you had both better get in and we can blues and twos it to the hospital,' he said. 'Get in the back. And er, can you sort of sit on that plastic sheet thing? I've only just got this car.'

As the car took off at a fairly speedy pace, with the blue light flashing on top, Hoagie wondered why the car had a plastic sheet in the back, but he thought it best not to ask.

'First time I've bin in a plod car when I haven't bin nicked,' he whispered to Leela, thinking it might cheer her up a bit.

The driver had radioed ahead, so Leela and Hoagie were quickly ushered in and Leela was given a wheelchair. They were rushed off to the delivery room. But before he knew what was happening, Hoagie was gowned and masked and taken through with a 'there you go, dad!'

'Wait!' said Leela. 'Can somebody call my husband? He's at this hotel. This is the number.' She passed the nurse a piece of paper.

The nurse looked at the midwife, then at Hoagie, then at the Doctor, who shrugged, then back at Leela. 'All right,' she said, and beckoned to a student nurse. She handed her the paper and said something to her. 'And be discreet!' she finished, glancing at Hoagie again.

And then they were off into the delivery room where it was suddenly all action.

'Dad, come down the business end and have a peep!' said the midwife, all excited.

'It isn't mine!' said Hoagie. But his protests were muffled by the mask and drowned out by Leela's screams. He was feeling very hot, sick and sweaty, and the one thing on his mind was that he really needed a hit. The methadone was wearing off, and anyway it was never enough to hold him. What was he thinking of? The idea that a few sips of a sickly dose of luminous green cordial could replace the sheer sweet fizz of a needle in a vein was ridiculous. They'd probably given him Night Nurse for all he knew! It wasn't just the drug he craved right now; it was just as much the using of it. Methadone was like owning a Lambo and choosing to drive a rusty Escort. And this! This was the worst. Fuckin' Jonesy! He'd kill him too.

Then he looked where the midwife was pointing. The room began to spin…and that was the last thing he remembered from the delivery room.

When Hoagie woke up, he was in a hospital bed, and his wrist was in a cast. His clothes were neatly folded on a chair beside the bed.

'What the fuck?' said Hoagie out loud. But all thoughts were interrupted when he realised he was desperate for a piss. He tried pressing the buzzer, but after 5 minutes, when no-one came, the situation was getting desperate. He decided to take matters into his own hands and wandered off to find the toilet.

'Ay, Ay! I know that arse!' It was Toad.

'What the fuck! I'm gonna fuckin' kill you mate!' said Hoagie. 'What d'y'mean, you know my arse?'

'There's a split down the back of that gown!' said Toad. And your tattoo – the one we got in Amsterdam, remember?

'Shit!' said Hoagie, pulling the gown round him. 'Anyway, I had to go in the bloody delivery room! That was NOT a pretty sight. Fuck me – like that Alien film where it bursts out of his guts.'

'Yeah, I know,' said Toad. 'The nurses are all talking about it! You passed out and you cracked yer wrist. I've bin to see Leela and Jonesy with their new kid.'

'Back to bed for a bit, Mr Hoag! Til the morphine wears off at least,' said a nurse behind them.

'Ah! Morphine! I knew there was something,' said Hoagie.

'He's not allowed to have morphine,' piped up Toad.

'Shut the fuck up,' said Hoagie between clenched teeth.

'Yeah, but it'll show up on yer piss test!' said Toad.

'At this point,' said Hoagie, 'I really don't give a fuck.'

As soon as Hoagie was back in bed, Jonesy showed up.

'Mate,' he said, 'what the fuck were you thinking of? Are you fuckin' stupid or something? Takin' a pregnant woman out on a fuckin' job? Let alone my fuckin' wife!'

'Look, mate,' said Hoagie, 'If you was at home where you should have bin, not on 'a course' which you and me know is really bangin' your bosses' secretary... I'm not stupid mate.'

'I was on a course...' said Jonesy.

'Whatever,' said Hoagie. 'Don't ask me to do you a favour again, right? You still owe me for the last time I covered up for you, and the fuckin' time before that.'

Jonesy fell silent.

'Come and see my kid,' he said.

'I saw it when it was fuckin' comin' out,' said Hoagie. 'That is not something I wish to repeat.'

'Ah come on, Leela asked for yer,' said Jonesy.

'I'll give it a look,' said Hoagie. 'What is it anyway?'

'It's a baby, you twat,' said Toad.

'You dickhead! What sex is it? Is it with or without?'

'It's a boy,' said Jonesy. 'Definitely with.'

'Bloody hell,' said Hoagie. I've just realised, you're a father. Shit!'

The boys were all crowded round Leela's bed that evening. Hoagie with his plaster cast and high on morphine, Toad's eyes bulging out even further than usual and Jonesy doing the awkward, proud father look. Leela looked a bit rough, dark under the eyes, but she seemed to have put on some lipstick, and she smiled at Hoagie.

'What you gonna call it?' asked Hoagie.

Leela looked him straight in the eyes. 'Well,' she said, 'we was thinkin', if you don't mind, we was thinkin' of namin' him after you, as you had some input into it.

'What, Hoagie?' said Hoagie.

'No!' Like, your actual name!! Or your middle name. Actually yeah. What is your middle name?'

Jonesy and Toad broke out into sniggers. 'It's Vincent,' said Toad. 'Like that bloke what cut his bloody ear off!'

'I'll cut both your fuckin' ears off if you don't belt up,' said Hoagie.

'Vincent it is then,' said Leela.

'Poor little fucker!' said Hoagie.

Burnt Lungs and Bitter Sweets

The Death of Some
Disco Wankers (1989)

Purple Haze (Jimi Hendrix)

Anyone who's been through the pain of withdrawal, and almost everyone who hasn't, will know that Hoagie's current attempt would feel like crap.

By the time Thatcher was reaching the end of her third term, Hoagie had been on smack for over ten years and the process of giving up was not unfamiliar to him. When he went to prison, it wasn't in the years they were sympathetic, holding your hand and wiping your arse, giving you medication to ease the symptoms. Oh no. Hoagie was chucked on the floor of the cell and left to sweat it out. To be fair, it did work.

But always, Hoagie was back on the gear in no time at all. And that meant more stealing and selling. He got another shitty flat, courtesy of the housing association helping out 'people like him', picked up his dole, went out nicking, bought his gear, got stoned and did it all again. He shied away from the pin for quite a while, enjoying it as he had when he was a kid with his friends from time to time, but mostly alone in front of his little tv, watching daytime soaps and night-time shit. TV got worse as the decade went on. He had his records, so it wasn't a terrible existence. He used to go with his mates down to a seedy little second had vinyl shop they nicknamed 'Smellies', on account of the owner stinking so badly it filled the whole shop. However, he'd had some great finds there.

But now, somehow, it was nearly the end of another decade and music was changing. Music, for Hoagie was a bit of a lifeline, like a soundtrack for his own life. In this decade, he felt like he was a bit schizophrenic, so it was quite funny that the music also seemed to be firmly split down the middle: shit and not shit. He daren't admit it to his mates, but he had quite liked the Smiths, especially the early stuff. The singer sounded like a miserable tone-deaf fuck, but some of the words were funny, mostly, and the guitar player was awesome. Hoagie smiled and put one of their songs on now, '*This Charming Man.*' It already sounded dated. How cool to have lived through the evolution of so many good bands. And now something else seemed to be on the horizon. People were buzzing about this new scene in Manchester (always fuckin Manchester, of all places!) and kids were goin' around wearing really baggy shit and T-shirts with smiley faces on them. Some girl had died after taking a drug called E and now everyone wanted to do it.

Hoagie smiled again. When the papers blew up a massive anti-drug campaign, it always had the opposite effect. There was this thing about heroin done in a kids show, *Grange Hill.* Yeah, he was too old to watch *Grange Hill*, but he totally loved it. It was like his own school days but a sort of sanitised version, fit for telly. But when it came out, everyone was pretty blown away by how 'shocking' it was. This series of episodes had a nice kid called Zammo shooting up and dyin' in a toilet! The slogan of the day was 'Just Say No,' and they even brought out a really shit song about it, which was guaranteed to send you straight out to score, it was so depressingly crap. Just Say No. Oh yes, it was all so fuckin' simple. Originally dreamed up by that death-on-a-stick Reagan bird in her 'war on drugs'. She looked like she said no to everything including food, Hoagie thought. Hoagie didn't often say no, and if he did, he really meant yes. But enough was enough. Something really annoying had happened. He'd been found a job. If he didn't take this job, his benefits would be cut. Then he'd have to nick more, and deal in the underpass, then he'd probably go back to prison. So, he'd taken this job. *Job*, a four-letter word. Well, you know what I mean. Work yeah. *That* was the four-letter word. All that time doing nothin' and now he'd been caught. Working, even for a few months, doesn't go well with having to score and fix up, so he had made the decision to go cold turkey. Again. Because if he told doctors and stuff, he'd be on a well-meaning path to get clean for life and Hoagie was never one to say never. He'd told Toad, who seemed to be able to use casually and never suffer, and Toad said he'd help him out.

So here he was. Today was day three and this was when the real storm would hit.

It started just before lunch. He'd had aches and a bit of a sniffle and all the usual crap he always managed to banish with a fix. But now there was no fix. He'd sworn off it. And now the aches turned to pain and the thick head turned to the worst cold and streaming nose he'd ever had. He was sneezing and yawning, and as the day wore on, he returned to his bed. And that was when the shits began.

143

Hoagie had a phone in the flat. (Mobiles, you understand, weren't a thing then). But he had to get out of bed to call Toad, who also had a shit flat now, and a phone, and also a shit job; a job under the radar, where he could actually shoot up at lunchtime! No more trips to the phone box for Hoagie though. He quickly wiped the thought of phone boxes from his mind. Phone boxes had bad memories.

'S'me,' he said to Toad. 'I can't get out of bed, and I need some of that shit stopping stuff.'

'Oh, fuck me,' said Toad, 'It's Saturday morning. The chemist is closed.'

'Well, haven't you got something'?'

'Maybe, but it's probably a bit out of date.'

'I don't care. If you don't get round here, I am gonna shit the bed.'

Toad, who was watching '*Going Live!*' shifted from his makeshift sofa and went to the bathroom. Under the sink he found a box of Imodium, probably used in his last clean up. It was out of date. He could hear the tinny voice of Hoagie shouting on the other end of the line.

'Are you there you wanker? Ah, my fuckin' head.' Toad picked up again.

'I've got it. I'm coming. What else do you need?'

'Lucozade? Paracetamol. Valium? He-ro-in? What are you watching? Is that Gordon the fuckin' Gofer?'

'Yeah. It's funny,' said Toad.

'If you don't get round here right now, I am gonna shove that little furry bastard right up your arse,' said Hoagie. Then he began moaning indecipherably.

'Someone's hand is on the end of it,' said Toad in protest.

'Fuckin' good for the gofer,' said Hoagie. 'Get here. Now. Shit, I'm gonna throw up.' The line went dead.

'It's fuckin' agony!' moaned Hoagie for the umpteenth time.

'I know. You said,' said Toad.

'Why aren't you like this?' sniffled Hoagie, kicking his legs about.

'Cos I'm not stupid,' said Toad. 'I've given up giving up. But I don't shoot up right now. Look, why don't you just have a taste, mate? I can work and use, so why can't you? It's not a problem unless you see it as a problem.'

'Because I don't want to use anymore. I'm done with this shit. I'm too old.'

'Then you'll suffer all week, won't yer?' said Toad. 'And we're not fuckin' old.' Toad hesitated. He wanted to say something, but the words would just not formulate. 'Mate,' he said again. 'Mate…do you remember…well…' he stopped.

'What?' snapped Hoagie, wriggling about under the blanket he had wrapped himself in, and then throwing it off in a huff.

'Look. All I'm saying is, look... remember Kecks.' There. He'd said her name. 'She did the same. But look how that ended. You have to be careful. After. If you use it again. You know.'

Hoagie could not believe Toad had brought that up right now. He exploded with expletives. Then he put the blanket back around him, shivering again.

'Just do not mention that, all right,' he said.

'Sorry, mate,' said Toad. 'Look, should I call yer mum?'

145

'Fuck off,' said Hoagie. 'Just…just stay, ok?'

'Yeah,' said Toad.

Hoagie went quiet.

'You still alive, mate?' said Toad.

'Just,' said Hoagie.

'Only a few more days and you'll be right as rain,' said Toad cheerfully.

Hoagie groaned.

'Tell you what,' said Toad, 'Why don't we go out when you're better? My mate Shawn said there's this party goin' on in Walthamstow, like near the dog track in a warehouse or somefing. He does a bit of DJing at The Cave – and they had flyers and everything. But you have to wait around in yer cars at the service station to find out where it actually is, like. Now, if you want a real drug that isn't actually addictive, and cause all this shit, you oughta drop an E. That's the way to go. Shawney can definitely get us some.'

'We haven't got a car,' said Hoagie.

'Jonesy?' said Toad.

'Doubt it,' said Hoagie, 'he's up to his neck in nappies again. How many kids is it possible for one man to produce? He must be a walkin' jiz bank.'

'He *is* a bit of a wanker,' said Toad. 'Nah, he's all right. I reckon Leela'll be glad to see the back of him for a night. Get rid of one baby anyway.'

'When is it?' said Hoagie.

'Next weekend,' said Toad.

'Ask Jonesy, and if I feel ok I might as well,' said Hoagie.

'If you're still in the land of the living I reckon it'll pick you up no end,' said Toad.

.

By the following weekend Hoagie was climbing the walls and he would have done anything to stop thinking about smack. A rave in a warehouse and the promise of a drug he had not yet tried sounded like heaven on earth. He'd downed half a bottle of cheap scotch from the corner shop and two codeine pills that he'd conned out of the doctors a month ago by telling them he had injured his back, before he heard Jonesy beeping his horn from the street.

'All right! I'm coming!' he shouted down from the window. He grabbed his jacket and ran down the stairs and out into the street.

'What the fuck is that?' said Toggie, who was in the front seat.

'It's me smiley T-shirt,' said Hoagie. 'Acid House and all that.'

'Hmph!' said Toggie.

The service station seemed to pulsate with a life of its own. A line of cars like a tremendous dragon lit by orange fire snaked its way along the road, causing a mile long horn-blaring tail-back. Jonesy's car was parked up, radio at full blast, listening for the signal that would give them the directions to their venue. Hoagie vaguely remembered someone, maybe his grandfather, whom he barely knew, listening to the shipping forecast. It seemed similar, like a kind of code for the in-crowd. A Pied-Piper call for those in the know. Now why would he even recall that? Where would he have been? And how old? He wiped the thought as fast as it arrived. Thinking about the past never did him any favours and what was the point of it?

'Got a fag?' he said. 'Or a bit of puff? I'm so fuckin' bored waitin' around.'

'Got a spliff, yeah,' said Toad. 'But the fuckin' law are about 'cos of this mayhem, so maybe not.'

'Fuck it!' said Hoagie. 'They're not gonna look for what they're not lookin' for.'

Toad lit the joint and took some very deep drags before he handed it over to Hoagie.

'Look at fuckin' Jonesy! Like a cat on hot bricks!' he said to Toad, and gestured to Jonesy, who was out of the car and was now hopping from foot to foot, occasionally reaching in to twiddle the volume of his car radio up and down.

'Stop playin' with your knob in public, Jonesy,' said Hoagie. 'Get back in the fuckin' car and have a suck on this!'

Hoagie held out the joint as Jonesy looked round in alarm. He flapped his hand about to get Hoagie to put it out of sight.

'Where's Toggie?' said Toad, suddenly.

'He's havin' a slash round the back I think,' said Hoagie.

At that moment, Toggie came back with a wide grin on his face.

'Got me some more disco biscuits,' he said.

'I thought we had some,' said Hoagie.

'Nah, these are better man,' said Toggie. 'This guy reckons they're so strong they could have you up on the ceilin' in minutes.'

'Fuck off they will!' said Hoagie.

'Less try 'em then,' said Toggie. 'Also, I've bagged enough to re-sell at the venue. You all in?'

'Yeah, I will,' said Toad.

'What the fuck? These are love hearts int they?' said Hoagie.

'Twat,' said Toggie. Although he wasn't completely sure.

All of them except Jonesy, because he was driving, said they'd try the Ecstasy, but before Toggie could tell Toad some important information about these little pills, Toad swallowed his.

'You idiot!' said Toggie. 'I was going to tell you that we should take 'em before we go in, so they can't do us, but a bit closer to the time. Even Jonesy can join in.'

'Wait? Innit like acid then?'

'No!' said Toggie. 'It starts workin' after a bit, but it don't last as long. Now you'll peak before we even know where we're goin' to!'

'I bet it's dud anyway. You've bin ripped off mate. This definitely looks like a love heart bin dyed,' said Hoagie.

'Look. This bloke says it's all right,' replied Toggie.

'Your bloke is a dealer,' said Hoagie. 'Really trustworthy I reckon!' He gave a low-pitched laugh.

'He's sound, man. Anyway, it'll wear off,' said Toggie. 'But there you go. I've got more.'

'Bet it's a dud,' repeated Hoagie.

Toggie rolled his eyes. 'It's what's new,' he said. 'Still, I'm going back to the bog. Got some smack as well and need to get it in me before we get to the rave.'

'Both?' said Hoagie.

'Yeah, not a bad mix,' said Toggie.

'I'm off it,' said Hoagie, though he could swear his veins actually started throbbing in anticipation at the thought of it.

He tried to think of something else. 'When the fuck do we hear about this rave thing?' he said, irritated.

'The call will come through the radio,' said Toad.

'Ah, fuck it,' Hoagie gave up and rolled the small pill between his fingers where it now nestled in his pocket. 'I'm getting out for some air.'

Whilst Toggie had gone to fix up, the others listened out for the announcement. The air was static with excitement. Over 40 minutes had passed and nothing.

'This pill in't doin' anything,' complained Toad. 'I've took another one.'

'What the fuck, Toad!' said Hoagie. 'That could be bloody anything Toggie's got ripped off with. I might not take mine. I won't take two that's for sure.' He considered for a moment. 'Mind you, I can wait and see what it does to you now, can't I?' he smirked.

Toggie returned with a smile of serenity.

'This wanker took two of them pills,' said Hoagie, jerking his thumb towards Toad.

'They don't work,' said Toad. 'Actually, I took three.'

'Twat. You're in for a fun night,' said Toggie. 'If you don't miss it altogether.'

And just like that, Toad was suddenly staring into space with an odd expression. 'Shit,' he said, 'I think they might be workin.'

And as he said that the call came crackling across the airwaves.

'Did you get that number?' said Toggie.

'No! I dunno! Maybe!' shouted Hoagie. 'Quick, quick, get to the phone box!'

Burnt Lungs and Bitter Sweets

'It's all right, that tosser there will call, and we'll follow,' said Toggie, pointing at some twenty-something hoodie in baggy jeans legging it towards the phone box.

The baggy jeans hoodie emerged waving a flyer. There was suddenly a lot of movement. People jumping into cars, slamming doors, honking horns.

'Go, Go, Go!' shouted Toggie, snatching a ciggie out of Jonesy's mouth and forcing him into the driver's seat. 'Follow that car! Always wanted to say that!'

'All right!' said Jonesy. 'Mind me head!' He started up and they joined the snake of cars heading up the dual carriageway.

'Fuck me,' slurred Toad. 'I love you mate.' He snuggled up to Hoagie.

'Fuck off!' said Hoagie.

'It's just the E talking,' said Toggie.

'What the fuck!' said Hoagie. 'I int takin' that.'

'You'll love it,' said Toggie. 'You won't care. Wait 'til we get there.'

'I am too old for this shit,' said Hoagie.

They slowly followed the glowing line of cars, which seeped smoke from every passenger window as if it were a giant metal dragon. Eventually they reached the site of a seemingly abandoned warehouse. But the building was already pulsating into life. All of them, including Jonesy, who had been assured it would wear off in time to drive home, swallowed their pills and headed for the door.

It was like entering a different dimension; no, a new galaxy. So, this was 'new earth', thought Hoagie. And from this glimpse of promise, he really believed he might like it. They strode into the belly of the beast; on a space shuttle to the sun; four friends with the world just as it should be for one night.

Hoagie and Toad headed for the bar. Unusually, it wasn't crowded.

'What they all doin' drinkin' water?' said Hoagie, entranced by the sight of thousands of already glistening people of all ages waving their arms about to the beat and swigging water from plastic bottles in time to the music.'

'Dunno,' said Toad. 'But look at your eyes, man!'

'I can't see me own eyes, can I?' said Hoagie. He peered at his blurry reflection in the metal-topped counter. 'Oh yeah!' His pupils looked huge. 'Like an acid trip. Except – hey do you remember that one where I thought my coat had vanished and there was egg boxes moving about and stuff? Like, an eggbox dragon or somefing?'

'Nah,' said Toad. 'I'm dancing.' He tripped off into the throng.

'Like yer hair,' someone said.

Hoagie turned round. 'Eh?'

A girl, probably around Hoagie's age, so more of a woman really, with long red hair, wearing a red velvet corset and cropped black trousers was touching his spiky style.

'I love your hair!' she repeated. 'You're like, a punk raver.'

'Yeah,' Hoagie was quite transfixed. She looked like a goddess, and her hair resembled flames. Like bloody Rita Hayworth!

It's your first time, isn't it?' she said. Her voice sounded exotic, like warm silk brushing his ears, he suddenly thought. Christ! His senses were all getting mixed up. He had to pull himself together a bit.

'What?' he said.

'I said, is it your first E trip?'

'Yeah, how do you know?' he said.

'Cos you just look, kinda still. Kinda *enraptured.*' Her tongue seemed to surround the word. There was some accent, but he couldn't place it in the noise which seemed to rise up and surround them.

'Whaa?' Hoagie's speech didn't quite catch up with the thousand sunny thoughts that were circling his brain like hummingbirds, and he was starting to drift off somewhere on the music. But this girl…

'Come and dance with me.' She took hold of his hand and led him serenely onto the dance floor where he floated off on the pulsing beat and there was no need for words. They communicated beyond words. Everything was good. Nothing mattered and it never would again.

Somewhere in the corner of the vast space, Toggie had been shifting the Es for £15 a tablet. It was a bit dodgy, as he could see that one of the bouncers had got him in his sights. He ducked into the corridor leading to the loo and kept his head down.

'Ow much?' said a skinny bloke in a neon t-shirt who kept nodding his head in time to the beat.

'15 Quid,' said Toggie. 'Get in 'ere.' He shifted the guy into the toilet. 'Want some for yer mates as well?'

'Yeah, mate, five.'

'75' said Toggie.

'What are these beans then?' said the noddy guy.

Toggie peered closely at his loot. 'Spotted fish, mate,' he said.

'Oh, oh right, yeah,' said Noddy. He paid up and took off back to his waiting friends.

Not bad, this, thought Toggie, who was also coming up on his own trip, and gently smacked up too. He thought he'd shift the rest, then get dancing a bit himself.

But the bouncer was heading his way. 'Fuck's sake,' he muttered and headed out and into the crowd.

Meanwhile, Toad, Hoagie and Jonesy were having a wonderful time on the dancefloor. Toad was doing some kind of dance only he knew about – one which involved pogoing up and down whilst also waving his arms up towards the light and gazing into the middle distance as if he had seen a vision. Even Jonesy had taken the drug, having been assured it would definitely wear off in time for him to drive home, and he was floating around in his own little crowd of admirers, running his hands over everyone who danced in his vicinity. And Hoagie could not keep his eyes off the beautiful redhead who seemed to have been sent to him from God. She waved around, seemingly in slow motion, making patterns with her delicate hands and spinning in a hypnotic whirl to the rhythmic pulse of the beat.

The disturbance started in a fairly low-key way. Just what seemed to be a minor scuffle on the edge of the dancefloor. But pretty soon everyone was crowding around two guys lying on the floor. They both seemed to be convulsing and, in his trippy state, Hoagie felt fascinated, as it appeared to be happening in slow motion.

Suddenly, he was grabbed by the arms and whisked away from the mayhem that was unfolding. It was Toggie.

'Mate, it's one of them blokes who sold me the pills. He's probably had too much of his own supply,' he said. 'We should stay out of the way. I've been selling the same stuff and it must be dodgy!'

'But what about us?' said Hoagie. 'We've had it too!'

And as he spoke, he saw Jonesy's legs begin to buckle and he crumpled down to the floor.

'Shit!' he shouted. 'Leela'll kill us!'

They both ran to the floor and dragged Jonesy away to the side, where they poured a jug of water over him. His eyes had rolled back in his head, but when the water hit, he sat upright and was promptly sick on the floor. He sat up, bewildered. And as soon as they breathed a sigh of relief, Hoagie and Toggie heard whistles and banging. The police came thundering in.

'Shit! Shit! We gotta go!' said Toggie.

'Fuck yeah!' said Hoagie, who had no intention of getting arrested. 'Fuck! Where's Toad?'

'No idea,' said Toggie. 'He can sort himself out. Let's go!' Toggie headed off without even stopping. He'd left Hoagie with Jonesy.

'This way,' said Hoagie, heaving Jonesy up with his arm around him. They headed for the fire escape.

Toad had been in the loo splashing his face with water when the commotion had started. It didn't sound good, and when he heard the words, 'Police!' he knew straight away that he ought to exit the warehouse. He'd headed out of the other fire escape. So as Hoagie was hobbling out with Jonesy, undetected, Toad was going in the opposite direction. Hoagie put Jonesy on the ground by the car, a safe distance away from the police raid and Jonsey babbled on incoherently about the lights and colours.

'Look, mate,' he said, 'I'm gonna go back to find Toad. You ok?'

Jonesy nodded, then he was sick again. 'I'm all right now,' he said, then his head drooped down onto his chest, and he appeared to have fallen asleep.

'Look, let's get you in the car,' said Hoagie, picking him up and manhandling him into the front seat. 'You can just look like you are asleep in there if anyone sees you. I'm goin' back for Toad. He might be ill too.'

Jonesy mumbled and then started snoring.

Hoagie headed back towards the fire escape he'd exited from. Meanwhile Toad had scarpered. Across the vast industrial area, over a fence and into some boggy marsh ground, where he lay low, feeling a bit unwell, but a safe distance from being picked up. He vomited and felt fascinated by the way you could always throw up diced carrots even when you hadn't eaten them since you were six years old. He moved away from his own vomit but remained where he was.

Back in the club, the lights were still not up and quite a few of the people had left. The chaos still reigned around the two guys on the floor, who looked very unwell indeed. Hoagie went over to see if he could do anything. One of them briefly opened his eyes.

'Help,' he rasped.

Hoagie's vision swam. There was no sign of Toad, so he hoped he must have got out. Toggie had long gone. This guy looked like he was dying, and his friend already looked dead.

People were screaming and someone was yelling to put the lights up. The cops were running all over the place and in the background, Hoagie could see that two of them were heading his way. He thought about giving the guy mouth-to-mouth, although he wasn't really sure how to do it. He thought about Kecks. He considered trying some other first aid of some sort, but he hadn't really got a clue what to do. Still, he might be able to help. Then he thought about Jonesy, also weak and ill and maybe poisoned on the same stuff this guy had sold him. He thought about the police approaching and the lights going up. And he thought about prison. He briefly glanced up and he saw that redhead. He made a decision. 'Sorry mate,' he said. 'Dodgy drugs I reckon,' he said to the crowd. 'Needs a paramedic.' He took hold of the redhead's arm and said, 'Let's get out of here!' They both ran to the fire door again.

They ran for Jonesy's car. It was far enough away to be a safe place, away from the scene. Jonesy was slumped, asleep, but probably out of danger, across the two front seats. Toggie was also there, sitting serenely in the back seat. There was no sign of Toad yet.

'I have to find my mate,' said Hoagie. 'I think the night is over for us.' The drug seemed to have all but worn off after the rude interruption, but Hoagie still felt captivated by the mysterious woman. 'Can we exchange numbers? What's your name, even?'

'I'm Emma,' she said. 'I'm from Liverpool, and this is my number.' She gave him a scrap of paper.

'Hoagie,' said Hoagie. 'James, really, but everyone calls me Hoagie. I knew there was some accent, but you don't sound like a real scouser?'

'I've travelled around a bit. I'm at the Uni. You'll find me, if you want to, but I have to go now!' She swept off into the night.

'Wait!' said Hoagie. But she had gone. 'Shit,' he said to himself.

He popped his head into the car. 'Look,' he said, 'I can drive us a safer distance away. Round the corner.'

'You don't have a licence,' said Toggie.

'Well, we don't have much choice, do we?' said Hoagie. 'Where the fuck is Toad, anyway?'

'Maybe he got picked up?' suggested Toggie.

'Look, let's get going, and we can find him later on,' said Hoagie. We only need to go round the corner. There's a little café thing which will be open at about 6. We can have breakfast and then go home when we're all sober. I reckon we can find Toad in the morning. If we don't go too far, he might find us.'

They moved the car into the next street, a dark side-street, and they slept for a while.

Hoagie was the first to wake. Someone was knocking frantically on the car window. Bang, bang, bang, bang! It was Toad, wild-eyed, damp and muddy with his hair on end.

'Let me in you bastards!' he was shouting.

'Toad! Where have you been?' said Hoagie, opening the door.

'Only sitting in some fuckin' bog land most of the night, then wandering round the streets lookin' for you!' he screeched.

'In a bog?' Hoagie burst out laughing. 'Good place for a Toad,' he said.

Toad reached into the car and got hold of Hoagie by his neck. 'I'll fuckin' strangle you!' he screamed.

'Get the fuck off!' said Hoagie and pushed him roughly away. 'And get the fuck in the car!'

Swearing and cursing, Toad climbed into the passenger seat. In the back, Jonesy and Toggie were stirring. Jonesy was asleep on Toggie's shoulder.

'What the fuck?' said Toggie, pushing Jonesy to the other side of the car.

'Well, Toad's back,' said Hoagie. He's been Toad in a hole all night!' He was nearly pissing himself laughing.

'Not funny,' said Toad, although even he was beginning to smile in spite of himself.

'How did you find us?' said Toggie.

'I lay low until all the fuss died down and then I went back to where the car was, but you'd gone, so I sort of wandered round the streets and I found you by luck,' said Toad. 'Bloody good job I did. What were you thinkin' of? Were you goin' back home without me? Did you even try to look for me?'

'We wouldn't have gone without you, Toad,' said Hoagie. 'We thought you might have been picked up.'

'Well lucky for us all I wasn't,' said Toad. 'What happened in there, anyway?'

'Those couple of wankers who sold the E's to Toggie,' said Hoagie, 'they was layin' on the floor and I think one of 'em was dead.'

'Really?'

'Yeah,'

'Do you think they did die?'

'I dunno, but Jonesy was really sick as well,' said Hoagie, 'and Toggie threw up later on.'

'So did I,' said Toad. 'Twice.'

'Well, fuck 'em then,' said Hoagie. 'Shall we go for breakfast in that café over there?'

'Yeah, let's go,' said Toggie.

The four of them sat around the Formica table and the waitress plonked four greasy looking English Breakfasts in front of them. 'Eh, did you hear all the commotion last night?' she said, pointing at the television.

'Nah, what's happened?' said Toggie.

'Oh, some blokes died at a rave round the corner, and the cops are lookin' out for anyone who was there. Drugs, I reckon. As usual.'

'Turn it up,' said Hoagie.

The news of the deaths, grainy images of the warehouse in darkness and the faces of the two dead dealers were on the screen, and Hoagie could swear he could see the outline of himself and the redhead making their way across the industrial waste ground to the car.

'Is that you, mate?' said Toad.

'Shut up,' hissed Hoagie. 'We should go home. Now.'

'Who's that bird you're with?' said Toggie, as they hurried out of the café.

'Met her in there,' said Hoagie. 'Name's Emma. I've got her number somewhere.'

'You gonna call her?' said Toad.

'Nah,' said Hoagie. 'I was just high. Come on Jonesy, start her up before that waitress notices we haven't paid the bill.'

Jonesy pulled out of the side-street just as the police car pulled in.

'Just in time,' said Toggie.

'Fuck them wankers,' said Hoagie, 'it was a good night otherwise. Come on Jonesy, step on it. Let's get back and get some real gear. None of them poncey pills.'

'I think you should phone that girl,' said Toad.

'Nah, I don't even know her last name. I was just high,' said Hoagie. 'Besides we've got bigger things to worry about.'

'Like what?' said Jonesy.

'Well, what you're gonna say to Leela when you get home for a start,' said Hoagie.

Jonesy suddenly looked very pale again.

Virginia Betts

Juiced (1994)

I Love to Love (Tina Charles)

Hoagie woke up with a cough. He didn't know where he was – he was lying in a bed surrounded by a lot of bright white everything and the sound of beeping. His throat was sore, and his head ached. His body felt like he had been run over by a truck. He tried to sit up and groaned. What the fuck had happened?

The last thing he could remember was being in the back of a van with Toggie and some other guy whose name he couldn't remember right now, but he would never forget his face because it was as scary as fuck.

Hoagie moved his arm and discovered he had some sort of tubes attached to him. What the fuck? There was a radio playing in the background, *'don't you forget about me'*. Then he was aware of someone sitting there beside him. It wasn't his mum. It was a woman in uniform. Police uniform.

Before he had a chance to speak, his mum bustled into the room.

'He's awake! Thank God for that! What the hell do you think you're doing?' said his mum.

'I dunno,' Hoagie croaked.

'I am literally gonna kill you!' she said. The policewoman started to stand up.

Hoagie thought that the best course of action at this point was to feign sleepiness. He had guessed by now he must be in hospital, did not like the fact that there was a policewoman beside his bed, and needed to get out of talking to his mum right now. So, he let his eyes roll back in his head a little and pretended to nod off. To be honest, there was not much acting required; he felt as if he might slip into sleep quite easily. But there was no chance his mum was letting him off that lightly.

'You can bloody well keep awake!' he heard his mum say.

'Mrs Hoag, James needs to rest as much as possible,' a nurse said. Then, to Hoagie, 'However, James, it wouldn't be good for you to fall asleep. Try to stay awake.' She had a quick word with the policewoman and they both nodded towards Diane Hoag.

'Mum,' said Hoagie, 'Whass happened?'

'The police want to ask you a few questions, Mr Hoag,' said the nurse, 'but they have agreed to let your mum sit with you for a bit while you have a rest.'

The policewoman and the nurse both left.

'You little shit,' said Diane Hoag. 'I've had just about enough of you. Another fuck-up I've got to sort out.'

'But what have I done?' said Hoagie. 'Why am I in hospital?'

'You really don't remember?'

'No. The last thing I remember is sitting in the back of a van,' said Hoagie.

'Well, for once it's a good thing you turned into a junkie again, 'cos getting *'stoned'* and *'high'* or whatever you call it, will probably keep you out of prison, for now at least. Even if you did nearly die.'

'What the fuck?'

'And stop swearing you little shit,' she said.

'Mum, can I just go to sleep for a bit?' said Hoagie, genuinely tired.

'No, you cannot,' said his mum. 'If you go to sleep you might drift off into a coma. If I don't murder you first.'

'Will I get me memory back?' said Hoagie, suddenly frightened. 'What if I can't remember anything ever again?'

'Won't make much difference to someone with NO BRAIN,' she hissed at him. "What the hell have I done to deserve you doing this?'

'Nothing. I was probably just bored. I *am* bored. All the time,' said Hoagie.

'Life *is* boring and then you die,' said his mum. 'Get used to it. What do you think? Do you expect to be entertained all the time? Why don't you try working?'

'No-one will employ me,' he said. Look, please can I just have a rest? Usually, you don't even want to talk to me, so why are you here now?'

'I'll go now, and if you're lucky, I'll come back later. You'd better start remembering, and get some sort of story straight, because the old bill out there are wanting to ask you about it all.' Diane got up to leave.

'Mum!' said Hoagie.

'What?'

'Nothing.'

He could hear her talking to someone out in the corridor, telling whoever it was that he didn't live with her, hadn't done for years, except for coming back once in a while to borrow money, but she hadn't seen him for a while because he was a drug addict again, and she couldn't have him at home. That was about right, he thought. The real reason was because she couldn't put up with anything about him, he reminded her of his dead dad, and when he was not living there, she didn't have to deal with any of it. Anyway, he wasn't a drug addict. He used drugs. That was the difference. Kecks had been a drug addict and the proof of it was that she was dead. He was not dead. But he suddenly felt very sleepy and started to drift off.

Hoagie woke again with a start. It was still bright and noisy where he was, in this airless room, but he could see through the small window that the night sky had grown dark. He must have been asleep for a couple of hours. No-one was beside him at the moment – good. They'd left a used paper cup there though, so he guessed they would be back. He began to get flashes of memories to piece together from the night before.

He'd made his way to Toad's, and they had gone to call on Toggie, with the intention of getting high, watching the football, and sinking a couple of beers. And they had done just that, because you could always rely on Toggie to provide good gear, beer and telly. Toggie had a mate round – some bloke called 'Hammers'. He'd arrived carrying copious cans of lager in a carrier bag.

'Have one,' he'd said to Hoagie.

Hoagie was high on heroin and weed and he wasn't really bothered about drinking but when he hesitated, straight away this bloke started taking the piss, so he accepted, and kept up the pace with him, can for can. Not many people could best Hoagie's ability to take his drink and drugs.

Hoagie didn't much like this bloke, Hammers. Hammers was short and squat, but he had a big frame. He was rather like a pit-bull in human form. He also had a face like a pug. He had a scar running the length of his left cheek and several tattoos on his forearms.

The conversation soon took a turn to robbery. It reminded Hoagie briefly of his dad.

'I reckon there's no time like the present,' said Hammers. I've got a van outside, the back is empty and I've the right tools for the job. I think we should just do it.'

'I agree,' said Toggie.

'What are we talking about?' said Hoagie, 'just so I'm clear.'

'Woolies!' said Toggie. If you think about it, it's a dream! Iss dark round the back, but there's no shutters on the windows, so we can always lob a brick at one. It's all fair game.'

'Are you really doin' this,' said Hoagie. 'Are you sayin' that your grand plan is to nick stuff from Woolies?'

'Yeah, Toggie's in, in't yer Toggie?' said Hammers. 'It's a gift. You in, mate?'

'I nick stuff from Woolies all the time,' said Toad.

'I don't think he means pick and mix,' said Hoagie, 'and yeah, I've nicked stuff from there too. When I was a kid. Sold some of it to get us to Amsterdam if you remember. Their security is lax to say the least. But don't you think you should take a bit of time to plan it a bit more?'

'Been planning it for weeks,' said Hammers.

'Oh, right,' said Hoagie. 'So…'

'More drink first,' said Hammers.

'Deffo,' said Toggie. 'Cheers,' he said, popping open another two cans and chucking the ring pulls over his shoulder like a medieval King with the bones at a banquet.

By the time they had climbed up into the van, Hoagie was completely pie-eyed, and pretty much up for anything. Toad had nearly chickened out, saying he had to get home for his dinner, and Hoagie wished he was in bed to be honest, but he went along with it.

They parked up at the back of the shop and staggered out. Hoagie had initially supposed it was just a drunken hair-brained scheme that they'd give up on, but this bloke, Hammers…something about him made the whole thing a bit more edgy. He reminded Hoagie of a gun with a hair-trigger. Bit like Toggie, but even more on the verge of going off on one. And the more they had drunk, the more doing it tonight had seemed like a good idea. Nevertheless, it had got to the point earlier where Hoagie had been thinking of an excuse to get going. He wasn't keen on going back to prison again.

Then Toggie had brought out more smack.

'Not for me,' said Hammers, holding his hand up. 'I only supply the stuff. I'm not into stuffing meself full of this shit when a few pints can do the job nicely.'

'Well, we like it, don't we boys?' said Toggie to Toad and Hoagie. He cooked it up, took off his belt and wrapped it round his arm, tightening it as much as he could. Toad didn't hesitate to share the needle.

'You?' offered Toggie.

Hoagie had been close again many times lately, but something had always stopped him because he'd managed to get back on the juice – the methadone – again, and even though that was a bit shit, it was pretty good with a bit of smack as well. He didn't want to tip the balance, though, even if he did have a miraculously strong constitution. And shooting up was not that interesting when there was no-one else around. Like drinking alone. These days, he'd become less and less bothered about anything. Even prison didn't really bother him at the time. Drinking alone had become more and more of a regular feature in his days. If he did it and died, really, who gave a fuck? He really couldn't care less at this point. Everyone just fucked off and died anyway, didn't they?

'You not shot it up before?' said Hammers.

'Yeah, quite a lot,' Hoagie gave a wry smile, 'but I'm good smokin' it these days.'

'Oh, mate, you don't know what you're missin', does he Toad? Good stuff, apparently,' said Hammers.

'Nah,' said Toad, 'This *is* good stuff. I think you should just do it.'

'Oh, fuck it, why not,' said Hoagie. It definitely appealed more than the alternative, which was returning to his empty flat, where Kecks' ghost still cast a gloomy shadow over him, even now.

The process was sort of therapeutic: the cooking, the drawing it up, finding the vein. Yeah, he liked that part. For Hoagie it was as if a light went on. It hit him instantly. There was no delay, like smoking the stuff, which he'd long become quite tolerant to, no burn in the throat, just a pure chemical rush. It was wonderful. It was the best thing he had experienced for ages.

And surprisingly, for one who had smoked and also downed a lot of alcohol, he wasn't sick. He just lay back contented for a while, and then suddenly he could not stop talking.

'Has that effect on some people,' said Hammers. 'Some people can't shut up. You're quieter, Toad. I can tell. More mellow, like.'

'My arse he is,' said Toggie.

'I reckon we could definitely do it tonight,' Hoagie was saying. 'Absolutely definitely.'

Hammers had given them each a choice to go 'tooled up', which Hoagie discovered meant baseball bats and pieces of lead pipe, not guns. He was too wasted to make any clear decisions though. They made their way over to the store.

The back door entrance proved more difficult to break open than they thought.

'How about we chuck a brick through the side window?' said Toggie.

'Have we got a brick?' slurred Hoagie, 'and what are we nickin' anyways?'

'Anything we can sell!' said Hammers, 'just go for the expensive stuff. And yeah, I have got a brick.' And with that, he lobbed it through the glass.

An alarm rang out into the night.

'Don't worry, once we're in we can disable it,' said Hammers.

Toggie gave a tribal yell, and ran into the shop, swiping up whatever he could lift and stuffing it into a large bin bag. But suddenly, all the lights came on.

What had happened after that? Hoagie's head began to pound again. He couldn't remember. It was like a dazzle of white light in his head, this memory, after the lights came on.

169

He breathed out slowly. Then he noticed that his bedside police companion was coming back into the room. He closed his eyes.

The next few days shed a bit more light on his situation. He no longer had his spleen, and he had unfortunately managed to overdose with a mixture of weed, speedballs and alcohol. He'd been grazed by a vehicle, and he'd also suffered a fall from a height, which he could only vaguely remember. What the hell was he doing up there? He was incredibly lucky, must have nine lives, they said. Ha! Like he'd never heard that before. Only nine? But he'd been lying half dead in the street near where 'a very serious crime' had taken place. Three of his friends had been picked up, and two people had been badly injured, one of them a minor, but no-one was really talking. It wasn't clear whether Hoagie had been involved or not. However, one of the group, Mark Hammond, had said he was with them.

'He's not my fuckin' friend,' growled Hoagie, thinking that anyone who dobbed him in definitely wasn't his friend and never would be. He *knew* he shouldn't have trusted that fucker.

A week later he was back with his mum for a while. Even David had popped in to see him.

'Bloody hell, I must have looked bad if you're here,' said Hoagie.

'Don't get used to being here,' said his mum. 'Let's just get you back on your feet and through the court case and you can get your arse back to that flat.'

'Feelin' *so* welcome,' said Hoagie.

'Don't push it,' said David.

170

'How's life, David?' said Hoagie, attempting to change the subject and make conversation.

'I met someone, and work's ok, you know,' said David. 'I'm not up on criminal charges, so on balance I'd say all was well.'

'*I'm* not up on criminal charges,' said Hoagie. 'I'm just under suspicion.'

'Do you remember anything else from that night?' said David.

Hoagie looked up at him. 'I only remember the bits I said already.' It was true, he had a very vague recollection of most of the events, and he'd told the police most of what he knew.

After they had broken in and the lights had come on, they had run around trying to disable the alarm and then gave up and began grabbing stuff. But a hapless security guard had come rushing in. As soon as he had seen him, Hoagie had made the decision to run as quickly and as quietly as he could. He'd headed through a door which he thought might lead him out of the building, but in front of him was a flight of grey stone stairs. He had headed up, but it led only to a shabby warehouse with broken windows and full of boxes and cobwebs. Hoagie had heard shouts and footsteps. He'd hidden behind the boxes. Shit. How would he get out? Now he heard the footsteps prowling round the area, and it was only a matter of time before he was found. He had edged back towards the door. Suddenly, he was illuminated by a bright torchlight shining in his face. There stood the silhouette of the security guard. 'Aha! Gotcha yer you shit!' said the guard.

Without thinking, Hoagie had run blindly towards the light in the direction of the door. He'd kicked it open and charged through. The Guard was right behind him, so Hoagie had mounted the handrail and begun to slide down for a quicker escape. Unfortunately, drunk and high, he'd lost his balance as the momentum built.

It had all happened very quickly. Hoagie had tumbled over the side and without any time to even yell out, he had landed with a crunch at the bottom of the concrete stairwell, having cracked his ribs on the way down. In agony, only slightly dulled by opiates, he had got up, aware that his back, ribs, ankle and wrist did not feel normal, but still set on escape. He'd dragged himself towards the door leading back onto the shop floor and went to go through it just as it flew open and smacked him in the face. Slightly concussed, shaking his head, which felt very woolly, he cursed Toggie as he rejoined him. But Toggie hadn't been listening anyway. Toggie had carried on with his own charge right up to the guard and then he had whacked him over the head with the iron bar he was carrying. The guard fell down backwards.

'What the fuck did you do that for?' said Hoagie.

'So we can get away you twat,' said Toggie. 'Come on! Van, now!'

They had bolted, or in Hoagie's case staggered, to their exit and piled into the van with a small haul, although it was hardly worth it.

'Now, let's pull away slowly, shall we?' said Hammers from the driver's seat, 'so's not to draw attention to ourselves.'

Obviously, it was too late. The lights were up; the police were on the scene. The game was up, but Hammers wasn't about to give up that easily.

However, Hoagie threatened to thwart his plans for a sharp get-away. The mixture of narcotics and alcohol, combined with adrenalin and injury had suddenly proved too much for him as his eyes rolled back in his head.

'Christ!' yelled Toad. 'Look! We need to get him help!'

Hoagie could only hear them from far away; it was like living underwater, and it all seemed to happen in slow motion as he faded in and out of consciousness. He had been aware of Toad's voice – Toad was saying something about calling an ambulance. Then there was another voice shouting at Toad. The next thing he knew was that he had the sensation of being bumped along the ground; he'd tried to get up and run at the side of the van, but the last thing he'd seen were the taillights of the van as it screeched away at top speed. He wanted to call out, 'Stop!' as he had seen, (or had he imagined?) a small, lithe figure hurrying across the road, holding a package. The figure had paused midway across, startled by the commotion, and stared at Hoagie. It had looked like a kid. But Hoagie was unable to call out to warn the figure, and instead, he had drifted away. The next thing he knew was when he woke up in hospital.

The courts were reasonable with him. He expressed remorse, and it was quite genuine: he really did regret ever going out with that lot when he could have stayed home and not ended up in this state. And after all, he wasn't really on the scene as such. He told the judge he had gone along with the hope of talking his friend, Toad, out of being mis-led. (he couldn't care less about Toggie, really, and certainly not that Hammers). They didn't buy it, but he was truly sorry about the security guard. No-one needs to whack a guy over the head with a weapon, he thought. Well, not a thing like that. The guy was in hospital a lot longer than Hoagie, and he was scarred for life. And then there was the kid.

The kid was a teenager, who had just gone out to buy fish and chips. Now he too did not have a spleen and was in a coma after being hit by the van which had sped away recklessly. It had only grazed Hoagie, but this kid – he might not survive. Hoagie was glad he had not been conscious enough to see the kid's face and he'd been avoiding the news, although it was difficult – the headlines, 'Teen still in coma', made periodic appearances in the newspapers and on television. It became shortened to 'Coma Teen'. *Coma Teen*. The headline loomed large in those wakeful moments at 2 am. He had enough nightmares to deal with lately without another face to be added to the gallery. Hammers got sent down and so did Toggie. Toad got a lesser sentence and he'd be let out soon. Hoagie's sentence was suspended on the condition he went to a residential rehab centre. Not quite prison, but nearly. And he was back on the methadone programme, would follow it up with regular support sessions and he had to stay with his mum for a couple of weeks. It was all so fucking *invasive.*

He'd never done proper rehab before. They did a lot of talking and stuff, but he hated joining in. He just couldn't see what they got out of it. Some of the 'inmates' were not even proper addicts; they were just there because their parents were a bit worried about them having a toot at the weekends and paid for them to have a week's holiday. Still, during the day, when time was filled by sessions and talking and medication, it wasn't too bad. In the daytime, he did drawings, attended his classes, met with a counsellor and even wrote a journal. The nightmares came when he was alone in his room and the lights went out. Apparently, his roommate had asked to be moved to a room on his own, because Hoagie's yelling out kept waking him up. Hoagie wasn't sad to see the back of the whining little git but alone, staring at the walls with no drugs to take him away from himself, he just felt nothing.

The weeks wore on; the weather got hotter, and the kid remained in a coma.

In the final week, they all filed in from the smoking area. The team leader of 'Sober Sharing', who was called Jez, had a forty-a-day habit, but pointed out that smoking was much preferable to his previous drinking and then shovelled a packet of jelly babies down his throat before shepherding his flock back inside.

'So, thank you so much for sharing earlier, Lottie,' he said. 'Does anybody want to go next?'

A mousey-looking woman, dressed as what can only be described as an ageing hippy, beads included, raised her hand. 'May I?' she said quietly.

'Of course, Trixie,' said the group leader. 'Shoot!'

'Christ,' muttered Hoagie, under his breath.

She shot him a look, then said, 'Hi, everyone, I'm Trixie, addict.'

'Hi, Trixie,' said everyone except Hoagie.

'Say hello, Hoagie,' said Jez.

'I've said hello,' said Hoagie. 'I've said hello to her every single meeting. We all know who she is by now. We get it. Her name is Trixie,' He suppressed a smirk, 'and she's an addict.

Except 'addict' isn't a word we should use because it isn't positive reinforcement, is it now?'

'Anything else, Hoagie,' said Jez, keeping calm.

'Nah, you're all right,' said Hoagie.

'Okey dokey,' said Jez. 'Shoot then, Trixie.'

'Except you shouldn't really say '*shoot*' should you,' said Hoagie. 'Not to a group where people shoot up and stuff, yeah?'

Toby, '*Cocaine Anonymous did nothing for me,*' who always sat with a permanent scowl on his face, gave a small titter. 'Oh, ya,' he said in his rich tones, 'he's so right. Hilarious.'

Jez was about to speak, when he started coughing uncontrollably. 'Sorry,' he apologised, still choking a little. 'Jelly babies…sugar rush.'

'Shouldn't say '*rush*' either, should yer?' pointed out Hoagie.

'Thank you, Mr Hoag,' said Jez, recovering. "Would you like to add anything else?'

'Nah. I'm good,' said Hoagie.

'So, I'm Trixie,' twittered Trixie, who was desperate to share. 'As you know I had a difficult childhood, and why we do what we do is the theme of today's meeting, so I thought I'd give it a go, sharing about it. It's quite difficult to do, actually,' she said, and then launched into a terrifying monologue about how she'd had an affair with her babysitter when she was only thirteen, which started her down the 'wrong path' and how she'd married an abuser because of this and lost her kids because she'd been drinking and finally went to prison for drunk driving, where she'd then become a drug addict, and for years she'd blamed herself but now she'd realised how it wasn't her fault and that she had forgiven the babysitter, who was a woman, but most importantly, she'd forgiven herself. She barely paused for breath.

'Let's all give Trixie a group hug, shall we?' said Jez.

Hoagie groaned but did it anyway. The guy meant well, even if he was now addicted to cigarettes and jelly babies. Not for long, mate, he thought. There's talk of banning fags from pubs and stuff. It's coming, whether we like it or not. Be the fuckin' Jelly Baby Police next. He heard his name.

'So, Hoagie, do you know why you do the things you do?' prompted Jez.

'Do you know, mate,' Hoagie replied, 'I haven't got a fuckin' clue.'

Back at his mum's, the final step before he could go back to his godawful flat, Hoagie was being spoiled rotten for getting clean. But she was on his case to get a proper job.

'Mum, no-one will employ me in a proper job!' he whined. 'Especially not when I have to go to the bloody chemist every day and get juiced up.'

'Well, whose fault is that?' she said. 'Look, you're worth something better. Employers will understand. You're trying to get off it. Oh, you were such a sweet little boy.'

'Oh, bugger off, mum,' he said. 'Anyways, I'm going out tonight. Toad told me about a good club, open late, and I'm gonna have one on him, as he can't, being banged up and that.'

'Are you ever, EVER, going to grow up?' said his mum.

'Nope!' said Hoagie and shot upstairs to find some clean clothes to wear. 'Where's my green t-shirt, mum?' he yelled.

'It's in the ironing pile, Jamie,' she yelled back.

'Thanks mum!' he shouted. 'Can you bring it up for me?'

The club was called 'Venice', and it was a sticky-floored, cheesy music mix of smoke, old and new music, and coloured lights, with a dancefloor the size of a postage stamp around which gathered the not-so-brave, and the downright ugly, watching the brave and the beautiful (or those who believed they were) strut their stuff. *Wonderwall* had just finished, the blokes swaying their beer-bellies to its anthem, and the DJ made an announcement for the next song as 'an oldie, but goodie – this one's got an edge to it. It's the Cardiacs – Is this the life!'

A life that's never home, thought Hoagie. Yeah. 'If this one's an oldie, I'm fucked!' he shouted to no-one in particular.

'I know that voice,' said a woman behind him, 'And I know that hair! Fancy a dance, punk raver?'

'Bloody hell! It's Emma, innit?' Hoagie was unbelievably delighted. "What the hell? What you doing here?'

'Hen night,' she said.

'Are those safety pins in your ears?' he said.

'Yeah. I was inspired by this bloke I met a few years back at a rave. I liked him, but the fucker never called me. You're not on E now, are you?'

'Nah,' said Hoagie, 'I wouldn't say that's my drug of choice. To be honest I'm on nothing. Well, except alcohol, and that's not going down that well right now. You?'

'No. Things change. You have to grow up, don't yer? Move with the times.'

'Do yer?' He smiled. 'Can I get you a drink,' he said, 'to say sorry about not calling?'

She held up a huge fishbowl cocktail. 'Best not,' she said. 'This is meant for ten people! But after, you owe me a dance.'

'Fuck it, dance now!' he said and swept her onto the floor. As they did so, the song changed. It was 'I love to love,' a seventies number by Tina Charles.

'Cheesy or what?' said Emma. They swayed in time to the music. Hoagie didn't care for once that it wasn't 'his' music. Emma was '*spinning like a top*', just as the song said, her distinctive red hair flowing like flames. But suddenly, everything around him felt false. Maybe she was right. You do have to move with the times. This club was everything about the past.

'Less get out of here,' he said, 'and I'll tell you what I've bin up to.'

'All right,' she said.

'I gotta go for a slash, but don't go, will you? Don't just leave and disappear again!'

'I promise I will sit here with me drink,' she said.

Hoagie hurried to take a piss, elbowing some weedy drunk out of the way, ridiculously excited to get back to Emma. When he did return, Emma had been joined by a middle-aged, scruffy looking bloke. Hoagie hurried over.

'I'm with him,' said Emma, giving a dazzling smile.

'Sorry mate,' said the bloke, as Hoagie scowled at him. 'I was just saying your girlfriend here looks like that Nicole Kidman or somefing. Sorry guv'ner.' He backed away.

'You come across as right flirty, but you don't realise. You gotta be careful, Emma,' said Hoagie.

Emma burst out laughing. 'Cheers, Dad,' she said, 'I'll bear that in mind. Anyway, do you know what he said to me? He said, *I want to lick your arse!*' she laughed.

'He said what? I should have decked him!' said Hoagie.

'No need,' she said. 'I just said to him that he really DIDN'T and that was the last place he'd want to lick!'

Hoagie laughed too. 'Genius,' he said. 'Well played. Still. Fuckin perv!'

'Indeed. Come on, let's get a kebab.'

'Girl after my own heart,' said Hoagie. 'Hey, you got any spliffs or anything?'

'No, I'm on a hen night, remember? I live in Liverpool! But I'm staying in a hotel tonight. If you want, we can get some booze and go back? We can walk it.'

Hoagie was definitely not going to say no. Juice or no juice. Emma would be worth missing his methadone appointment; he wasn't going to let her slip away again.

In the kebab shop, they talked, and Hoagie told Emma a bit about what had happened. 'So, I have to go and get my juice in the morning,' he was saying. He glanced up. The tv was on mute. Hoagie looked at the words on the screen: '*Coma Teen injured in robbery dies.*' The room started spinning. *Oh my God, oh my God*!

'I need to score,' he said.

'No, you don't,' said Emma. 'You really don't. Come back to my room. Just come with me.'

Then she kissed him and the moment between them was the most electric he'd ever known. Even more electric than the hit he had thought he needed a minute ago.

'I like you,' she said. 'I like your crazy hair, and your stupid gappy grin and I think you're funny. Come back with me, and don't use drugs. At least not those ones. You can do it.'

Hoagie suddenly had a moment of clarity. 'Emma,' he said, 'it's over for me here. I know this sounds crazy, but after the hotel, yeah, like tomorrow, can I come with you to Liverpool?'

She had her back to him, sipping her coke through a straw. Shit, he thought. Blown it. Then she turned.

'Yeah, why not?' she said.

Virginia Betts

Fin de Siècle (1999)

End of a Century (Blur)

It had been five years now. Five years since he'd been living in Liverpool. Five years doing work, (on and off), staying clean, (sort of) going to the gym; the same routine every day and it was great. He even had a cat.

And he was so lost.

After all this time and at whatever the hell age he was, (bloody 40!) he still didn't know who he was and where he was going. Hoagie wondered if everyone felt like that, or whether it was just him. Everyone else, maybe with the exception of Toad, (and even he had a job and seemed content just living day-to-day), they all seemed to be able to just get on with it; move on. But here he was still the same, asking the same questions. Maybe he just overthought everything?

It had taken him ages to get round to tracking down Emma after he'd met her at that stupid rave, and then she was with someone else. It took a while for the universe and a bit of effort to put things to rights, and after that he had really surprised himself by moving to Liverpool. When they finally 'got together,' they'd tried the long-distance thing, but that wasn't really working out for him or Emma, and when she gave him an ultimatum, he just up-sticks and left his life to be with her. Totally out of character, but he came home to a girl, a woman, who was fun and up for a party, didn't do hard drugs and called him by his first name, just like his mum. He hadn't seen his mum, his brother or his mates from home for at least three years, but tonight Toggie, Toad, Jonesy and his missus, and even his younger brother David, were all coming up for the party and the band, and Emma was downstairs with a playlist that she'd recorded onto a CD. Blur's 'End of a Century' had just finished and now it was the great Robbie, with 'Millennium.' Prince was on the playlist too; she'd had the CD on all afternoon while she steadily sipped from an expensive bottle of champagne she'd saved for three years, occasionally yelling that tonight they were gonna party like it was 1999, because it actually *was* 1999. Bloody hell! When did that happen?

And now Emma was yelling up to Hoagie, 'Jamie! Are you nearly ready? What are you doing up there?' which reminded him of when he'd shouted up to Kecks in the bathroom with the bare bulb in his rented flat decades ago. Unbeknown to him, Kecks was probably injecting heroin in the bathroom that night. How could he not have known? He wiped the thought away. Because Emma didn't realise either.

It had all started when he met Silas. Silas had joined Hoagie's NA meeting. Yeah, he even went to those. He kind of felt obliged; Emma had been great and had never judged him. But they both knew that a lifelong smack habit was not likely to end well. Emma was never interested in it, and when he'd moved to Liverpool, part of it was to get away from everything in his old life, as well as be with her. He'd pretty much stopped anyway, but it just made the break, and he hadn't thought about it for ages. Both he and Emma were pretty heavy drinkers, but she found it easy to be dry for weeks on end. She had what he called a normal relationship with it. Lately though, Hoagie needed a drink every day. The first thing he did when he came

183

home from his work at the gym was to pour a glass of something alcoholic. He knew full well that one addiction tends to replace another and having spent most of his youth on various drugs, and then various programmes to get him off them, he thought he knew quite a lot about '*addictive personality types*'. So far, he thought he had escaped being a *proper* alcoholic, but the tipping point was never far away. He said so at one of the meetings, and everyone gave him the very helpful and sincere platitudes that they had probably learned from the book of 12 steps. And he smiled and took it, then decided to go home and have a beer. But outside, there was the new guy, Silas, and straight away Hoagie's radar was alerted.

'Wanna come for a beer then?' Silas had said. And Hoagie, intrigued and desperate for a new friend who was a kindred spirit, said yes. Because, let's face it, if trouble walked into a room full of people, it would find Hoagie within less than a minute.

Inside the pub in Matthew Street, where the Beatles used to drink, Hoagie had taken the opportunity to study his new mate as he queued at the bar. He was a scouser; he was short and about Hoagie's age, maybe a little younger, and he had spiky hair. He was a bit like Robbie Williams in fact – gappy teeth which gave him a laddish, cheeky charm. He had a running top over a sleeveless vest thing, which he removed after he had plonked two pints down in front of them, and Hoagie had straight away clocked the track marks. Presumably that was why he'd joined the meetings.

'Listen mate,' Silas had told him, 'I gotta be honest wid yer, I'm not really into them meetings.'

'Nah, me neither,' Hoagie had admitted. 'But they do keep yer on track. You just have to ignore the simpering God shit.'

'That's one way of putting it.' Silas had laughed. And they had bonded, like proper mates. Like the sort of mate he'd been missing when he'd left Toad behind. And they'd loved going to the NA meetings and sharing knowing raised eyebrows and sneaky cynical smiles about anything they regarded as 'shit.' They both noticed that people often went to boast about their pasts and gain a sort of fucked-up one-upmanship about who was the worst addict, who'd done the hardest drugs, who had been abused, and who had suffered the most in withdrawal or rehab or whatever the fuck else they did. That was the druggie hierarchy. The 'real' druggies – the hardcore – made out that the weed smoking or weekend whizz dabblers were lightweights; like they weren't bad enough to be there. It was good to meet someone who shared the same opinion about this bullshit; someone to talk to properly, outside meetings. Hoagie even told Silas the 'dead rats' story and Silas had roared with laughter, 'Fook me? Really? Like actual rats? You couldn't make that shite up! Like, thas like out of a book, like!'

And at first, they had just started dabbling by getting hold of prescription pills, from another mate Silas knew. To break the boredom. It didn't take long for Hoagie to be popping codeine and diazepam on a daily basis, but he told himself they just kept him on a nice calm level, so he functioned better. Dope smoking was a given, and it didn't count; even Emma was fine about that. And then the occasional sniff of the old chop crept in. But one evening after the meeting a couple of weeks ago, Silas had told Hoagie he knew where to get some good gear if he fancied a taste again. Well, of course he did. The pills just weren't cutting it anymore, but he still had withdrawal symptoms when he didn't use them. It was getting boring. A bit of H would go down well, and he could just do it when he felt like it.

Now, Hoagie was sweating in the bathroom, twiddling the little wrap between his fingers and getting the syringe in and out of his jacket pocket. He'd had both wrapped in a piece of tissue and hidden in socks at the back of a drawer in the bedroom for the last two weeks. He had been in two minds. Firstly, it had been so long he'd have to be careful not to OD. Secondly, it had been so long that he'd be breaking his clean time and have to start again. Maybe he'd get a habit again. What would Emma think about it. He longed to tell her, but something in him held back, because deep down he felt there was this unspoken thing: this would be a deal breaker.

But surely, a little taste wouldn't hurt. Just once, for old time's sake. Take him into the new century with a bang and start the new year on a high. And technically, it would be done in the old year, so it wouldn't count. Just once. Not all the time. Not ever again maybe. But here it was, right here in his hand, too good an opportunity to waste, surely? He put both in his inside pocket. Not now. Not yet. He needed to think about it.

'Come on, Jamie! Get the fuck downstairs!' Emma was yelling over the music. 'Got a glass waiting for you!'

'Coming!' said Hoagie. He'd wait. Perhaps he didn't want to use it after all. Why fuck things up? That was the sane side of his brain talking. The sober side. But he wouldn't throw it away. Not yet. Just keep it in case – like insurance. He whacked in 4 codeine tablets and a diazepam to kick-start the party and hid them back in his washbag's zip compartment.

He ploughed down the stairs and whisked Emma up into the air, whirling her round. 'Happy New Year!' he said.

'Not yet, idiot!' she said. 'Here,' she handed him his glass of champagne which he knocked back fast.

'Oh!' she exclaimed. 'Oh, you needed to make that last! The rest is just fizzy wine.'

'Well, we're goin' out int we?' said Hoagie.

'Yeah. When are your mates and David coming?' said Emma.

'Any minute I hope,' said Hoagie. 'I can't wait to see 'em to be honest, it's been so long!'

And at that moment, the doorbell rang. Hoagie and Emma winced simultaneously. Both of them hated the sharp sound of the doorbell intruding in their lives.

'Bloody hell! It's you!' exclaimed Toad. 'You've no idea how long it took me to get here and then the taxi to find this place, I had to book it about ten fucking weeks in advance and even then, the bastard took me the long way round. What the fuck you doin' movin' to this dive? Nice house though, by the way.'

'And hello to you, Toad,' said Hoagie. 'Emma, you remember Toad?'

'How could I forget,' said Emma. 'And presumably, this is Jonesy and Leela comin' up the path?'

'Yeah, yeah,' said Hoagie excitedly. 'And there's Toggie! Goin' to the wrong house! Oi! Toggie you wanker!'

'You look well, Hoagie,' said Leela as she hugged him.

'What have you done with your kids?' said Hoagie. He noticed she had short, bobbed hair and it was pitch black again, and straightened, swishing about her face like silk curtains.

'Sold 'em,' said Leela. 'Nah, Grandma and Grandad have them so we can have a no-holds-barred par-tay! Where's the booze?'

'Leela,' said Jonesy.

'Aw, shut up you old fart,' said Leela. 'We're all friends here.' She winked at Hoagie.

'What are your kids' names again,' said Emma. 'I can't remember.' She took Leela into the kitchen.

'Well, there's Vincent, he's the eldest, then Rhys, Shannon and Miles are twins, and last but not least, Brooke.'

'Jesus!' said Emma. 'That's quite a lot of kids!'

'Yeah,' said Leela. 'We didn't have a telly for ages, that's why.'

'Huh? Oh! I geddit,' said Emma.

'Seriously, I get knocked up so easy,' said Leela. 'But Danny can't get me pregnant again,' she whispered, and Emma could smell she had already been drinking. 'He's had the chop. My dad paid.'

'Well, thank goodness for that,' said Emma.

'You two gonna have kids?' said Leela, as Emma poured her a drink. 'Because you need to get a move on? How old are you now?'

'Thirty-three,' said Emma. 'The last time you saw me was on my 30th, remember?'

'Oh, yeah, plenty of time,' said Leela. 'But still...'

The boys entered the kitchen. 'What are you goin' on about?' said Hoagie.

'Havin' kids,' said Leela. 'I told Emma she should get a move on, although she's younger than us lot.'

'I don't think I can,' said Hoagie, smiling as if in jest, 'after all the chemicals I put in me,' he winked at Emma, and she half-smiled back. It was only partially a joke. Hoagie's fertility had been impaired by his heavy drug use, so he'd been told. That was why they never bothered about contraception. And that was why Emma was now pregnant, although she hadn't told him yet. She was still a little in denial and determined not to miss out on a few drinks this evening. Time enough for that conversation in the year 2000.

'Better get going soon,' said Hoagie. 'I booked a big people-carrier cab, as I thought this might be one night Jonesy isn't gonna drive us.'

'Bloody right,' said Jonesy. 'Got the fuckin' train this time. Hotel's nice though.'

'It's shit,' said Leela. 'Anyone got a fag?'

'What about yer brother?' said Toad. 'When's he coming?'

'He's meetin' us there,' said Hoagie, handing Leela a cigarette. 'This cab will be here in about half an hour. Glad you got here on time!'

'Why don't we have a bloody 'nother few drinks then?' said Toggie, 'and where's yer bathroom?'

'Upstairs, first on the right,' said Emma.

'For fuck's sake,' said Jonesy, 'he can't go five minutes without doing coke.'

'Oh, he doesn't have to use the bathroom,' said Emma. 'Toggie, just do it down here.'

'Excuse me, but I need a piss,' said Toggie. 'But I will do the coke down here. Want some?'

'Yeah,' said Toad.

'Nah,' said Hoagie, 'I'm clean.' The lie bit at him. But at least he hadn't touched the gear yet.

'You?' Toggie gestured to Leela and Emma. 'I know you won't, Jonesy.'

'Yeah, why not?' said Leela, 'it's Millennium after all.'

'No, it's ok,' said Emma. 'Not me.'

'Coke? Seriously?' said Hoagie. 'Who do you think you are? Gordon Gekko?'

'Who?' said Emma.

'He's a banker. Like Jonesy,' smirked Toggie. 'Off a film from the 80s. I said *banker*,' he smirked again. 'Nah, one of me mates got it for us. A posh knob. He shifted some cars and stuff for me.'

'Oh, ok,' said Hoagie. 'Still no. It's probably Vim.'

The taxi turned up after half an hour and they all piled in, already tipsy. It drove at a break-neck speed into the city centre, and Leela noticed Emma was as pale as a sheet.

'You all right,' she whispered as they made their way towards Pier Head, where they were meeting David, Hoagie's brother.

'Not really,' said Emma, 'I feel a bit sick. That driver.'

'You look like I did,' said Leela, 'when I was first up the duff with Vincent.' Emma looked startled. 'It's all right, I won't say anything,' said Leela. 'It's your business.'

Emma flicked back her flame-coloured hair. 'Thanks,' she said. 'I will tell him, but not tonight.'

'Aw, he'll be fine,' said Leela. 'You know he delivered Vince?'

'Yes, I know,' said Emma, 'but there's something going on with him. And I'm just not sure if this is the right time.'

'Never is,' said Leela, 'And there's always somethin' goin' on with him.'

A special venue had been constructed for the celebrations and there were thousands of people already gathering at Pier Head to see The Lightning Seeds, Orbital, Space and Cream. All eyes were on London, but the real party was about to begin in Liverpool.

'How the hell are we going to find David?' said Toad.

'He'll be by the hotdog stand over there,' said Hoagie. 'We can go and wait for him. Then we can get a good place to be for the bands.'

'We're so early!' moaned Toggie.

'Need to be,' said Hoagie. 'So many people.'

'This is massive,' said Emma. 'This is history, this is.'

Hoagie looked over at the hotdog stand, and he saw his brother, David, standing there in a long trench coat, looking awkward. David worked as a solicitor now, and he had a wife and two children. Hoagie went over to him.

'Mate!' he said. 'How's it hangin'?'

'Jamie,' said David. It's good. Busy, but ok. I've got quite a lot to fill you in on.'

Hoagie and David were not close. They hadn't been since Hoagie was a teenager and his behaviour had got David taken away for a short spell in a foster home. To be fair, that was probably his old man's fault as well. But he was dead, and his mother seemed to have got over it all. Mostly. He was glad his brother had agreed to come up and see him at the turn of the century.

'What's mum doing?' said Hoagie.

'She's on holiday,' said David. 'She said she wanted to be away to properly celebrate.'

'Fine. Dunno where she gets the money.'

'I think they both saved it,' said David. 'She deserves it.'

'If she's got any spare, she might give some to me,' said Hoagie.

'You're all right, aren't you?' said David.

'Yeah, s'pose so,' said Hoagie. 'Emma earns more than me though. It's not the first thing people like to see on a job application – time in prison; history of so-called drug addiction. Mind you, If I could fuckin' not do any work at all…'

'You're 40, it comes to us all,' said David. 'You still, you know, *all right*?'

'What, clean?'

'Yes,' said David. 'Stupid bloody word, really.'

'Yes,' said Hoagie. 'And yeah, I suppose it is.' But there was that little twinge in his guts of the lie again. And yet, it wasn't like he was addicted to anything. It was just pills. And all the other stuff was not regular. And weed was practically legal. So, it didn't count. Except the little wrap and the syringe were still in his pocket. Maybe he'd just sell it on to some punter tonight. That would be best. Tell Silas he wasn't into it anymore.

But he'd thought about it, and it ignited a little battle in his head once again. Distraction, he decided. It was fuckin' Millennium Eve for fuck's sake. That had to be enough distraction. They headed over to the rest of the group.

'I think you know everyone,' Hoagie said. 'Here's David, everyone!'

'Let's get this party going,' said Toggie. 'I got some of them little hats from that bloke over there, and glow stick things.'

'Er, thanks,' said Emma.

Someone handed David a drink and the music started up. By the time the first band came on, they were completely shoulder to shoulder with a heaving throng, swaying in time to the music.

'You want another drink?' said Hoagie to David.

'Yeah, I'll give you a hand,' said David.

At the bar, David looked decidedly awkward.

'Spit it out,' said Hoagie.

'How did you know?' said David.

'You're my brother. I know the look – you look…cagey,' said Hoagie. 'And I'm an expert in hiding things int I? What is it that you're hiding?'

'Too noisy,' said David. 'Later. Back at your place. Hey, I *am* staying with you, right?'

'Er,' Hoagie had actually thought he'd be in a hotel. 'Yeah, course! Only a camp-bed though. There's a boxroom, but it's full of boxes.'

'Great,' said David. 'I didn't bring much, just this rucksack.'

'Yeah, it's a pain in the arse,' said Hoagie. 'You look like a fuckin' terrorist. But tell me, otherwise I'll wring your neck. I can't stand waiting for anything.'

'I can't,' said David. 'It's too…big.'

'What the fuck? Tell me!'

'All right. Shit I'm gonna regret this. Just remember, this isn't the time or place.'

'Is it mum? Is she dying?'

'No! Not that!'

'Well fuckin' what then?'

'Jamie, do you remember when dad died?'

'What the fuck? No course not. What do *you* think?' Hoagie's voice dripped with sarcasm.

'Yeah, yeah. Well, what if I said he wasn't actually dead?'

'What the fuck are you on about? It's New Year, not fuckin' April Fool's!'

'Shut up and listen for once. You were not speaking to any of us really at the time, and you were, you know, *on drugs*. Mum didn't know what to do.'

'What?'

'He isn't dead, Jamie. He lives in London. Mum told us she didn't know where he was because she didn't. Not for ages. Then she told us she'd heard he'd died of a heart attack because she thought it was kinder. Well, you remember. He wasn't a very nice man.'

Hoagie couldn't take it in properly. 'What the fuck? Are you saying, mum told us he was dead, but actually he's alive and well and living in London? For twenty odd years? What the fuck? What the fuck?' Hoagie started pounding his fist on the side of his own head.

David looked alarmed. 'It's ok!'

'In what kind of fucked up world is that ok, David?' Hoagie stared at him in disbelief. 'Did you know? Did you know? Why are you telling me now?'

'I swear I didn't know. Well, not until a couple of months ago. And out of the blue, I got an email from him. I told mum someone was scamming me, and she suddenly broke down, and she told me. She made me promise not to tell you. But I couldn't not.'

'I wish you hadn't,' said Hoagie.

'Sorry,' said David. 'You know I had to.'

'That total bitch!' said Hoagie.

'Oh, come on! That's not fair,' began David.

'She let us mourn him. She let us think we missed his funeral and that she didn't know where he was, and she thought it was KINDER?'

'She didn't know where he was.'

'But she's a liar!'

'We're all liars, Jamie,' said David. 'You more than most. I can see you're on something, even though you say you're clean. I know the look. I know the eyes.'

'I am on prescribed drugs,' said Hoagie.

'Yeah, except who are they prescribed for?' said David. 'You used to nick scripts. Fill 'em in for yourself. I know you, Jamie.'

'That is not the point. This is about our actual father being actually living and breathing when I thought he was rotting underground for two fucking decades and you choose to tell me on Millennium Eve!'

'I didn't. You made me!'

'You sound like you did when you was a kid! *Jamie made me do it*! Fuck's sake!'

'Look, I had to tell you. It's the right thing to do. Mum said not to, in case it sent you over the edge, but I told her you'd understand.'

'I don't understand. I don't get any of it,' said Hoagie. 'Fuck you! Get a hotel or piss off back home.'

'Don't shoot the messenger,' said David.

'Fuck off, you University twat!' said Hoagie. He suddenly decided that he had to get away. Go anywhere, he didn't know where, but not here. 'Look, I gotta go to the toilet,' he said. 'Take the drinks back.'

'Jamie…'

'It's fuckin' HOAGIE!' he shouted. 'No-one calls me anything else, except sometimes Emma and the fuckin' police, and you and mum can fuckin' well call me Hoagie from now on!' and he walked off into the crowd at a pace.

'Where's Hoagie?' said Toad.

'Loo,' said David. But he looked worried.

'Really?' said Emma. 'Hope he gets back soon. It's really busy.'

An hour passed.

'Do you think you ought to look for him?' said Leela.

'Oh, he'll be dancin' somewhere,' said Emma. But all the same she seemed a little serious. Toad supposed that was because she was not pissed. 'Have another drink,' he said.

'No, I'm ok. Antibiotics,' she said by way of explanation.

But another half an hour passed, and Hoagie had still not returned.

'Shit,' said David. 'I told him somethin' tonight. I think I upset him. I'll go and look in the toilets.'

'But then you'll get lost too!' said Emma.

'He'll be back,' said Toad. 'He's bullet proof, him. Toggie's gone off somewhere as well. They've probably met someone they know.'

'Probably,' said Emma. 'That's what's the most worrying I suppose.'

'I think you should look, David,' said Leela. 'I can come with you.'

'But the fireworks are soon!' said Toad.'

'Let's just have a look,' said Leela.

Leela and David went around shouting Hoagie's name. They were pushed and jostled by the crowd, and it was almost impossible to make themselves heard. They decided to split up.

'I'll look in the disabled toilets,' said David.

'I'll look in the other Portaloos,' said Leela.

When she reached the Portaloo, it was locked.

'Been in there for fookin' ages!' said some bloke in the queue. 'Fookin' miss the fookin' fireworks. I'm gonna piss in a bush. Fook it!'

Some sixth sense in Leela knew. She started kicking at the door 'Help me!' she cried.

'Someone's desperate for a piss,' commented a woman passing.

Leela saw David running towards her. 'I think he's in here!' she shouted.

They both kicked at the door.

'Oi!' a policewoman came running over, just as the door gave way.

There was Hoagie, slumped sideways, turning blue, a syringe hanging out of his arm and foamy spittle dribbling from his lips. His eyes were turned up in his head.

'Shit!' said Leela. She immediately began trying to resuscitate him, whilst David stood there white faced, and the Policewoman radioed for back up.

'Don't die you fucker!' Leela said, tears running down her face. 'Don't you fuckin' die on me!'

Suddenly there was an almighty bang and a flash of light. The first fireworks were going up and as they rocketed skyward, Hoagie's body jolted back to earth. Leela quickly turned his head sidewards as he threw up all over her and began to shake violently.

'You fucker!' she shouted, as the ambulance arrived.

And just like that, as the new century dawned, Hoagie was carted off to Liverpool General with Leela in the back holding his hand.

Don't Eat Goat (2000/1978)

Back from the Dead (Babyshambles)

The train journey had been uncomfortable, like the awkward and bitter farewell with Emma. Hoagie was trailing his worldly goods with him, such as they were, and most of the way he'd had to stand. He'd missed his vein trying to shoot up in the tiny, disgusting toilet when the train jerked round a sharp corner, and he now sported a painful swollen lump in his arm. His drugs had run out; his pockets were nearly empty of cash; his bank account was definitely depleted, and his stomach was growling.

'Happy Fuckin' New Year, you twat,' he said to his sorry reflection in the carriage window.

He hadn't been surprised when Emma had told him it was over.

'I'm so sorry, Jamie,' she'd said. 'I just can't do this anymore. I still love you. But I can't.'

'I'm not gonna change, Emma,' he'd said. 'I have tried, I have. And I did clean up my act, you know I have done. But I can't make any promises I can't keep.'

He didn't have much stuff to call his own; it was surprising how little he'd accumulated even after five years, so it didn't take long to pack. Most of his records were still back at his mum's house in the loft, so it was just a couple of bags to lug with him. He was so tired of it all – the pretending. That was it; always just on the edge of a life, but really, he was just an observer. He didn't know how other people did it. 'Adulting' was too exhausting for him. Perhaps it was his so-called problem, or perhaps it was just everyone else's problem? Maybe everyone was pretending all the time – get up, go to work, do the laundry, send the kids to school, mow the lawn, feed the cat etc – when inside they were just dying to get whacked out of their heads and sit on their arses all day eating junk food? He reckoned it was quite likely. So, he hadn't put up much of an argument with Emma. He figured he would do her a favour and get out while the going was good. He was still alive, and more importantly, so was she. He'd kissed her on the cheek, and then he had left without looking back.

Just before leaving, he'd made two calls: one to his mum, who'd wished him well, but said there was no space for him there, (cow!) and one to Leela. There had been no answer from her. He decided to take his chances anyway and go to Jonesy and Leela's place that evening, when Jonesy got home from work. Perhaps they'd find space for him. It didn't appeal, having to share with Jonesy and five kids, but Leela was always soft on him, and in the dire straits he was in, he didn't have much choice. Toad's place was cramped and Toggie's place was unsavoury, even for him. He wasn't that desperate! First, though, he had to have something to eat.

He headed for the first place he clapped eyes on. It used to be a chippie, but now it seemed only to be offering some sort of Asian Street food. Hoagie was hungry, strung out and still dazed after the overdose ordeal, and perhaps he was more wounded by his break-up than he cared to admit or even understand. Just another fuckin' disaster. He should be used to it by now. And as he hit the streets under the weight of his bags and his misery, the rain fell.

'For fuck's sake!' he said to no-one in particular. 'Give a man a break!'

Inside the takeaway, he asked what was on the menu.

'Try our special,' said the helpful man serving. 'Goat Curry.'

'What the fuck?' said Hoagie.

'Special price.'

Hunger got the better of him. 'Oh fuckin' go on then,' he said, and handed over the last of his cash.

He perched on a high stool in the window and looked out. The rain cast a greyness over the street, making the area seem unfamiliar. He suddenly thought of Kecks. Him and Kecks running, not quite hand-in-hand, to this very place when it was the chippy; Kecks with her duffel coat held high over her head and wobbling on high boots, trying to stay dry in a sudden shower. Her mascara had run down her cheeks and both of them were high and hungry. He had spent the last of his cash then as well, and they'd sheltered in the chippy until the storm passed, stabbing chips with wooden forks. Then they'd splashed back home through the puddles and spent the rest of the day in bed, smoking heroin and weed alternately. God! He'd done a lot of smack in them days, he thought to himself. He smiled. A day in bed might sound salacious, but when you have a body full of opiates, the only seduction you have any real interest in is the seduction of the drug. They had lain semi-conscious, libidos flatlined; surrounded by foil, cans and the litter of discarded sweet wrappers. It had been a good day. Later that evening though, they had got into a spot of bother.

Oh yes, he remembered it very clearly; he was right back there.

'I wanna go out,' Kecks said.

'Where?' said Hoagie, 'We haven't got much money. We blew it on gear.'

'Well, we'll have to get some money,' said Kecks.

'How?' Hoagie said.

'Oh, I dunno,' said Kecks, 'perhaps one of your mates will buy us a drink?'

'Yeah, I'll go and give Toad a ring, and Jonesy. See if they'll sub us 'til Friday,' said Hoagie. He didn't hold out much hope though, as Toad had quit his job, and Jonesy was on a YTS. Toggie wouldn't part with cash if his life depended on it, even when he had any. They were all skint. But Hoagie had enough change for a couple of phone calls, and it was worth a try.

And sure enough, Jonesy came up trumps. And he said he would drive, so a night out was on.

They met at the Grinning Rat, as usual.

'Dead in here, innit?' said Hoagie to Kecks. 'What'll it be?'

'Vodka and orange,' said Kecks.

'Fuckin' no chance. Lager's cheaper,' said Hoagie.

'Why did you ask then?' said Kecks, huffily.

'Oh, have the bloody vodka then,' Hoagie said. 'I just thought you could have another couple if you saved on that. Anyway, this is the only one and the last one until Jonesy gets here with the sub, so make the most of it. I'm gettin' this in early before I end up havin' to buy a full round.'

But it was too late. Jonesy sauntered in. 'Mine's a pint of shandy,' he said. 'Getting you to buy one before I have to buy the rest.'

'Defeats the object,' said Hoagie. 'The more I buy now the less money I'll have, and then you'll end up having to give me more so we can have more. Booze, that is.'

Jonesy and Kecks looked at each other. 'There's some logic hidden in there somewhere,' said Jonesy, 'but I can't for the life of me see it.'

'Oh fuck's sake,' said Hoagie. 'I'll get 'em in. NOT vodka,' he added and Kecks stuck her tongue out.

'Fuck!' exclaimed Jonesy. 'When did you have your tongue pierced?'

'Couple of weeks ago,' said Kecks.

'Bloody hell, did it hurt?'

'Horrible! Like, really bad.'

'Shit!' said Jonesy.

'Ay ay!' said Toggie, entering the pub. 'Mine's a pint.'

'Fuck,' said Hoagie.

'Put your tongue away, girl, unless you wanna use it on me?' said Toggie, with a salacious grin.

'Fuck off,' said Kecks.

Two drinks down, they began to think about what the night held for them.

'I have got a plan,' said Toggie. 'A plan that might make our night a bit more interesting.'

'I'm not putting fireworks up a cat's bum,' said Hoagie.

'No way!' said Kecks, 'I like cats!'

'What the fuck?' said Toggie, grinning a wide, gappy grin.

'Oh, come on,' said Hoagie, 'don't tell us those was just rumours.'

'Fuck off,' said Toggie, 'otherwise I'll put a firework up your arse. Anyways, I like cats too.'

'But you did do it?' said Jonesy.

'Might've,' said Toggie and shrugged.

Perhaps it was one of those urban myths, Hoagie thought to himself. He hoped it was.

'Ok, what's the plan then?' said Kecks.

'I think we should break into cars – steal stuff and sell it,' said Toggie. 'It's easy.'

'Oh, I know how!' said Kecks. 'You get a bit of wire and push it through that rubber bit in the window. I've done it – you wiggle it a bit, then you can sorta hook up the lock and you're in.'

'When?' asked Toad.

'Look,' said Hoagie, 'Shall we go back to mine and get wrecked and work it out there?'

'Who's got gear?' said Toad. 'Because I need to go shopping.'

'I have, and you can buy it off me,' said Toggie. "I seen Big Adam.'

'Let's go then,' said Hoagie. 'Except you'll have to sub me, mate.'

Back at Hoagie's they all got high, except Jonesy, who said he'd just drink and then he could do the driving.

It wasn't the most co-ordinated plan. They drove into the town centre, parked in a side street, and then proceeded to try out the wire on half a dozen cars. Hoagie finally managed to get into a brown Cortina using Kecks' fool-proof method of hitching the lock up with the wire, at which point Toggie whipped out the car radio and put it into his loot bag and they legged it off down the street and into the pub again. They collapsed in a corner with stifled snorts of laughter.

'Tha' was so funny!' said Kecks. 'Told you it'd work.'

Toggie put his bag on the tiny table, and they all peeped in the top to look at the goods.

'We gonna sell it?' said Toad.

'We need more than one!' exclaimed Hoagie. 'That's ridiculous! How's that gonna be any use?'

'That was just a practise run,' said Toggie. 'Next time we go out when it's a bit darker and we do loads.'

'But we tried loads today, and we only managed to get one car open,' said Toad.

'We'll have better luck in the night, when people are a bit pissed and forget to lock their cars,' said Toggie.

'Then we just have to open the door,' pointed out Hoagie.

'I still have to get the thing out,' said Toggie, 'or whatever else we see in there.'

'You're gonna need a bigger bag,' said Toad.

'What you puttin' that voice on for?' said Toggie.

'In't you seen Jaws?' said Toad.

'No. I don't like Stephen King,' said Toggie.

'Iss not Stephen King! It's Stephen, oh whass his name?'

'Spielberg,' said Hoagie. 'I'm bored now. What shall we do next?'

'I gotta go home,' said Toad. 'Me mum's got me dinner.'

'Wanker,' said Hoagie, cheerfully.

'We'll go out again,' said Toggie. Let's go back to my place for a bit. I'll give one of me mates a call on the way home. I know this guy who'll be up for it.'

'I'm in,' said Jonesy, as he opened another can of lager.

It turned out that Jonesy was very talented at breaking into cars. In fact, Jonesy was very talented at stealing the whole car.

'What the fuck?' said Hoagie when Jonesy rolled up. 'Is that a Merc?'

'Yeah,' said Jonesy. 'I sort of borrowed it.'

'But you can't steal a car!' said Hoagie. 'I mean, that's a little bit bigtime, innit? I reckon the owners might miss that.'

'I haven't stole it,' said Jonesy, 'I just borrowed it for a drive around in. Then I'll put it back and no-one will be any the wiser.'

'I don't like it,' said Hoagie.

'You don't have to ride in it,' said Jonesy. 'I met this bird, and I reckon she'd like a ride in it.'

'Yeah, in more ways than one,' said Hoagie. 'I know what you are!'

Jonesy gave a lecherous grin. 'Toggie, what do you think?'

'Whatever,' said Toggie. 'If you can nick cars that easy, I reckon you might have a future career. Shall I put you onto this bloke I know?'

'You'll have to put it back,' said Kecks. 'So, it doesn't count.'

'Too right it don't count,' said Hoagie. 'Well go on then, take us for a spin in it.'

'But what about Julie?' said Jonesy.

'You can have '*Julie and Jonesy*' stuck across the windscreen for all I care,' said Hoagie, 'but while you've got it you might as well get us out cruisin' in it first. We can go and pick up Toad on the way out.'

Burnt Lungs and Bitter Sweets

Toad's mum and dad stood at the front door open-mouthed as they watched him pull away, hanging out of the window of a packed Mercedes, shouting something unintelligible as he went.

'Whooah! What you bin drinkin', Jonesy?' he yelled.

'Anything I can!' Jonesy yelled back, swerving all over the road.

'Shit! Shit! Slow down! Pull over!' shouted Hoagie from the back seat.

'What? Why? It's fun!' Kecks shouted, hanging her hand out of the window and letting the wind trail over it. 'Go faster, Jonesy!'

'That actor in that film – Michael Caine – he got his hand chopped off doin' that!' yelled Toad.

'What the fuck?' said Hoagie. 'Nah! Pull over – there's a cop car ahead!'

'Jonesy screeched to an abrupt halt at the side of the road and Kecks shot forward.

'Fucking hell!' she said. I nearly went through the window screen!'

'It's 'windscreen', like a screen from the wind,' said Hoagie. 'Oh, never mind. Look, you can't drive like that, or you'll get pulled over. Then what?'

'You have to drive then,' said Jonesy.

'I can't drive,' said Hoagie.

'Well, I'm pissed, and they'll notice me more,' said Jonesy. 'Toad can't drive and I'm definitely not letting Toggie drive.'

'What about me?' said Kecks.

'You can't drive,' said Jonesy. 'And anyway, you're a woman. Women are terrible drivers.'

'Fuck you,' said Kecks, taking a swig of her bottle of vodka. 'Male chauvinist pig.'

'But I'm high,' said Hoagie.

'Yeah, well,' said Jonesy. 'I don't think there's a law.'

'Dunno,' said Hoagie. 'Oh, go on then. Less have a go.' He hopped in the front and Kecks got in the back seat. Jonesy shifted across to the passenger seat, and put his feet on the dashboard, leaning back.

'So,' he instructed, 'you put it into neutral – yeah that's right, when the knob goes all floppy.'

Kecks giggled.

'Shut up,' said Hoagie, amiably.

'Then you put both feet on the two pedals. The left one is the clutch. Oh, no the left one is the brake. No I was right.'

'Jesus!' said Toggie. 'You did pass your test, yeah?'

'It's hard telling someone else; I get mixed up with me left and right,' said Jonesy. 'The brake is in the middle, so you put your foot on the brake and clutch. Yeah, right down. Now look, it's in Neutral, so you need to try to move away. Put your foot on the clutch and keep it there. Select first gear –

'I've had some gear,' piped up Toggie.

'Me too,' said Hoagie.

'Shut up!' said Jonesy. 'So, put it in first, like this, see.' He manoeuvred the gear stick into place. Now press the accelerator pedal a little and at the same time bring the clutch up really really…'

The car kangarooed forward in a leap, then stalled.

'Yeah. Like, I was gonna say, slowly,' said Jonesy. 'You have to find the biting point, see.'

'Oh fuck off,' said Hoagie. 'All right let's go again.'

Eventually they got on the road with Hoagie at the wheel. He seemed to be getting the hang of it, but then they approached a roundabout.

'Shit! What do I do? What do I do?' he panicked. 'Oi! What do I do?'

Jonesy made a lunge for the wheel. 'You're supposed to look to the right,' he said, as the oncoming car narrowly missed them and honked its horn.

Hoagie pulled over and hit the brakes. Everyone lurched forward in their seats.

'Not too bad,' he said. 'Do you want a go, Kecks?'

'Yeah,' said Kecks. So, they swapped places again, Jonesy beside her. Kecks made quite a good attempt at driving the car and the boys were all impressed.

'Look,' said Jonesy. 'There's Julie at the bus stop. Pull over, Kecks.'

'Is that her?' said Toggie. 'I know her!'

'*How*?' said Jonesy. 'You know bloody everybody.'

Didn't she go to school with us?' said Hoagie.

'Nah,' said Jonesy. 'She's too young.'

'Have you sin her in daylight though?' said Kecks.

'Ooh! Bitch!' said Toad.

'I've seen her in the chippy,' said Hoagie. 'Go on then – pick her up!'

Jonesy leaned out of the window. 'Oi! Julie! Do you wanna lift?'

Julie moved closer to the car. 'Oh! It's you! I thought it was some pervert.'

'It is!' chorused Toggie and Hoagie.

'Take no notice,' said Jonesy. 'Do you want a lift home? Or you can come back with us?'

Julie hesitated. 'Why aren't you driving?' she said. 'Who's this?'

'Oh, it's just Kecks,' said Jonesy. 'Hoagie's bir – er, girlfriend.'

'I will, but only if you drive,' said Julie, 'so I can sit in the front.'

After they had all swapped places, lit cigarettes and opened more lagers, Jonesy sped off with a wheel-spinning screech of tyres to impress Julie, who clung onto the dashboard tightly. As they raced through the dark streets, Hoagie lobbed an empty can out of the window and it smashed a streetlight. Kecks applauded this new sport they'd discovered, and tried it herself, but unfortunately, she missed, and Jonesy had to step on it as they all turned to watch the stricken face of the woman she'd hit shaking her fist at the retreating car. Julie began to rummage through the glove compartment.

'What are you doing in there?' said Jonesy. 'You're putting me off – I just run a red light!'

'You've run all the red lights!' she protested. 'And I *knew* this weren't your car! I *know* this car!'

'Whose is it?' said Hoagie.

'It's my mate's dad's car! He's the one who owns the chippy – you know – Tony!'

'Fuck's sake, Jonesy!' said Hoagie. 'You have to put it back!'

'But I found it in town, near the pub,' said Jonesy. 'It weren't nowhere near the chippy!'

'Well maybe he was out for a drink, you prat!' said Toggie.

'Hey,' said Kecks, 'How come he can afford a car like this?'

'Have you seen what he charges for fish and chips?' said Toad. 'I swear it's different every time – it's a right rip-off!'

Hoagie smiled at the memory. They'd got it back to the chip shop and Jonesy had got off with that Julie for the night. Tony was probably wondering how his car got back home on its own to this day! He yawned. He couldn't stop yawning. It was almost nine o'clock when he landed on Jonesy's doorstep and by that time, he was a shaking, sweating mess, having spent most of the evening trying to score and failing; trying to get across town with no money and a couple of heavy bags, and knowing he was about to enter withdrawal yet again with no help in sight. He rang the doorbell. Vincent appeared. God! He'd got tall! A man, really.

'Uncle Jimmy!' he said with affection. 'Mum! It's Uncle Jimmy at the door!'

Hoagie winced at being called 'Uncle Jimmy', but he gave his middle-namesake a weak smile. 'You've got tall,' he said, 'thought you'd have left home by now.'

'Don't be silly, Uncle Jimmy,' said Vincent, 'I'm in sixth form.'

'Oh,' said Hoagie, 'we didn't do that when I was at school. Well, not my school. Well, I didn't do it anyways.'

'I'm at your old school,' said Vincent. 'Mum!' he yelled again. 'Are you ok, Uncle Jimmy?' he said.

'Yeah. I had a goat curry,' said Hoagie. 'Feel a bit sick. Hey, do us a favour will, yer, just call me Hoagie, yeah?'

'Righto, Uncle Jimmy,' said Vincent. 'Mum!'

Leela appeared at the door, holding a glass of wine in one hand and a cigarette in the other.

'Jesus! Hoagie,' she said, 'what are you doing here?'

'I'm out, Leela,' he said. 'Emma and me are over. Can I crash here for a few days? Just 'til I get meself together and all that.'

'I dunno, Hoagie,' said Leela.

'I won't be no bother,' he said. 'I can babysit and all that.'

'We've got five kids, Hoagie, 'said Leela, 'and I reckon *you* need the babysitter.' She told Vincent to go and put the kettle on.

'You can come in,' she said, 'but Hoagie, seriously,' she hissed, 'you cannot bring drugs into this house.'

Hoagie pointed at her cigarette with one finger and the wine with the other and raised his eyebrows.

'You know what I mean. These are legal,' she whispered, 'and fuck knows I need 'em. But you can't shoot up here, or whatever the hell you do.'

'I'm clean, Leela,' he said, 'after the OD.'

'Yeah, looks like it,' said Leela.

'Please, Leela!' said Hoagie. 'Me mum's not speaking to me after, well, you know. And last time I er, well, I nicked her rings and sold them, so she's 'specially not speaking to me. I got them back though, so I don't see why. And David hates me as well, so if you don't let me stay, I'll end up detoxing on a park bench.'

'I thought you said you were clean?'

'I was. I am. That's what I mean. This is the last time, I promise.' He looked up at her with what he hoped was a winning grin, albeit a little gap-toothed.'

'You say that all the time. Every time. Look, Have a cup of tea. I expect you can put up on the sofa tonight.' God, that grin always got her.

'Thanks, Leela.' He was relieved. 'To be honest, I thought you might say no, given the look of me.'

'Well, you do look a bit sick,' she said. 'Look, I honestly don't mind. Have you had anything to eat? You can have something with us.'

'Oh God, no,' said Hoagie. 'I had a bloody goat curry of all things, from what used to be the old chippy. Bloody horrible. Put me right off anything else.'

'That does sound a bit revolting,' said Leela.

'Do you need to run it past Jonesy?' he said, as he dragged his bag into the living room and began to unload.

'He'll do what I tell him to do,' said Leela.

Later Hoagie could hear them in the kitchen, arguing in hushed voices. About him.

'No,' Jonesy was saying, 'no he can't stay here, Leela. He od'd last time we saw him and whilst he's me mate and all that, enough is enough. And if he stays here, he'll end up robbing us blind. I know, because even I've done stuff I don't want to think about with him. He's an addict, Leela. We've got five kids anyway. There's no room. I'll be tearin' me hair out with another 'baby' in the house.'

'He'll have to sleep on the street!' said Leela.

'Well, that should tell you somethin', that even his mum don't want him now. He stole her mother's rings from her, Leela. I love him, but you can't trust him.'

'Just the night. Or two,' said Leela. 'He's not so bad.'

213

'What *is* it with you and him?' said Jonesy. 'You fancy him or something?'

'You can talk,' said Leela. 'I don't know where you are half the time.'

'At work, Leela. I am at work,' said Jonesy.

'So you say,' said Leela.

Jonesy ignored her remark. 'I'm gonna tell him to leave,' said Jonesy. He headed for the living room, where Hoagie was slouching on the sofa, watching the football.

'Hoagie, mate,' he began, 'listen, er,'

Hoagie looked up at Jonesy, then he threw up all over his shoes.

'Christ's sake! What the fuck is that?' said Jonesy. 'No, wait, I know what it is. Fuckin'…he's cluckin' for drugs. Look at him! He can get out. Now. I'm not havin' him detoxing all over the place in here. We've got kids, Leela.'

'No, I know what that is!' shouted Leela suddenly.

'Leela…' Hoagie looked up at her with pleading eyes. 'I'll get me stuff together,' he said, defeated.

'It's the goat curry,' said Leela, wildly.

'What?' said Jonesy.

'Goat curry!' He had it before he came here. I told him it couldn't do him any good. Probably got poisoned.'

Hoagie looked up at her, wide-eyed. She gave him a small shrug.

'Yeah,' he said, uncertainly, 'it might be.'

'Bloody goat?' said Jonesy. 'Who eats that? They're like the bloody devil, with their horns and little beady eyes. I got butted by one once. Where did you get that?'

'Old chippy,' said Hoagie.

'Ah well, that explains it,' said Jonesy. 'I had food poisoning from there once.'

'I think he ought to stay,' said Leela, 'at least until he feels better.'

'Really?' said Hoagie.

'Yeah,' said Leela. 'You need to *get better*.' She put the emphasis on the last two words.

'I still think he oughta get on his way,' argued Jonesy.

'Do you know, Jonesy,' said Hoagie, 'There was one good thing about goin' to that chippy. I had this moment of nostalgia when I was eating that shitty goat curry. I was thinking about that time when we all went out on the town, and you somehow came home with the wrong car. Do you remember that?'

Jonesy looked at his wife in panic. Then he said, 'Yeah, mate. We did have some good times.'

'Cor, I reckon Leela would love to hear about that night,' said Hoagie.

Jonesy looked slightly sick himself. 'Nah,' he said, 'I am sure she'd be bored by our daft stories. Hey, right, look, we can catch up tomorrow, yeah. You look tired. Why don't you stay, all right?'

'I don't know what to say,' said Hoagie. 'Actually, I do. I feel like, really shit. And I think I need to use your toilet. Now!'

'That way!' said Leela.

No-one wanted to hear it, and everyone pretended they couldn't hear Hoagie emptying his guts.

'What's wrong with Uncle Jimmy,' said Brooke, Jonesy and Leela's youngest child, who had wandered in rubbing her eyes.

'He ate goat,' said Jonesy.

'Urgh!' she screwed her nose up. 'Goats stink.'

Hoagie emerged, sweating. 'Sorry, Leela,' he said. 'I cleaned it up as best I could. Oh, shit I feel fuckin' sick.'

'Well, you know the answer to that, don't you?' said Leela.

'What?' Hoagie groaned.

'Don't Eat Goat,' said Leela, meaningfully, 'especially not under my roof.'

'Yeah,' said Hoagie, with a weak grin. 'I think I've decided to stay off the 'goat' for life.'

'We'll see,' said Leela with a sigh. 'Come on, let's get you another blanket.'

Burnt Lungs and Bitter Sweets

Underpass (2000)

Going Underground (The Jam)

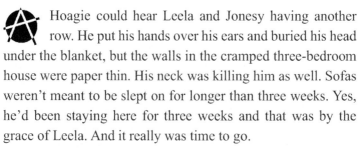 Hoagie could hear Leela and Jonesy having another row. He put his hands over his ears and buried his head under the blanket, but the walls in the cramped three-bedroom house were paper thin. His neck was killing him as well. Sofas weren't meant to be slept on for longer than three weeks. Yes, he'd been staying here for three weeks and that was by the grace of Leela. And it really was time to go.

But go where?

Maybe he could convince his brother to let him stay there? But then again, he was still pissed at him for telling him that thing about their dad not being dead. And David probably hated him anyway. Or maybe Toad would finally get off his backside and sort himself out so they could share. More sofa surfing. Toad was getting a place, so he'd heard, but Toad hadn't been around to see him yet and he'd been sick for two weeks out of the three. This was the last time he decided. No more drugs. Just weed. He'd sort himself out once and for all. Probably better not share with Toad on second thoughts.

Hoagie could hear the row still going on. He wasn't certain it was about him. He heard Leela scream the words *'flowers'* and *'receipt'*, and he bet this little drama was to do with Jonesy and some woman at work as usual. He thought it might take the heat off him at least so he decided to listen in on this little drama and went to stand halfway up the stairs.

'I found it! In your bloody pocket!' screamed Leela.

217

'It's for the team!' shouted Jonesy. "Someone at work was ill, and we had to send flowers to their house, and I got the job of buying them.'

'We've got five kids!' screeched Leela. 'Why did *you* have to pay. And anyway, I don't believe you. It's that bitch, innit?'

'Leela, I'll get the expenses! It's no-one. I promise!' said Jonesy.

Hoagie had covered for Jonesy before, and he hated doing it, but what Leela don't know, he thought, won't hurt her. He had hoped Jonesy had changed, but he didn't believe him either. The biggest surprise was that he would buy flowers for some tart. The little rat. And Hoagie would never have put him down for a flowers type. He thought he'd talk to him about it later. But then again, he and Jonesy weren't exactly getting on with him sleeping on their sofa. It was about time he got out and went to see Toad. And he knew where he might find him.

At 11, Hoagie shouted up to Leela, 'Just goin' out for a bit!' She didn't answer. She'd started shouting about one of the kids now.

'She's not goin' to that party, and that's the end of it!' she was saying.

Just before he was about to leave, he heard Shannon join in. 'I can hear you! And I *am* going!' She came thundering down the stairs, so he dashed back into the living room and pretended to be thumbing through the Jonesy's stash of Vinyl.

'Did you hear that?' said Shannon.

'No,' lied Hoagie.

'It's so unfair,' she said. 'It's just a party, with friends. I'm old enough, and Miles is allowed to go out.'

'He's a boy,' said Hoagie. 'It's different.'

'No, it isn't!' she replied. 'What's that one?' she pointed at the record Hoagie was holding.

'It's…bloody hell! He kept them all!' said Hoagie in wonder. 'Jeez, this takes me back!'

'Pass it here,' said Shannon.

Hoagie handed it over.

'*The Sound of the Suburbs*,' she said. 'This is dad's? Who's it by?

Hoagie gave a small cough. '*The Members*,' he said.

She giggled. 'Put it on.'

'I'm going out,' said Hoagie.

'I will then,' she said, and put it on the turntable. It blasted out. 'It's all right,' she shrugged.

'It's bloody brilliant,' said Hoagie. 'Smells like teen spirit.'

'That's Nirvana,' she said. 'But Kurt Cobain's dead so that's old now.'

'This is older,' said Hoagie. 'But better.'

'Oi!' shouted Jonesy from upstairs. 'You touchin' my records?'

Shannon took the record off the turntable and put it back in its sleeve. 'I AM going out!' she shouted.

Hoagie took his chances and slid towards the front door. The shouting began again. He slipped outside, closed the front door quietly and gave a sigh of relief.

Hoagie made his way to the river where he thought Toad might be, and sure enough he was loitering on the riverbank, waiting for his dealer.

'Ay aye!' said Hoagie.

'Shit! You made me nearly piss me pants!' said Toad. 'How long you bin back?'

'Three weeks,' said Hoagie. 'I'm stayin' at Jonesy's place.'

'What, with all them kids?' said Toad.

'Yeah, on the bloody sofa,' said Hoagie, 'but it's all right. Only place I've got.'

'I've got a flat by the river,' said Toad. 'Got put in it by the social. And I'm doing odd jobs down the dock and a bit at the factory.'

'Fuck me! Working?'

'Yeah, I know. I had to 'cos they stopped me benefits. But I was plannin' to have an injury to me back soon.' He winked.

'Yeah, well. I suppose I'll have to get off me backside and do somethin'. But I've got to get a script sorted for the juice again. And probably get movin' out of Leela and Jonesy's soon,' said Hoagie. 'You got space?'

'Yeah, mate,' said Toad. 'I can give yer a mattress on the floor for a bit,' said Toad. 'You sure about methadone? I'm getting' some good gear in a minute.'

'Oh, go on, cut me in and I'll get on the methadone tomorrow. I int had any for all the time I've bin here,' said Hoagie, 'and I'm still rattlin' bad.'

'Knowin' you, you'd be on both anyway,' said Toad. 'Never known anyone neck back so much shit and stay upright.'

Except at New Year, thought Hoagie, but he didn't want to think about that. 'You'll have to sub me, mate,' he said. 'Just til I get something sorted.'

'No worries,' said Toad. You could always rely on Toad. Toggie wouldn't be as helpful.

'Anyways,' Toad continued, 'I might be able to help you there. I've got this mate, Sonny. Sonny Cloud his name is.'

'Sonny Cloud?' interrupted Hoagie scornfully.

'I dunno, it's not his real name is it!' said Toad. 'Look, let me get on with it. He's a dealer, right, and he's always looking for someone to help him out. Pays.' Toad looked triumphant.

'Yeah. Yeah,' said Hoagie, rubbing his chin, 'All right.'

'Come back to mine, for a bit, and you can meet him,' said Toad. 'He's a bit of a character though, I warn yer.'

Toad's place was near the river and part of a grey, graffitied concrete block of flats. It looked depressing. But it was somewhere to stay which was not on a sofa in a house filled with kids and shouting.

Sonny Cloud was an arsehole, thought Hoagie. Typical arrogant swaggering twat, probably as he had once been. No, he considered. He hadn't been like that. This guy had been watching too much *Withnail and I* and was more like a caricature than a 'Character'. But it was the chance of badly needed cash. And it would get him out of the house.

'Look, I'll go back later and then I'll tell 'em I'm moving out next week or something,' said Hoagie. 'I can't go straight away 'cos they've been really good to me, but I expect they'll be glad to see the back of me. Why don't I come out with yer tonight, er, Sonny?'

For the time being though, they got high and chased the afternoon away, letting the day drift into evening.

Dealing in a dripping underpass near the river was not exactly what Hoagie had in mind, Sonny Cloud stood at one end of the underpass, dealing with his regular customers, selling them Beak and H mostly. Hoagie was more-or-less employed as a look out, and he was told he could have a small percentage, like a wage, for helping out. Sonny had been nicked recently and wanted to avoid it again at all costs.

The customers were mostly a sorry little bunch, skinny and pale. There was the occasional posher type, buying coke for the weekend. Then he saw a young man with a girl who looked familiar. Hoagie marched over to the couple.

'Does your mother and father know you're here?' he said.

'Uncle Jimmy! What the fuck?' said Shannon.

'Does she know you swear like that as well?' he said.

'Look here, what's going on?' said Sonny Cloud.

'You can't serve this pair,' said Hoagie.

'Uncle Jimmy, it's not for me, it's for our friend,' said Shannon.

'Don't give me that fuckin' bullshit,' said Hoagie. He stared at the boyfriend. 'And you are? No don't tell me, you're just a mate, *you won't tell anyone, will you*? and *it's for a friend*. Maybe your fuckin' *friend* had better buy their own shit, don't you think?' He turned to Sonny. 'This is my, er, niece, and she doesn't want anything from you, and this is her soon-to-be-flattened boyfriend if they don't clear off out of here right now.' He turned back to Shannon. 'Go and shit away from your own doorstep at least,' he said to her. 'I don't want to see you down here buying this shit again.'

'But Uncle Jimmy, you're dealing the shit,' Shannon pointed out.

'I'm looking out for the bloke who's dealin' the shit, yer cheeky bint,' said Hoagie. 'Look, just don't get into it, yeah. I won't say anything, but don't get into it. I know what I'm talking about,' he sighed.

'We're going to that party in Vermont Close tonight. Mum thinks I'm at my friend, Daisy's house. I'll be back at around midnight. I won't tell on you either, but let Aaron take his gear, and cover for me, yeah. It's just a little bump, bit of a whizz, for the party, yer know. *I* won't use it. It isn't *heroin*, Uncle Jimmy, it int *addictive* is it?' She looked at him all pleading and young, and maybe a little bit defiant. It suddenly startled him, the way she reminded him of Kecks at around the same age, sticking out her chin, and he felt ancient.

'I ain't got any right to say don't do it, Shannon, but just go easy.' He sighed again. He turned to Aaron, who went quite pale. 'And you,' he said, 'if anything happens to her you're history, mate.' He grinned widely. Aaron looked as if he might be sick.

'Maybe we'll just clear off?' he offered. But, of course, he already had the stash in his pocket because he'd parted with the money.

After his shift, Hoagie went back to Toad's again and helped Toad out with his stash. It would be rude not to. He almost forgot he was still staying at Jonesy's place, and he didn't arrive back at Leela and Jonesy's place until 1 am. Police cars were outside.

'Thank God you're back!' said Leela, whose face was streaked with tears and black mascara. 'The police need to talk to you, and I had no idea where you were.'

'I was with Toad,' said Hoagie, 'but I wouldn't say now is a good time to talk to the police.'

'Shannon's gone missing,' said Leela.

'What?'

'They want to talk to everyone who has seen her today.'

'What the hell?' said Hoagie.

And at that point, a tall, thin policeman, introducing himself as 'Inspector Dean', leaned in and addressed Hoagie. 'We need to speak to you about Shannon Jones. When did you last see her?'

'I saw her this morning, briefly,' said Hoagie. 'On the landing with her mother, I think. I'm stayin' here, see, on the couch, just until I get a place.'

'Would you be willing to come down the station and conduct a more formal interview?' said the inspector.

'Yeah, but I don't see I can be much help,' said Hoagie.

'Get your coat, Mr – er – Hoag is it?'

'Yeah,' said Hoagie.

At the station, Hoagie was ushered into a small room.

'So, Mr Hoag,' began the Inspector, 'we already know you have seen Miss Jones, because we have arrested a friend of yours. We have some CCTV footage of this friend, er, Mr Cloud, and Miss Shannon Jones with a young gentleman who is unknown to us at present.' He paused.

'Oh yeah?' said Hoagie. 'So, what makes you think I have seen her then?'

'Mr Sonny Cloud says you were there, and the footage does reveal the back of a gentleman matching your description,' said the Inspector.

'But you can't see if it is actually me?' said Hoagie.

The inspector left it a beat. 'No,' he said.

'Because I wasn't there,' said Hoagie.

'Mr Hoag, I have to tell you that Mr Cloud was arrested for dealing drugs and supplying them. He says you were there helping him out.'

'Well, I weren't,' said Hoagie. 'Prove it. 'Cloud', my arse,' he muttered under his breath with a snort.

'Mr Hoag, on the CCTV footage…' began the Inspector, ignoring Hoagie's snort of derision over the name.

'Does it show anything like my face on it?' said Hoagie, praying it didn't.

'No,' admitted the Inspector. 'But it certainly looks like you from behind and the figure in question has your distinctive hair and has quite a long chat with your, er, niece, is it?'

'Er, Goddaughter,' said Hoagie, not knowing again what to call Shannon. 'Look, I'm telling yer, it in't me. Can I go now? Please,' he added.

The Inspector looked weary. 'Not yet. But we'll take a break for now. If you think there's anything you can tell me about where your Goddaughter might be…' He tailed off. He could tell he was getting nowhere. Put the scumbag in a cell for the night; see if he coughed anything. The inspector's professional ambition had been ignited – finding a missing teen and bagging two dealers in one night if he pulled this off. He had Hoagie led away to a cell. He hadn't charged him, but he was sure this guy knew something. It was bloody obvious it was him on the grainy image. If only he could prove it, it would be one more off the streets – and much kudos to him. He'd probably get a promotion.

The time dragged on. Hoagie had been in a cell before, and he had no wish to return for a longer period. He could deal with a few hours. They had nothing on him, and he wasn't about to give up his freedom for some daft teenager's antics with her weedy boyfriend. He didn't give Shannon any drugs himself,

225

and he certainly couldn't stop her. At least, he told himself, this dodgy Cloud bloke wasn't the worst dealer she could have gone to. He'd sampled the goods, and it seemed all right to him. She was probably having a brilliant time and would be home soon enough. But as the time ticked by, and he lay with his knees drawn up, facing the grey walls, his thoughts began to wander to the darker corners of his memory. With his last fix wearing off, and desperately tired, he drifted in an agitated half-dream state. In his mind, Shannon's face morphed with Kecks. It was Kecks in the underpass; Kecks he had allowed to leave with the dopey boy and the pocket of drugs; Kecks looking defiant as she walked away: 'It's not *addictive,* is it?' Cheeky mare! And yet…and yet…

Where had she said they were going? Think Hoagie, Think! Vermouth? Vermont. Vermont Close. He was the only one who knew where she was. But if he said he knew, it would be a dead give-away. Nah, he'd stay quiet. They'd figure it out.

'Mr Hoag?' came a voice. 'You're out of here.' They were releasing him without charge. Leela was waiting for him at the front desk.

'Still no word,' she said, and she began to cry again as they left. "Best get home. Perhaps you can stay at home while we go looking for her. Oh my God, if we could just know where she'd gone…'

'Hang on a minute,' said Hoagie. He went back into the station.

After Hoagie had confessed what he knew, the team of officers had swooped on Vermont Close, surprising most of the neighbours and not least Shannon, who'd been lying semi-conscious in a bed with her drippy semi-conscious boyfriend.

226

Burnt Lungs and Bitter Sweets

They couldn't prove Hoagie had been an accomplice to Sonny's crime – just because he was in the underpass and had spoken to Shannon when the other guy was dealing, it didn't mean he was also dealing, or even the lookout. He didn't have a really good explanation as to what he was doing there if he wasn't helping Sonny Cloud to deal his drugs, but coincidence is a funny thing. It's not illegal to talk to a mate you've happened to run into. He himself was not dealing drugs, he told them indignantly. But there was his past record and his recent overdose, and, well, you join the dots. The police weren't stupid. They'd definitely be on his case now. But Shannon was brought home shame-faced and most importantly safe. She didn't end up in a bloody body-bag outside a telephone box, so maybe it was worth it.

'You can't stay here, you know, not now,' said Leela, as they both stood in the kitchen at daybreak, unable to sleep. 'Danny won't have it. Not with the kids and that. I mean, it's pretty obvious what was going on in that underpass, even if you have got away with it.'

'I know, Leela,' said Hoagie.

'I'm glad you've got away with it though,' she added.

'I know, Leela,' said Hoagie.

'Where will you go?'

'I dunno. Toad's floor for a bit? Prison?' He attempted a grin.

'Oh, stop it! They won't send you to prison! I'd always speak up for you. We all would. It's just…'

'I *know*, Leela.'

'When did all it stop being fun, Hoagie?' she said sipping her coffee and pulling a face.

'For you, on your wedding day,' he joked.

'Fuck off,' she said, 'you know what I mean.'

'Should have stuck to one kid,' he replied. 'Jonesy's still a big kid inee? Still goes out on the lash, yeah?'

'Well, he's got a good job and everything. Oh God, I'm just so, so, I dunno, bored or something with it all. When do you become a *real* adult, do you think? Like our parents? When is it that you start feeling like you're actually an *adult*, and you know what to do and stuff?'

'I have no idea, Leela,' said Hoagie. 'I was thinking about that on the train down here. And if you mean *my* parents, well, you're picking the wrong example there.' He stopped. 'Leela,' he said, 'what if I told you something about my dad?'

She looked at him, intrigued. 'What?'

He blew out his cheeks. 'Nothing,' he said. 'Nothing.'

'I know he died of a heart attack, didn't he?' she began.

'Yeah, yeah. He's dead. Yeah,' said Hoagie.

'So?'

'Honestly, forget it,' he said.

'Well, I think there's something I need to tell you,' Leela began. 'It's…well, you remember Millenium – '

'Not really, Leela,' he interrupted.

'Oh yeah,' She gave a weak giggle. 'Sorry. Inappropriate,' she said, continuing, 'It's just that…'

At that point Shannon came into the kitchen. She could hardly meet Hoagie's eye. Leela caught hold of her dressing gown. 'Oi, haven't you got something to say? To your uncle?'

'He's not my real uncle,' said Shannon. Then she half-looked at him. 'Sorry,' she said grudgingly. Leela gave her a look. 'Well! He can't talk!' Shannon added. 'I know, I know – he delivered Vince!'

'At least you're back home,' said Hoagie.

'Yeah, but it was a bloody good party as well,' said Shannon.

'You can thank me later,' said Hoagie. Bloody kid. Just like Jonesy. Can't take any responsibility. Ungrateful. He could have gone to prison 'cos of her! Or got a hefty fine or community service or something. Probably the last one, he thought. He'd had 'good behaviour' for so long, and they really hadn't got anything concrete. He'd seen it before – sometimes you were offered a choice – 'compulsory volunteering.' What a joke! It was the sort of scheme some politician might dream up someday – probably try to bring back National Service or something to get the unemployment figures down. May be better than prison though, he supposed.

Jonesy appeared in the kitchen.

'I'm packed already,' said Hoagie. 'I'll go to Toad's for a bit, just til I see what's what.'

'Sorry mate,' said Jonesy, 'but you know we can't have you here any longer.'

'I'm already gone,' said Hoagie. He turned to go into the living room, where his bags did indeed sit packed and ready. Leela put her hand on his arm. She had decided not to tell him about Emma after all. Emma probably didn't keep the baby anyway and there was no sense making things worse by causing more heartache. She put her hand on his arm and then she kissed him on the cheek.

229

Virginia Betts

'Thanks, Hoagie,' she said, 'thanks.'

'Pleasure,' he said. He turned to leave, but impulsively he turned back, took Leela's face in both his hands, leaned in, and planted a soft kiss on her lips. Her cheeks flushed bright pink.

'Have a good one,' he said. And with that he'd grabbed his bag and was off into the early morning street, to the sound of rattling milk bottles and the distant echo of a train on the tracks.

Daylight Robbery (2018)

Is this the Life? (The Cardiacs)

The bus pulled into the grey concrete station, bringing him home as the early morning sun struggled into sight. It was raining – that fine, misty drizzle that soaks everything. To Hoagie, even the air seemed heavy as he stepped off that bus. Everyone else seemed to be going about their business, unaware of this invisible and oppressive tension; they shopped, they laughed, chatted over coffee and went to work. But Hoagie could feel it. Perhaps it was because everything had changed here but then again, nothing had really changed. Despite its pretentions of being an up-and-coming, new-housing, new-flats, waterfront-and-wine-bar place, the town was really a series of unfinished high-rise projects, hairdressers, mobile phone shops and chain pubs. And God, it was so dark. Perhaps there was a tax on daylight now? Or maybe it was just him – wet, grey and miserable.

After his latest stint in the nick, he'd decided to come back and talk to his mum about finding his dad. Make his peace with him before he popped his clogs or something like that. To be honest, he couldn't think of anything else better to do, which was a sad state-of-affairs. And he missed Toad. Toad – still living the same life. Still single; still shooting smack and still alive. Fuckin' miracle. Come to think of it, he couldn't remember Toad ever having a girlfriend for more than about ten minutes. There was that bloody excuse for a human back at the Wimpy, but other than that…Or a boyfriend – well you have to think about that kind of thing these days. Not that it bothered him. Live and let live. He smiled to himself. Toad was someone he'd known literally all his life, and yet he couldn't really say with any confidence that he knew that much about him on any deeper level, apart from the fact that neither of them could drive! They had always been too busy working out where the next score was coming from to discuss the state of the universe or anything. But here he was, back to where he started and none the wiser about anything.

The other reason he'd come back was because he was forced to. Conditions of his freedom were to remain in his hometown and attend those bloody meetings, counselling sessions and drink that piss-water methadone everyday again. All the chemists round here knew him on sight by now! *Here's your little drink, Hoagie, how are you keeping, mate,* and all that. Very familiar with him. Well, he'd been back a few times now, and never missed. Course, they didn't know he was topping it up with the real stuff as well most of the time. It was pretty rare for him just to be on the juice. He thought of it as 'extra' rather than 'maintenance' therapy. Like a free gift on the NHS. This time he had to be good, or at least definitely not caught being bad, because he might be on his final life now. And he'd had quite a few near misses in his time.

He thought he'd go and see Toad this morning. Or maybe it was afternoon now? Who knew? He knew exactly where he'd find him – Toad was pretty predictable. He didn't work on a Wednesday, and it was likely he'd be down by the river, meeting up with his dealer, Dave. But first, Hoagie thought to himself, he needed to get some new trainers. He glanced miserably down at the current ones. Once gleaming white, they were now a dirty grey. He'd bought them in 1982, and they were so old now that they were now considered 'retro'! He had a couple of other pairs of shoes, obviously – boots and stuff, but these were his favourite trainers. He'd moved away from the punk image a bit, you had to move with the times and all that, although he couldn't quite let the hair go. Lucky he still had hair, he thought, thinking of Jonesy's slightly receding hairline, and Toggie, who insisted he chose to have a 'skinhead' but was, in reality, bald. Toad still had his colourful mop though. The two of them could still ruffle a few feathers out and about.

Outside the shoe shop, he wondered whether to get the same type of trainers or something different. It used to be a question of two or three stripes that made all the difference to whether you were cool or not so cool. Today it was more about cash, or lack of it, which would determine the purchase he made. He decided he would be paying for them, not just spiriting them out of the shop because, well, it just wasn't like the old days with cameras literally everywhere now; he couldn't afford to get caught for a petty crime. Plus, every Tom, Dick and Harry knew the ins and outs of everyone's arseholes now. You'd be all over Twitter before you'd left the bloody shop these days. It was so hard to break the law now. Hoagie sniffed his armpits. Hmm. Not so great. He checked his reflection in the shop window and ruffled his hair a bit. He'd pass, but perhaps he should be on the safe side. Boots was next door to the shoe shop. He sidled in, and squirted himself with the tester sprays, then on the way back he sauntered down the accessories aisle and ran one of the combs over his unruly, and somewhat spiky bleached mop until it was a little flatter. He pocketed the comb and left the store. Now he was ready to be a customer in the shoe shop.

The assistant eyed him suspiciously. There was no hiding the fact that the current trainers he was wearing were not only grey and holey, but the sole of the right foot flapped about like a kipper. He told them he was just browsing but then, feeling scrutinised and under pressure, he told them to find a pair similar to the ones he was wearing, in a size 9.

The assistant re-appeared with six pairs.

Hoagie sighed, and began the charade of trying them all on, mincing about in them and admiring them in the long mirror. He tried to avoid looking at his reflection above the feet, as it reminded him of how old he was getting. Inside he still felt 17, if a little bit bruised and battered around the edges. It was always a surprise seeing the old git who resembled his father staring back at him. He wasn't fat though. He'd kept his fairly trim build, although he supposed that was fairly easy when you didn't really eat much. He'd definitely rather have a drink than food, that was for sure.

He settled on a pair of trainers he liked. Then he looked at the price tag. *Fucking daylight robbery*, he thought, outraged. Still, it was wet and miserable, and he could no longer ignore the holes in the old ones, so he'd have to get them. He was so tempted to simply run out in them, but no, he'd turned over a new leaf. And then there were those cameras.

At the till, the assistant went to package them up, but he asked if he could just keep them on and put the old ones in the bag.

'Are you sure you don't want me to, er, dispose of the old ones for you?' she asked.

'No thank you,' he replied. Cheeky mare!

'That will be £35, please,' she said.

Now Hoagie knew that wasn't the price on the tag. It was at least twice that. So, this left him with a little dilemma. Did he say something, and then have to pay through the nose, or did he keep quiet, and then risk her realising and knowing he was not an honest person? See the thing is, faced with that situation, what would any of us do? Is there a person alive who hasn't got an unexpected yet dishonest bargain and kept quiet? And even if they chose to be honest, surely the thought would have crossed the minds of the saintliest shopper?

Hoagie reasoned that shops must plan for this sort of mistake and factor it into their budget. It wasn't as if he was shoplifting – he intended to pay, but let's face it, the shoes were a fucking rip off in the first place, and obviously the gods had intervened and decided he could buy them at a more accurate price. So, he paid the £35, (which hit hard enough) and walked out with his new trainers on, exalted at his good luck for a change, and failing to notice the enormous neon sign stating '50% off all trainers'. He binned the old ones the moment he left the shop and headed for the river.

He was quite right – Toad was hanging around, as usual, waiting for Dave to turn up. When he saw Hoagie, his face lit up.

'Mate! Where you bin?'

'In the nick, mate,' said Hoagie.

'Really? Again? It's bin ages! What you doin' back here?'

Hoagie didn't really have a good answer to that. It was probably a mistake coming here at all. But he smiled and said, 'Missed me mates, didn't I?'

235

'How did yer know where to find me?'

'You actually have to ask that question, Toad?'

'Nah, s'pose not. Hey mate, where you stayin'?'

Hoagie hadn't really thought that through. But Toad must have seen his face. 'Stay at mine, yeah? Be like old times – we can get some booze and gear in. Have a party.' He offered Hoagie a cigarette, which he gratefully accepted. They sat down on the bank and blew smoke rings to the clouds.

Hoagie had to admit, it did appeal, staying with Toad, having a good old chat about old times. 'Well, I'm supposed to be a good boy, but fuck it,' he said. 'Hey – you don't still live with your mum, do yer?'

'You know I don't, mate – flat round the corner from here. You know that! You've bin there!'

Hoagie blew a particularly impressive smoke ring. 'I was thinking, on the bus here,' he said, 'how fast time goes, yer know.'

Toad nodded blankly.

'Ah, you don't realise, mate. You haven't changed much. And neither have I to be fair, but everything around us and everyone around us – it's like we got in this time warp and the world kept turning, and we sorta of missed it. Ah, I'm not really explainin' meself too well.'

'Yeah, I fink I know what yer mean,' said Toad. 'Like, when Toggie got out of jail, even he changed – moved away, yer know. And Jonesy, well, you can't really count Jonesy, he's always bin a bit of a wanker. But he's still a mate, so, you know. But he had grey hair the last time I saw him.'

'We don't change though, do we?' said Hoagie.

'Nah, not really,' said Toad. 'You got fatter though.'

'Cheers!' said Hoagie. 'You got stupider. If that's possible.'

Toad thumped him, 'Oi, fuck off,' he said.

'Seriously though,' said Hoagie, 'you know when we was 17, and we had everything to come – like, you thought we'd be in a band and we'd be famous and rich and get all the girls after us, and all the booze and drugs we could take…'

'Oh, yeah, well, we did get them, didn't we?' said Toad. 'Talkin' of which, Dave'll be here in a minute.'

'Don't you ever think about it though?' said Hoagie.

'Wass got into you?' said Toad. 'You're not normally this miserable.'

'Oh, I dunno. I'm not, really. It's just I thought I would have found whatever it was by now.'

'What?'

'Well – '*it*', you know, whatever it is you're supposed to find by my age. I s'pose it's cos I'm thinking of catching up with mum and dad…'

'Like, do you know where his grave is then?' said Toad.

For a moment Hoagie was confused, then he realised he'd never told Toad about his dad being alive. 'No!' he said, 'look, Toad, there's something I'm going to tell you.'

But Toad had hopped up onto his feet. 'Hold on, mate – hold that thought – I just got to catch up with me man Dave.' He disappeared into the grey concrete jungle beside the river.

Hoagie sighed. He finished his cigarette, and decided he'd keep any deep and meaningful thoughts to himself in future. Getting high with Toad was the best offer he'd had for ages, and suddenly he wasn't really bothered about much else. Mind you, he'd better stock up on fags, and he was quite hungry, so maybe some chocolate. When Toad returned, grinning, he showed him his shoes.

'Yeah,' he said, 'and the best part was, they undercharged me!'

'Finders keepers!' said Toad.

'Well, I didn't find 'em but... oh, never mind,' said Hoagie. 'Can you cook it up here?'

'Yeah, I reckon,' said Toad. 'You just stand up and shield me a bit and make sure no-one'll notice. Oh, I got you some, you'll have to pay me though.'

'Just don't fuckin' push me in the river like normal,' said Hoagie.

'You can swim, can't yer?' said Toad, with a menacing look on his face.

After about an hour, Hoagie was beginning to get cold and hungry. 'Look,' he said, 'I've got a couple of things to do – get some fags and booze for us, and I'm starvin'. You want anything?'

'Nah,' said Toad. 'Thought you was goin' to catch up with yer mum?'

'Oh, I can wait 'til tomorrow,' said Hoagie. 'Tell you what, I'll just nip to the paper shop, and I'll meet you back at yours.'

'All right, mate,' said Toad, 'catch yer later, yeah?' He gave a mock salute as Hoagie headed for the tiny shop just outside the town centre.

Hoagie plonked a six pack of lager on the counter. It irritated him that he had to ask for the tobacco, kept locked up as if it were the crown jewels.

'Pack of Amber Leaf, Packet of Rizlas – yeah, the big ones, mate – oh, and a Marathon,' said Hoagie to the assistant, pointing at the chocolate.

'It's a Snickers,' said the young assistant, looking puzzled.

'Not in my world it isn't,' said Hoagie. The assistant looked at him as if he were from another planet and put the items down on the counter.

'You oughta try vaping, sir,' said the assistant. 'It's healthier.'

'Is that what you do?' said Hoagie.

'What, no! I don't smoke, or vape – I don't even drink,' said the assistant.

'How old are you?' said Hoagie.

'Twenty-two,' The assistant replied. 'And a half,' he added.

Bloody hell thought Hoagie. How BORING! He was trying to think of something he hadn't done at twenty-two. He couldn't think of a single thing.

'That'll be £17.50,' said the assistant.

'Daylight Robbery!' said Hoagie. 'Again! What is the world coming to? Oh well, here you are.' He was about to hand over the money, when he remembered he needed something else.

'Oh, mate,' he said, 'have you got a lighter? One of them cheap plastic ones?'

The assistant turned back to get one from behind the counter, and as he did so, two police officers walked in.

Shit! The shop called 'em about the trainers! Without thinking, Hoagie grabbed his marathon and tobacco, knocking

239

the beer to the floor with a smash. He pushed past the police officers and legged it out of the shop.

'Oi!' shouted the shop assistant, 'he took the stuff without paying! Oi! Shoplifter!'

The police officers, who had only come in to get a couple of sandwiches and a packet of Monster Munch each, sighed as they realised that they had just lost their break, and took off after Hoagie.

Hoagie knew he was being pursued and all he could think about was that his freedom was at stake but even more importantly, his night of fun with Toad was under threat. He took a detour down by the river. He'd reached a particularly wide stretch, but he decided to go for it anyway, knowing they were still in hot pursuit and on the radio for back up.

The water was unusually high and the cold shocked his body like a thousand tiny needles. He thrashed about, trying to keep his head above water, realising that his shoes were getting heavier, but unable to kick them off.

Toad knew Hoagie wasn't the most reliable of people, so he wasn't that worried when Hoagie didn't show up. He knew he'd turn up eventually, especially with the promise of a good session. He could hear a bit of a commotion going on outside, down by the river near his flat. He looked out of the window, but he couldn't see anything. 'Probably some dosser gone for a swim,' he thought. He took a swig of his little bottle of vodka and began to skin up.

Dead in the Water

(2024/2019)

Ashes to Ashes (David Bowie)

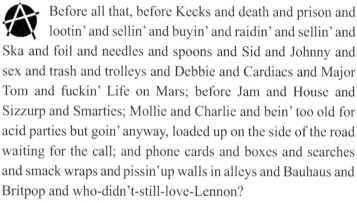 Before all that, before Kecks and death and prison and lootin' and sellin' and buyin' and raidin' and sellin' and Ska and foil and needles and spoons and Sid and Johnny and sex and trash and trolleys and Debbie and Cardiacs and Major Tom and fuckin' Life on Mars; before Jam and House and Sizzurp and Smarties; Mollie and Charlie and bein' too old for acid parties but goin' anyway, loaded up on the side of the road waiting for the call; and phone cards and boxes and searches and smack wraps and pissin' up walls in alleys and Bauhaus and Britpop and who-didn't-still-love-Lennon?

Before all that, and more, there were two skinny boys, eyin' each other up warily over a milk crate in a grey classroom that smelled of floor polish and chalk in the decade of shootin' up into space to reach the moon.

'What's your name?' I asked him and he told me: James Vincent Hoag.

And the other kid, me, spat his milk all over him. And Hoagie, he said, 'Well you look like a fuckin' Toad!' And that's my name from then on.

And we giggled, and I shared my straw, as later I would share a needle the first time we fixed up together.

Watched him glide seamlessly up and down the outdoor pool, sun on his lean back; always faster than me. More daring hair. Divin' in recklessly and never botherin' where he might land.

First time we saw Johnny at a college in London. And Rotterdam in '77. Got over there by boat with him hangin' over the toilet, arse in the air. So sick. Locked me out of the fuckin' cabin. I had to freeze on deck. Twat. His hair, man. Then on to Amsterdam, swearin' that's where we'd move; that's where we'd end, swaggerin' along Kanaalstraat (anal street, he called it) at 3 am, faces lit up in neon red, with the tarts glaring aggressively out at two skinny high boys with bright spiky hair. Getting those tattoos. We'd never seen nothin' like it.

I remember holding him while he writhed in withdrawal, sick and sweating and throwin' up. Aching in agony. He did try. We all did. His heart was never really in it though. Is it really *decades* of love-hate with heroin? Longest fuckin' relationship I've had. It can be done. Yeah. Really. Look at me. Did Hoagie ever stop? Sometimes.

We all went to the funeral. Luckily, he died before lockdown, or I doubt many people would have been there. Jonesy read about what happened in the paper. We often read about Hoagie in the papers over the last few years: 'Drug dealing addict, James Hoag, arrested and charged… sentenced'…yeah, yeah. He became a headline with a dodgy mugshot. But who was he really? Hoagie with a heart? Hoagie the scumbag? Rogue? Villain? Even I was never really sure. But if you knew, you knew. You couldn't miss him. You gotta love him.

242

Jonesy arrives first at the funeral. Well, after me, but first of the four. With Leela. Kids at home, naturally. All grown-up now I s'pose. He looks sheepish, like, guilty for moving on; getting on.

'Mate,' I say.

'Mate,' he replies.

'Hello, erm, Toad,' says Leela. She looks older, slightly rounder in body and face, but still quite pretty, if you like that kind of thing. 'It's Peter, isn't it?'

'Yeah,' I say, 'but nah, Toad is fine. Toad is who I am.'

Then bloody Toggie bursting through the door.

'Gotta nip into the toilets boys,' he says, 'gotta get the security tags off of me jacket. Nicked it this morning before I come.'

'Fuck me, Toggie,' says Jonesy. 'Hoagie would have loved that.'

Leela rolls her eyes but nods, 'Yeah. He would.'

'So, how did it happen?' asks Toggie. 'And, well, excuse me, but what the fuck? We're all still alive! It's a miracle innit?'

'Ever the tactful, Toggie,' I say. 'I dunno. I hadn't seen him for a while. Then he turns up that very day. But it was over somethin' really stupid. Word is, as far as his brother says, he nicked a Marathon – he never would call 'em Snickers – said it sounded like knickers – and a packet of fags from the shop but he was caught out, see, and 'cos he was on parole again, supposed to be clean again – on the script yer know – and he was carryin', 'cos of that, he ran I s'pose. And they bloody chased him, really like a fuckin' film, like keystone bloody cops, and he jumps into the river and tries to swim, and ditch the gear, but the trainers he only bought that day filled up with water and dragged him down.'

'But he was always swimming?' says Jonesy.

'Yeah, but he was so high, man,' I say. 'He lay there ages before they pulled him out. Apparently.'

We are ushered in. Hoagie's depressingly aged mum files slowly in, and his little brother, all white-faced and drawn. No-one walking behind a coffin then. Some in long black coats; some in football shirts. Some aging punks; some grown up to be normal with proper jobs and a house and things; even bloody Big Adam had snuck in at the back, good job Toggie hadn't seen him, and some mystery woman with red hair that no-one knew, there at the back, all exotic lookin', talking to one of his other schoolmates. And – wait – was that Hoagie's *dad*? Nah, he's dead, surely, isn't he?

It's so bloody weird when the music strikes up – *Ashes to Ashes* – I applaud whoever chose that, as I always sing that to meself when they do a formal committal – Ashes to Ashes, *Funk to* ... well you know the rest. Maybe not the most appropriate, singin' about Major Tom bein' a junkie, but somehow the *most* appropriate at the same time. Anyways, time for a bit of a snigger from Toggie. And they carry the coffin in. Hoagie was never big. Always quite lean. He filled out a bit as he got older, from time to time, 'specially when he'd been in prison and off the gear, but not big. This box is fuckin' massive though. Why so big? Me? I'm goin' in a cardboard box, and they can chuck me on the skip. It all goes up in smoke anyways. I'd rather keep the money, so to speak.

'Hey, I read about this guy,' whispers Jonesy, 'he recorded a message so it plays in the crematorium from the bloody coffin, *Help! Help! Let me out!* Fuckin' scared the shits out of everyone. But what a joker!'

'Shh,' says Leela.

'Just tryin' to lighten the mood,' says Jonesy. 'It's what Hoagie would have wanted.'

'I heard you can get yerself pressed into a vinyl record – yer ashes, yer know,' I say.

'Hoagie goin' round and round to *God Save the Queen* or something, with a needle in 'im! 'Bout right,' says Jonesy.

'It's no age these days,' whispers some old bird next to us, to her husband.

'Tell you what,' says Toggie, 'I reckon we could all smoke his ashes and be high for a week at least! Be a shame to waste 'em.'

Leela glares at him. 'I had quite a soft spot for Hoagie,' she whispers. 'Have some respect.'

'Leela,' says Toggie, 'you hated him, hated us all from the moment you met us!'

'Yes at first,' she admits, 'but after that holiday…'

'You mean our honeymoon,' interjects Jonesy.

'Yes. After that, I thought he was all right. Didn't really want him around the children though.'

'Ay, ay,' whispers Toggie. 'I never did find out exactly what happened on that holiday.'

'Nothing much,' says Leela, too quickly. 'I just found out he was…*nice*, in a way.'

'Yeah,' I says. 'I remember that one time, when I was datin' this girl called… called… shit, I forgot her name!'

'I know the one,' says Toggie. 'What *was* her name?'

'Ah, it don't matter, it was years ago,' I say. 'Anyways, she had this kid, and I do remember *her* name. It was Hayley. And it was bloody awful. She left the kid with us all and – do you remember Jonesy – you were there – and we were chasin' and…'

'And I'd like to point out that I wasn't', says Jonsey, his eyes flitting wildly to his wife.

'Yeah, yeah,' I say, 'no, you *weren't*,' I rolls me eyes at him, 'but the point was that she didn't give a fuck about her kid getting burned, or in pain, or us usin' smack in front of her, and he *saw* that. Hoagie didn't like that.'

'He was no saint,' says Toggie. 'Look at his mum. Look at his brother. They look terrible. Still…'

'Yeah,' I say. 'I remember…'

'What?' says Leela.

'Nothin.' I say, but I did remember. I remembered Kecks, and that night. And what we both did. And how we ended up in the river. Another funeral, years ago. Both of us high then, and in denial. But we both knew. And I have thought about it so many times over the years – and I know Hoagie did, although it was unsaid – replaying the incident over and over, playing it out in different scenarios – what if we did this, what if we did that? But you can't change it, and we wouldn't have done it any differently anyway. *God grant me the serenity to accept the things I cannot change.* That's how it goes. Any day now. Still workin' on it.

The music stops. The vicar makes his speech. A bit about his life. Jobs he supposedly had (it's amazing how a job that lasts two weeks before he was kicked out for skinnin' up on the premises can sound so good) and how he led an *enthusiastic* life. He *liked a party, sometimes a little too much.* Yeah.

So, it skips over most of his actual life, but it catches the essence of him well enough. He was...fuck me, *likeable.*

And two of his other friends get up at the front, forget what they want to say, obviously already pissed or somethin' and ramble a bit then nearly fall over gettin' back to their seat. And then it's all over and Hoagie goes out to the most common song played at Funerals: *My Way.* But not the Sinatra version. Only the bloody Sid Vicious one! Good Old Hoagie. Or maybe his brother got mixed up? Either way, thank fuck. Any aging relative who deigned to be present tutting with pursed lips and hurrying out. Hoagie would have loved that. Singin' about killing a *cat* at a funeral. Fuck me, Hoagie, was this in your plan?

Then the wake. That's when the real stories come out. Too many of 'em. You've heard some of em' from me. Last man standing. I always thought it would be him. Not bullet-proof then after all.

This mystery woman, can't be no more than, God now I look, 18 or 19 tops, is standing at the bar on her own, ordering a pint of water. It don't suit her. She's more like a G and T girl.

'Who do you reckon that is, Leela?' I ask.

'I dunno,' says Leela. Then she stares at the young girl and looks back at me. 'It can't be, can it?'

'What?'

'Do you reckon she's something to do with Emma? Like her kid or something?'

'Yeah, but Emma didn't have a kid,' I say stupidly.

'Toad, I'm gonna tell you something now,' says Leela. 'Emma was pregnant when Hoagie left.'

'What the fuck? No way?' I say.

'Yeah, she told me on that night. Millennium.'

'And you're telling me this now?' I say. 'Did he know?'

'I don't know.'

'So, what are you sayin'? I say. 'That she's the kid?'

'Well look at her,' says Leela. 'She looks just like Emma.'

'I'm goin' over,' I say. And I get up and join the young woman at the bar.

'Hello,' I say cheerfully. And I dive right in. 'How did you know Hoagie then?'

'Are you the one they called Toad?' she asks me. She's got a right funny accent.

'Yeah,' I say, 'and they still do, mate.'

She laughs, and her eyes have this mischievous sparkle. And there it is. Right there. Hoagie, just as if he'd crawled out of his coffin and returned as a female. Yes, she looked like Emma, but she was unmistakeably Hoagie.

'I'm Victoria,' she says. 'I'm his daughter.'

'I guessed as much,' I say. 'I mean, you're just like him. I just heard about you – like, this minute.'

'Am I? Like him I mean? Everyone says I'm like my mother. I've only seen a couple of photos of him recently, but I can't really see it,' she says.

'It's your eyes. You'd have to have known him when he was young.' I feel awkward. How's Emma?' I ask her. 'I mean, Your mum? God that sounds strange.'

'She's gone. She died a couple of years ago. Cancer, you know.'

'Shit,' I'm genuinely shocked. 'We lost touch, after she and Hoagie broke up. I never really knew what happened. Shit, I liked Emma – what I saw of her – and I always hated his girlfriends. I hated 'em breaking him and me up, yer know. Not like I'm queer or anything,' I add.

She giggles. 'You can't say that! Anyway, it wouldn't matter if you were.' I feel old.

'We moved away when I was quite young,' she says. 'We went to America, actually. But we came back to Liverpool three years ago. She wanted to come home when she got ill. She didn't last that long, but she told me a lot about him not long before she died.'

'What did she tell you?'

'She told me...nice things. But she told me it didn't work out. She told me she found out she was having me after he'd gone, but she didn't tell him. She said he was always a bit troubled, and it was probably best not to go find him now. And yet I had a feeling she thought I should. Too bloody late though.'

'Did she tell you he was a heroin addict most of his life?' I say straight out. That surprises me. It isn't a word I normally say. *Addict*. We always say *user* lately. Neither word are those Hoagie would ever have used about himself. I don't add that I am still a user. An addict, probably.

'Yeah. She did. And I know he went to prison and stuff. It sort of explained a few things.'

'Huh? I say.

'I've had a few issues myself.' She sees my face. 'Oh, I'm fine. I'm training to be an addiction counsellor in fact.' She smiles at me.

'Christ!' I say. 'Fuck.' I really don't know what to say. 'Hey, do you wanna proper drink?'

'Er, I don't drink now, Toad,' she says.

I don't know what to say to that, but she laughs. A really hearty laugh, just like Hoagie. 'Are you an alcoholic?' I say, unnecessarily. Then I really feel stupid.

'Sorry,' I say. 'I'm an idiot.'

'Yeah, because heroin is so... what is it again? *Passé?*' she laughs again. 'See? I knew you'd get that! I've got great taste in music.'

'We all do,' I tell her. 'We went to see the Sex Pistols a couple of times. Me and Hoagie. Your dad. Fuck tha's weird sayin' that. Yeah, he called Sid Vicious a tosser. To his face!

'Jesus! Really? No! Look, I've got to go,' she says. 'Long way back to Liverpool. I've got a son. He's with my sister at the moment. And I thought I might call in on my grandmother and uncle I've never met at some point.'

'Son? You started young!'

'He's only a baby!' she protests.

'Sister?' I say.

'My mum got married. My sister is my half-sister. Mum got divorced years ago though. He's still in the States.'

'Nah, but wait, can't yer stay a bit?'

'I'd better not. I didn't know him. Not like you. Look, that's my mobile number; give us a call and we'll chat about it more.' And then she's gone. Like her mum in that way, I reckon. I remember the night Hoagie met her at that bloody rave. Took ages to try and track her down. Then he just runs into her! I go back to me mates and we all just get pissed. Leela asks about the girl. I say nah, just a coincidence. A cousin of his twice removed. I can tell she don't buy it, but she says nothing.

I never did go and see Victoria. Maybe you shouldn't open cans of worms. Well, I've still got her number, so there's always time. If I can afford the train fare. Maybe Jonesy'll drive me?

So, here I am. Still here in 2024! Survived lockdown! This story does not begin, 'Once upon a time' and it does not end 'happily ever after.' It just goes on, backward and forward, forward, and back. It goes on. Bloody Hell! There are so many more stories to tell. Maybe I will get in touch with Victoria after all.

I think I'll go back down to the river. I'd better go and see if my man Dave is there. See the man about the dog, you know, 'cos I'm back here again, stuck staring at the four walls in this godawful flat with the graffiti on the side, and there's this need, this skin crawlin' need still, after all this time. And when I look in the mirror, I still see that 20 something boy. And I can see Hoagie's face, behind me in the mirror grinnin'. Not as he was the last time I saw him, mind, but as he was then. I'll go to the river. Now they have probably cleared away that dead swan. It proper got to me, that swan. Hoagie. Like that bloody swan. Half the people constantly trying to save him; half of em' couldn't care less. Sometimes, he let them save him for a while. But always with a wink. His heart wasn't in being saved. I think he enjoyed himself too much.

Burnt Lungs PLAYLIST:

The soundtrack to a bittersweet life.

What A Waste - Ian Drury and the Blockheads
Virginia Plain - Roxy Music
Shot by both sides - Magazine
Call me - Blondie
Alternative Ulster - Stiff Little Fingers
Anarchy in the UK - The Sex Pistols
Lipstick - The Buzzcocks
The Sound of the Suburbs - The Members
White Punks on Dope - The Tubes
I wanna be Sedated - Ramones
The Young Offenders Mum - Carter USM
God Save the Queen - The Sex Pistols
Jubilee - Blur
Rock the Casbah - The Clash
Pretty Vacant - The Sex Pistols
Corpses in their mouths - Ian Brown
Rat Trap - The Boomtown Rats
Sleeping Pills - Suede
The A Team - Ed Sheeran
Ghost Town - The Specials
White Wedding - Billy Idol
The Passenger - Iggy Pop
Going Underground - The Jam
California Dreamin' - Max Martis and Haluna
Public Image - Public Image Ltd (John Lydon)
Voodoo Ray - Tall Paul
Blue Monday - New Order

Step on - The Happy Mondays
Purple Haze - Jimi Hendrix
The Death of a Disco Dancer - The Smiths
Golden Brown - The Stranglers
Queen Bitch - David Bowie
Hey Ya! - Outkast
This Charming Man - The Smiths
I love to love - Tina Charles
Millenium - Robbie Williams
End of a Century - Blur
Back from The Dead - Babyshambles
Is this the life - The Cardiacs
In Pursuit of Happiness - The Divine Comedy
Ashes to Ashes - David Bowie
My Way - Sid Vicious
Not if you were the last Junkie on Earth - The Dandy Warhols

About

Virginia Betts is a tutor, writer, and actor from Ipswich. She has had three books published, *The Camera Obscure* (supernatural and gothic-noir stories) *Tourist to the Sun* and *That Little Voice* (both poetry collections). She has also had numerous award-winning poems and stories published both in print and online journals and magazines, with her poetry and prose being performed regularly on stage and BBC Radio. Her poetry has been described as "combining the directness of modern poetry with the musicality of traditional verse."

Her most recent stage roles have included Kate Bush, Mary Boleyn, Elizabeth Barton, Maud Gonne and Patricia Highsmith, and she has also co-directed, produced, and written for the stage.

Burnt Lungs and Bitter Sweets is her debut novel.

Virginia is a member of The Writer's Guild, Equity, The Poetry Society, The Wolsey Writers, The Dracula Society, and a trustee and Stanza Representative for The Suffolk Poetry Society. She writes a monthly column for the 'Felixstowe Magazine App' and 'Author's Electric' and runs the book club at David Lloyd Gym.

virginiabetts.com (website)
@WriterGin900 (X)
ginnb900 (insta)
virginiacbetts (facebook)
Threads ginnb900

Also Featuring Virginia Betts

An Anthology in aid of FIND - Helping Families in Need

Urban Pigs Press presents a collection of 23 stories by 23 different authors inspired by the prompt HUNGER. From gritty crime, realism, horror and everything in between. All profits will go directly to FIND - Families in Need to help tackle the global issue of hunger.

A collection of stories that are as close to the bone in literary class as they are in their scathing analysis of a broken society.
-Stephen J. Golds
Author of Say Goodbye When I'm Gone

Part social commentary, part linguistic showcase, the authors of Hunger share such thought-provoking stories of a feeling that no-one is alienated from.
Some will leave you angry, some will leave you grateful and some will leave you with questions.
I would say it was a joy to read but more accurately, I am a more rounded person for reading it.
You're about to go on a journey. Where to? You will know when you get there.
- Rob Jelly

Featuring the talents of Sophia Adamowicz, LG Thomson, Jacko Pook, Mathew Gostelow, Paige Johnson, Matthew McGuirk, Virginia Betts, Marek Z. Turner, David Cook, Neda Aria, Eddie Generous, Ann Hayton, Russell Thayer, James Jenkins, Bam Barrow, Sebastian Vice, Cassie Premo Steele, A.J. Stanton, Mark Burrow, Tabitha Bast, Rob Walton, Tom Leins and Jude Potts. Front cover by Jo Andrews (Mojo Art) and inlay by Cody Sexton (Anxiety Press). Foreword by Andrew Marsh of Dial Lane Books.

urbanpigspress.co.uk

Also Available From Urban Pigs Press

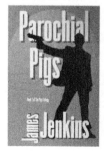

urbanpigspress.co.uk

Printed in Great Britain
by Amazon

53697504R00149